The Mysterious Disappearance of Santa Claus

A Holiday Story By
Kelsie Washington

THE MYSTERIOUS DISAPPEARANCE OF SANTA CLAUS

First edition. September 6, 2024.

Grams the Great

Santa Claus disappeared in the year 2025, gone from the memories of the people and taking with him the beloved holiday known as Christmas. There were no more stockings or toys, no Christmas trees with lights, no parties or feasting. And the world had not seen the wonder of snow for eighty-two years. Not a single snow flake. His legend did not fade as time passed, but rather the people forgot that he ever existed. Eighty-two years of no Santa Claus, no Christmas, no delight. The people had forgotten it all. But I knew all about him. I knew because Grams the Great was 127 years old, and she remembered. Santa Claus was a saint who had been granted long life and magic. Yes, magic. No one believed much in magic or saints anymore, but I believed.

Grams the Great was born in the year 1980. She said back then the grown folk had already stopped believing in magic but any kid worth their salt believed.

Kids back then, she said, believed strongly. Santa Claus would fly to their rooftops in a magical sleigh pulled by enchanted reindeer and leave toys, real toys, and never gadgets. Grams the Great hated gadgets. Gadgets were, said Grams, not toys but devices that turned your brains to mush. Real toys inspired you to imagine and dream. Santa Claus left beautiful toys, crafted by elves who lived with him at the North Pole. Just think about that. A toy, made by an elf, flown to your rooftop, and placed in your stocking by a magical saint. Of course your imagination would be inspired! Oh, how I longed to be gifted a toy made by an elf that smelled like fresh wood, snow, and magic, and gave me room for all my hidden dreams.

So many times, I begged Grams the Great to tell me about Christmas toys. I wanted to know everything there was to know about those magical wonders crafted by elves. Toys were not permitted in my childhood, or anyone's childhood. We had to work, learn, strive, but never dream or imagine. Never play. She said she was too old to remember any of them, but the toys were never that important. She said I was focusing on the wrong thing. Grams the Great said that what she remembered about Christmas was the whole season, the weeks before where you sang in a Christmas pageant at church, cut down a tree and decorated it, shopped for gifts, ate too many sweets, and took days off school and work to revel. Yes, revel. The whole world was full of lights and tinsel and people would sing on the streets.

Grams said the best part of Christmas morning was the feeling you had, when you woke up, never entirely certain if Santa Claus had come, and then there, right there in a stocking you had hung above your fireplace, were toys. Stockings, she said, were like giant oversized socks decorated to look pretty on a fireplace mantel. Grams said it did not matter what you found in your stocking. It was the magic of the nighttime delivery that made you fall in love instantly with your new toy.

My grandmother had twenty-two cousins and, on all holidays, after presents were opened and breakfasts were eaten, they would drive to her Grandparents' house, and they would play all day. Then eat, play some more, sing carols, and then have pie. And they would build people out of snow by rolling up balls and stacking them on top of each other and name them things like Frosty and Crystal.

Also, sledding. Flying down a hill on a toboggan, snow in your eyes, cold biting your cheeks and crashing and rolling in piles of soft, wet snow. Can you even imagine? She said there was a hill just outside her Grandparents' house and they would drag sleds to the top and fly down the hill and land in soft snow. I have never seen snow, but Grams described it to me so many times that sometimes I could feel it's wet softness on my cheek. Sometimes I could hear it crunching beneath my feet. It got so cold in our city, so cold, but never snow. I thought I could love the cold if it came with snow.

I dreamed of a white Christmas, cold and snowy, starry night skies where reindeer pranced, a Christmas where people felt joy. I did not believe people felt joy any longer, not like the way Grams described it. Snow and food and play and merry and the brightest joy. But when Santa Claus disappeared, the magic of Christmas went with him, and was replaced by drudgery and gloom and work, always work. It was all the people knew. At the mention of Christmas, their eyes would sort of cloud over and they just looked at you blankly. There were no gifts. There were no celebrations like what Grams the Great told me about from when she was young. I longed to taste a sweet potato pie, Christmas hams and turkeys, mashed potatoes slathered in gravy, rich green bean casseroles and stuffing even though I was not entirely certain what stuffing was. I wanted a real tree, with lights and dazzling bulbs, that left a piney scent wafting through your home. Grams always breathed in deeply when she talked about the trees like she was remembering the smell, and I always breathed in too and tried to imagine it.

I had been into the forest. There were not many left, but I had been and smelled that piney smell before. Grams the Great made mother take us. She said her old legs would not let her hike like she used to do out in the woods with the bears, bobcats and sasquatches, but old age could not keep her from ordering her family around and sitting out there on the edge of the forest and breathing in that smell. We brought branches home with us and Grams kept them in her room in vases for longer than the smell lasted. After that, she kept the old, dried things under her bed and only set them out in December, when Christmas used to be celebrated. I told Mom over and over we needed to get Grams fresh branches, but she was too busy all the time to make the trip. I think she was more worried about the sasquatches than taking time off work, but Grams the Great said no sasquatch had ever caught her in 127 years of tromping around the woods, so they must not want an old hillbilly like her.

I tried to tell my classmates at school about Santa Claus, but they just rolled their eyes at me and would later forget the whole thing. Each time I brought it up, it was like I was telling them something they had never heard before. They were wholly unimpressed with his flying reindeer, certain it was just a regular auto and no magic. Grams told me autos when she was young could not fly. They drove on roads and were mostly called cars. She said her grandparents rode in wagons pulled by horses and when Santa Claus delivered gifts to them the only way he could have flown to their rooftops was by magic. My classmates thought I was embellishing, crafting stories, which, I must admit, I had told a few tall tales to them over the years. Those were stories though. I had never insisted they were true. Santa Claus was no invention of mine. This was no fairy tale. Not that anyone read fairy tales any more either.

My hope was that if I continued telling people, kept reminding them of Christmas, maybe, even though Santa Claus was gone, we could at least bring back some of the other traditions. It seemed to me that Christmas was bigger than Santa Claus and even though he had disappeared, we could still celebrate. We could still gather with our loved ones and eat and dance and give each other gifts. If I could just help people remember the magic, but Grams said that you can't help people remember something they never knew.

Even Mom and Dad seemed to think, when Grams was telling her tales, that Christmas was some kind of story Grams made up, and then minutes afterward they forgot entirely. But I remembered. I could not seem to get it out of my head. Mistletoe and eggnog, gingerbread cookies and gumdrop houses, carolers, and mint hot chocolate. Can you just imagine it? Mint hot chocolate, as much as you could hold. And jingling bells and a soft white blanket of snow. Christmas.

Grams said people were just lighter, happier, and kinder to each other every year around Christmastime. But every year since Santa Claus was lost, the people have become meaner, grouchier, less kind. Grams said all the grey we wore, our brooding homes, the lack of color, all came into fashion after Santa Claus disappeared. Everywhere you looked things were painted gray, black, beige, drab, brooding, and Grams said it made us heavier. Mom and Dad said Grams was just a batty old lady. And she kind of was. But when she talked about Christmas something changed. Her battiness felt like joy, not lunacy. She simply became an old woman nostalgic for a more beautiful time, a time lost to all memories but hers. You believed her when she reminisced, and you believed in Santa Claus. Or at least I believed. Mom and Dad paid her no mind.

"Eve, my love, come over here!" Grams called out to me, interrupting my daydreaming about peppermint candy canes with red and white stripes. I was named Eve because I was born the day before Grams the Great's birthday, the eve of her birthday, and she thought it would be a clever way to name me after her, rather than using her actual name. She never liked her name and did not think it was one worth passing on. Grams the Great's name was Carol. Super old fashioned, but I wouldn't have minded. It's kind of Christmas-y, bell-like and musical. Mom and Dad agreed to her suggestion because they thought Eve was pretty and while Mom liked to argue with Grams, like a lot, Dad just could never say no to her.

"Leave that gadget behind!" she added. My 'gadget' is my gamma worn on my wrist, but Grams can never remember that it's just my school issue computer and most people never take theirs off. I need it for homework, but Grams never cared when I tried to tell her that. She just muttered something about pencils and paper and if you can't use a pencil, it's probably not real math anyway. I used to hope if I made it to 127 years old I would be a little less grumpy about missing the way things used to be. But I supposed if you could remember Christmas and homework with pencils and national forests you could walk around in without getting snatched by a sasquatch and it was all gone, it would be difficult not be a bit salty about the loss of it all. Plus, Grams used to be a mathematician and Mom said she probably missed it, but her brain just wasn't as sharp as it once was.

"It's like mush in there," Grams said once and I wondered if maybe she was right about gadgets, but what could I do. Homework must be done. I didn't remove it or leave it behind as requested because I lost things, and if I lost my gamma Mom would have a fit. But I did silence it and hoped that Grams would not even notice it sitting quietly on my wrist.

"Eve, be a dear and find me my fuzzy slipper socks," Grams asked in her soft, tired voice. Her toes were perpetually cold, and she had way too many pairs of brightly colored slipper socks, but I must admit they were really soft and warm. And I loved the way the color peeked out from her standard grey old lady sweatpants and sweater. I often thought they would be fun to wear, but the pairs Grams had were over eighty years old and I doubted they were any longer available for purchase. Anywhere. I shuffled down the hall to her

7

room and went straight for the basket beside her bed where she kept her ridiculous sock collection. Her room was a bit untidy, always clean, but little collections of things everywhere. Organized chaos she called it. She knew exactly what was in all her piles. She said a room needed to feel lived in, otherwise guests might think less of you. Mom disagreed. Wholeheartedly. She cleaned the strangest things when we were about to have company. But she tried to tidy in Grams's room once and it was pretty much a terrible disaster. You simply didn't mess with her organized chaos. Eventually, Mom decided when we were having company, she would just shut the door to Grams the Great's "eyesore of a bedroom," and make sure it remained closed.

"Here you go Grams," I said, handing her a bright red pair with green stripes. They had stood out among the beige and grey and were not difficult to find in her room.

Some of Grams' things were as old as she was, which is why I was so happy when Mom stopped messing around in her room. It left me room to explore the treasures she held in there. Under her bed was one of my favorite spots to sneak peeks. I loved to spend time in her room on a quiet day off from school, looking through her piles and listening to her stories, immersing myself in all the color of the past. She had kept so many bright and beautiful things that you simply could not find in our modern, drab world. Her old photographs were my favorite. She had real printed pictures you could hold in your hands and imagine what life had been like before you were born.

"Ahh, the Christmas ones. Perfect. I made these myself you know. Crocheted them before my fingers knotted up and became too gnarled to work properly. If I could, I would make you a pair," she said as she eyed my plain white socks. "It is already the first week of December," Grams bemoaned as she slowly bent over and struggled to slide her socks on. "See. Still spry enough to put my own socks on."

I quietly helped her pull the second one all the way up because I knew she hated it when they drooped, but it was hard for her to stretch all that way.

"How's school then?" She never got angry like Mom did about my grades and she never tried to push me to take on subjects that weren't interesting to me. Mom wanted me to go into science, but I wanted to write stories and create things. No math. No thank you! I wanted adventures and beauty! But this dreary world did not love art like it did when Grams was young. And in that moment, I had no energy to talk to Grams about how difficult school was, how much I wanted to write stories and make the world beautiful again. No one saw the value in art anymore. Grams had been a mathematician, but she had taken art classes and creative writing classes in school. She called it being well-rounded. No one cared to be well-rounded any longer.

"Grams, why do you think Santa Claus disappeared?" I asked because it was the one subject I knew would make her forget my poor math skills and even though she wasn't Mom, I still did not want to talk about school. I had asked her that question a million times before and I got a different guess every time. Some were a bit boring, he just got tired and old, or some dull thing like that. But some were wildly interesting, aliens and such, especially if Grams had snuck a bit of something out of Dad's special cabinet.

She always left him a note, I think so he would not suspect me. 'Just a swig James, cheers!' Totally off limits, that cabinet, as if I would have wanted to drink whiskey anyway, but Grams got away with anything with him. Poor Dad.

But she was tired and quiet and completely whiskey free, and not much for chatting. I considered, if only very briefly, suggesting I pour her a glass, but ultimately, I decided against it. Grams was hit and miss, you know. Could have found myself in a lot of trouble making that type of suggestion. She was humming some jingly tune and rocking in her old, comfy chair that Mom thought ruined her whole aesthetic, and she did not look like she really wanted to talk about Santa Claus or much of anything really. I spread a soft blanket over her lap because I knew she was always cold. She said when she was fifty, she was always too hot, but that was so long ago she could barely remember what it was like not to be cold. She said ancient folks like her just have poor circulation. I could remember her apartment was always roasting before she moved in with us. She would laugh and say my great grandfather would be turning over in his grave if he knew how high she kept her thermostat. Then she'd laugh some more and call him a penny-pinching old grump who could take his sweaters and sleep outside with the racoons and then her eyes would get watery and far away looking. You could always tell when she was missing him.

Grams seemed grateful for the blanket and tucked it in close around herself so no drafts could get in. "Your great grandfather was a very skilled bedmaker," she told me with a wink. "I would always get the babies ready for bed, read to them and give them their kisses and hugs, but when I was done, he would come behind telling me they were tucked in all wrong and were going to freeze in the night. Then he would tear all their covers off and remake the entire bed while they squealed and laughed, layering each blanket precisely, telling the children how it was important to properly layer everything to retain the most heat. I always thought to myself he could just give us a few extra degrees of heat, but he never did."

Whenever I started to think I had heard all Grams the Great's stories, she would share some new memory and I would be grateful. Even for simple stories like how my great grandfather used to make beds. I tried to picture my Granny as a child and Grams the Great just my mother's age, but I couldn't, even though I had seen all the pictures. They had both only ever been old in all my memories, so those pictures just did not feel real to me, just like the world had only ever been grey in my memory and Christmas did not feel real. I knew I might not ever be able to do more than imagine Grams young, but I really hoped that someday I would see a real Christmas holiday. No. Hoping was not enough. I had to believe it. I believed I would see a real Christmas, bright and there, and nothing like a faded photograph.

"Grams," I pressed again. "What was it like in 2025 when Santa Claus disappeared? When you woke up that Christmas morning, what was it like?"

Grams tucked a piece of snowy white hair behind a droopy and rather large ear and narrowed her watery green eyes at me. I could tell she was tired. "You always ask the same question my little snow angel," she said but she did not sound annoyed. "Well, let me see if I can find a new answer that will satisfy you today. You know, I was only forty-five years old when Christmas left our memories. A long, long time ago. I was still raising my children. It's all so very cloudy. We were all just so busy, and then........ Santa Claus just did not come that year. We just forgot. Our beloved Santa Claus disappeared, and the world just forgot. It was so very strange, Evie Pie, because all the people adored him, adored Christmas, and then he was gone, the holiday spirit was gone, and it all happened so quickly. We woke up expecting Christmas, but when it did not come, instead of feeling sad or curious where it had gone, instead of celebrating without Santa Claus and gifts, we just forgot. The polar ice melted overnight, and we became preoccupied with that phenomenon instead of the loss of magic. Science took over with explanations for the melting of the ice, but Santa Claus and magic were never mentioned again. Maybe it was just too difficult, too crushing for us to think about." Grams looked thoughtful and then narrowed her cloudy green eyes. "Or maybe it was something more, Eve?" Her voice dropped to a conspiratorial whisper, and she looked around as though she thought someone may be spying on us. "Maybe it was some sinister force that stole our holiday and stole the magic from the world? Maybe we've all been enchanted to forget?" she said suddenly, her eyes brightening as though she had just realized something she had not thought of before.

That was new. A sinister force robbing the world of holidays and magic? An enchantment, and not aliens, or a retirement, or death from old age?

"Grams," I breathed, excited for this new bit of information, "Grams, what kind of sinister force? And if that's true, why do you remember?" My heart was beating rather quickly now. An enchantment would explain why, whenever I tried to speak of Christmas to anyone but Grams the Great, they simply could not focus on the story I was weaving for them, and within seconds it was as though I had never mentioned Santa Claus.

"Well, my darling Christmas Eve, you know I've completely lost my mind," she said with a casual shrug as though that would explain everything.

"Grams, what if Santa Claus was kidnapped?" I proposed then. I wanted to keep her talking, keep her going on this new idea. "You always talk like he left, disappeared, but what if it was not his choice?"

"Why my little Evie Pie, look at your imagination running away with you. Do you see what happens when you put your gadgets down!" I rolled my eyes because if Grams knew how much more reliant on 'gadgets' my classmates were than I was, she would have been so impressed with me. "Kidnapped? I had not thought of that before," she said tapping a gnarled finger against her chin.

"Well, something happened to him! I really don't think he just one day died of old age after hundreds and hundreds of years of magical existence!" I said in exasperation.

Santa Claus's disappearance was a mystery I had been pondering since Grams moved into this house and began telling me all the stories. It drove Mom bananas, as she thought I really needed to focus on school and things that mattered. But magic mattered. Santa Claus mattered. Math......well......I suppose I could see its importance, but look, it was just not my cup of tea.

"And Grams, if he did die, or just decided to retire, why has the world forgotten him and forgotten Christmas and magic so completely?"

13

"Evie pie, I have no idea what happened to him and since I'm 127 years old it will be a miracle if I live to find out."

Grams. Grams. Why did she always have to point out to me that her time was short? I never really wanted to think about that. To me, she was the only magic left in a dull, dreary world. Or at least, the only one who remembered that magic once existed. I wanted her to live forever.

Then I had a thought. "What if we could bring it back, Grams?" I whispered, almost afraid of the thought, afraid to hope, but thinking that when Grams did finally have to go, because that is the way the world works, if there was some other magic in the world it might be more bearable. "What if we could bring magic and Santa Claus and Christmas back to the world?"

Grams the Great narrowed her rheumy eyes, once brightly green like a Christmas tree, but now faded with age. She leaned in close to me. "Well, my darling candied apple, I think you are just young enough to try it."

I smiled. A real smile, even though I was suddenly overcome by a nervous, wiggly feeling. Grams the Great was the only person I knew who believed kids could do more than adults. She said a magical maker of movies made her believe this when she was a child, that children were far more suited for adventure and daring than any grownups ever were. I began working up the beginnings of my own adventure. I began to think that I, a scrawny twelve-year-old girl, might just be daring enough, brave enough, wild enough, to actually have a magical adventure. And I told Grams this. Her eyes narrowed again, and she looked very, very thoughtful.

Finally, after a long time, she spoke. "My little Evie Pie, my little cool breeze, you are fierce and brave. You are daring and wild, courageous and spirited. But you must be more than a breeze to take on the kind of adventure you are speaking about. You must be a storm. A bluster. A blizzard. A real winter fury. You must be a force so strong that the magic cannot help but make its way to you. More importantly, you must believe, believe that Santa Claus and all his magic is real and if you believe hard enough, then maybe, just maybe, you will get your adventure."

Natalie Blackwood

I took what Grams the Great said to heart. I spent my days believing. I believed so hard sometimes I thought I heard bells, hints of music in the air. I believed so hard I felt snow in my lashes. I believed so hard, but nothing happened. I stared at myself in the mirror measuring my skinny frame, my dark eyes, my brown skin, my thick curls. I did not look like a storm. I looked more like a bedraggled kid who had been caught in a storm. I did not look like the kind of kid who could save anything. But Grams had always told me it was the inside that counted most. It was the outcasts, the underdogs, the 'no one would have ever suspected' kids, who pulled off the most derring-do in all the old movies I had watched with Grams from her youth and in all the old books she had given me to read. Could I believe big enough, could I be strong enough and brave enough? Could I do what it would take to bring Christmas back to the world?

I spent my time at home researching, combing through archives, coming up with new search terms, but I found nothing. It was like the net was wiped clean of Christmas. Reindeer would pop up - extinct nearly 20 years, once inhabited the arctic tundra, ate moss, leaves, and fungi, related to deer who do still roam the warmer forests. They were not known fliers. Narrowing my search to flying reindeer yielded nothing. Enchanted reindeer. Nothing. Santa Claus and reindeer. Nothing. I tried a million different phrases and search terms. Nothing. There was simply no information available on magical, flying, Christmas reindeer. When the image of the extinct reindeer floated up from my gamma I would imagine them in flight, and it was beautiful. I pictured their full winter coats, whites, tans and greys, flowing about their necks in the wind. I pictured silver bell harnesses that sang through night skies. I could hear their snorts and see their hot breath misting about them. Thanks to technology, I could see an extinct reindeer standing right in front of me, but I had to use my imagination for the rest, and I think Grams the Great would have been proud of the images I worked up of flying Christmas reindeer pulling a brilliant red sleigh full of toys.

It was the same with elves. Mythical beings, forest dwellers, but elves and toymaking? Not a thing. Spirits, capricious, elusive sprites in human form but smaller and with pointed ears. Related to fairies and leprechauns, but not real, just mythological troublemakers. They popped up in stories, books, and various mythologies from different cultures around the world. But I could find no mention of toys, toymaking, or Santa Claus in any elf literature I had been able to find.

All this research and I had found nothing. As I was doodling pictures of elves the way I pictured them at the North Pole, of reindeer pulling a sleigh across the moon, it occurred to me that no adventure story Grams had told me about ever started with research. There was, of course, always a smart kid, whose genius abilities would inevitably save the day, but the adventures always began with leaving home, embarking on some journey, with no adults. Just kids and guts and an adventure.

I tried to find flights to the North Pole, or at least close to where it once was. I thought if I could get there somehow, maybe I could simply look about and find Santa Claus. I know that sounds ridiculous, but that's how so many adventure stories began, with just a child having a look about. But the North Pole had melted into the sea over eighty years ago. Could I just hop on a boat? What ship captain was going to let a twelve-year-old hoping to discover a magical saint just hop on their vessel and sail?

I think before the melting of the ice, the North Pole was difficult to get to, but people went, they explored. Grams the Great said no one ever found Santa Claus's home, but she also said the people who went to the North Pole were never really looking for him. They tended to be scientists interested in studying the arctic, not magic. Folks blamed global warming for the disappearance of the ice and I'm sure that didn't help. But what if Santa Claus kept the ice alive? No one lived there, at least no known people. It was too harsh, the ice moved too much. These were the types of things I could research. Arctic facts. The ice was barren, it was dark from October through March with the darkest part of the year falling in December. Can you imagine, no sunlight all winter? I pictured Santa Claus's village covered in darkness and it did not feel right, but then I remembered Grams' stories about Christmas lights, and I pictured an entire village lit up by twinkling, starry lights and that felt perfect. I made myself believe in that sparkling Christmas village. I absolutely believed I would see it one day. Grams had said it was important to believe, it was the most important thing.

There was a documentary about the Arctic Circle and all the strange things that had happened there. Grams the Great and I watched every episode until Mom found out. We were both in trouble then. Mom thought all that mystery and death was too frightening for an eight-year-old. I was not scared. Only fascinated. And now I am wondering if the sinister force Grams mentioned might have something to do with the strange disappearances, sinking ships, crashed helicopters and other tragedies. People had eventually begun to steer clear of the Arctic Circle, but somehow, I had to figure out how to get there. I thought if I could make it somewhere at least close to the North Pole I might be able to find some answers. I found myself wishing Grams was just a bit less old and crazy so she could just take me. Of course, we would have had to take Dad's auto, because Mom, well.......it was always better to upset Dad than Mom.

I was packing my school bag for the day when I heard Mom begin to shout. "Let's go, up and out, you'll miss your transport! Today's the day, Eve!"

I sighed. School. Math test today, but Mom liked to remind me that every day was 'the day.' I'd have to sit next to Natalie again and hopefully she would keep her arm down so I could glance at her screen, as usual. Nat is my cousin and she's absolutely brilliant. She was the smart kid I planned to bring on my adventure. Unlike me, she did inherit Grams the Great's mathematical genius and every other genius ability as well. With a little luck, and a little help from my very generous cousin, I hoped to pass sixth grade math. I yelled down the hall to Mom that I was coming, so she would not lose her mind in a fit of rage about my lack of responsibility, about my inability to seize the opportunities that had been granted me, and I hustled to the front door. I tried to paint my face with eagerness for Mom, tried to look excited for school and the opportunities Ad Prima Academy was providing for me. She probably wasn't fooled, but at least she did not begin to lecture me that morning, and she did tell me she loved me and that I was going to ace that math test. Poor Mom. She was dead wrong.

Natalie was on the transport already and she had saved me a seat. She was munching on some delicious looking something or other and my mouth began to water when I saw it. Her dad, Mom's brother, was an absolute genius in the kitchen. Family gatherings were always at his house because he liked to do the cooking for all of us. My grouchy Mom who could not cook and her easy-going brother who made his living cooking (he had a real show on the net and several bestselling cookbooks) were such opposites. The biggest mystery was how Nat became such a genius though. Uncle P.J. had developed his cooking skills when he realized school was not for him and he had become something of a celebrity. Natalie's mother had skipped town, left when she was a baby, and Nat doesn't know much about her. From what I've heard, she married Uncle P.J. for his fame and money, but was not cut out for motherhood. It was whispered she was as dumb as a post but really pretty. It was also whispered that when she left, he gave her everything she asked for as long as he could keep Nat. She had agreed and no one ever saw or heard from her again. So, Mom stepped in to be a mother figure to Nat as well. And Uncle P.J. thought Mom put way too much pressure on both of us to be successful. But Uncle P.J., Mom, and Dad were solid adults, and Nat and I were always loved and cared for. Which was why I did feel kind of bad about the adventure I intended to rope Nat into. It had the potential to be dangerous, and I did not want to see any of them worried.

I plopped myself down next to her as the transport lifted off and happily took the still warm pastry she offered. Sometimes I think Mom forgot that a proper meal would only help me achieve my educational goals throughout the day. Uncle P.J. always sent Nat with extra, though. He said the processed junk in Mom's cabinets was no kind of breakfast for a growing girl. We did have a lot of food in wrappers, quick, easy, but never delicious. Uncle P.J. called himself a pioneer, bringing back the old foods, real food, with real nutrients, instead of all this easy food the modern folk had become accustomed to. He created an entire real food movement and had gotten quite rich doing it. I pictured him whipping up a festive Christmas dinner, and I wondered if I avoided the word Christmas and tried to explain to him what I was envisioning....... roasted chestnuts, cream pies, a giant turkey or a prime rib and mashed potatoes and sweet potatoes on one plate.........maybe he would be able to put it together and I could call it Christmas dinner just to myself. Or maybe, if I could bring Christmas back, I wouldn't have to be sneaky to get Uncle P.J. to make our holiday meal.

"Nat, we have to talk," I said, wiping a bit of fruit compote from the side of my mouth. She eyed my sleeve where a trace of raspberry red lingered, standing out brightly against the muted grey of my uniform and she rolled her eyes. I ignored her. I had more important things to talk to her about than the lack of care I took about my personal appearance. "Christmas, Nat. I am going to bring it back."

She gave me that blank look everyone gave me when I spoke of Christmas. "Nat, we have talked about Christmas before," I sighed. "Santa Claus, reindeer, presents, elves, snow....... come on Nat!" I was filled with exasperation. I was excited for my adventure, but every adventurer needed companions. I needed Natalie to be by my side. The smart one, the responsible one, the voice of reason. I think I was actually counting on her to keep us alive.

She rolled her eyes. "Oh, are you going on about that silly old myth of Grams' again? Eve, did you study for the math test?"

I put my hands on her shoulders and gave her a rough shake, just to get her to pay attention, just to shake some of the enchantment off her (because at this point, I was beginning to believe an enchantment was the only explanation). "Natalie!" Her beaded blondish braids clacked as I shook her, and I hoped I had not been too rough. "I need you to listen to me. Christmas is real. Santa Claus is real. And I need you to help me bring him back. Please!"

Her eyes focused on mine, and she started to nod. I thought for a second, I had gotten through to her, after years of trying. But then she put her head down and started muttering about studying for her math test. Ugh! Plan B.

"Nat," I said casually. "I've been thinking." She looked up warily from her math book and I had to stop myself from rolling my eyes. She is literally a genius and has been able to do the stuff she's studying since second grade. "Remember that documentary about the mystery of the north, all those people that disappeared, the melting icebergs?" I asked her, remembering she had caught a few episodes with Grams and me. She nodded and so I continued. "What if we could solve the mystery?"

"How could two twelve-year-olds solve a mystery that adults have been unsuccessfully trying to solve for over eighty years?" Her tone was perplexed but not annoyed and I began to feel hopeful that I could convince her. Maybe.

"Don't you remember what Grams the Great said about grownups? They have no sense of adventure. They've lost the ability to think outside the box. A mystery like this needs young people! Plus, you big dummy, you're a genius. You've never met a puzzle you couldn't solve." Flattery was at least one tool I had up my sleeve. Nat was modest, but she did love to be smartest person in the room, even if no one knew it but her and I.

"Eve, Grams the Great IS a grown-up," she replied, ignoring my comments about her being a genius. Flattery was failing me then.

"Not really," I argued. "She's too old to be a grown-up."

"That makes absolutely no sense, Eve. Besides, Grams is crazy."

"Precisely!" I replied.

"Why?" Nat asked, deciding to stop arguing about Grams and get to the point. I had known she would get there eventually, wanting to know the reason behind my curiosity, my desire to solve this particular mystery. Yet, I was still not prepared with any kind of answer. Telling her I wanted to find Santa Claus and bring back Christmas would not be the way to convince her.

"Don't you want to know?" I said trying to put magic and intrigue into my voice, trying to make her feel the urgency I was feeling to find Santa Claus even if she was too enchanted to understand my urgency had nothing to do with the Arctic Circle mysteries.

Nat shrugged but I thought I could see some kind of shimmer in her eyes. "C'mon. It will be an adventure. It will be fun. You and I can solve this mystery, prove that you're a genius to the world, and maybe my mom will stop pressuring us to take our lives more seriously. Maybe we could even take a trip, a vacation. Wouldn't your dad love a vacation to Scandinavia?"

Nat rolled her bright green eyes at me. Again. I did not like that this was becoming a habit. It was not usually this difficult to talk her into one of my adventures, but researching the Arctic Circle must not have sounded that appealing to her. She flipped her perfectly plaited hair over her shoulder. She was pretty, like her mother must have been, but never tried to show it off. She was always tidy, but never flashy, and kept quiet, in the background, like she was trying her best to go unnoticed. Most of the kids at our school had no idea how absolutely, insanely smart she was. Not even all the teachers had figured her out.

I was waiting for her to agree to my plan, I really could usually talk her into to anything, but she narrowed those green eyes at me, Uncle P.J.'s eyes,

Grams the Great's eyes, and she did not even try to let me down gently. "You are crazy, Eve. I have way too much to do to be working on an unsolvable and completely unimportant mystery right now. And no, to answer your question, I do not think Dad would want to take a vacation to Scandinavia of all places!"

I was crushed. Not only was she not in agreement with my plan, but her tone towards me was not one I was used to. I could only hope she had not grown tired of my antics.

I glanced over at a boy I had not seen before, feeling eyes on me, and wondered if he had heard me begging my cousin to do ridiculous things, because that is how it would have sounded to anyone around us. I had not noticed him sitting across the aisle from us and I felt my cheeks warm a little at the idea that this kid was probably thinking I was a whacko. We made eye contact, but both looked away quickly, each pretending not to have noticed the other. A new kid. Ad Prima Academy was a small school and new kids stood out. He was tall and lanky, with dark skin and short, closely cropped hair. I noticed the other kids on the transport were staring openly at him as we whipped through the gloomy fog and clouds on our way to school, so I made a point not to look at him again at all for the rest of the trip to school. I had been the kid getting those stares and I refused to join that party. Besides, I thought as I slunk down in my seat and crossed my arms over my chest, I had some planning to do and maybe a little sulking. Natalie was not making this easy on me.

"You know," Natalie said, interrupting my sulking and planning, "Auntie Celine is not wrong. If we don't take our education seriously, where will we end up?"

"Oh, I don't know, maybe rich and famous like Uncle P.J. with our own cooking show," I said sarcastically and a little cross that she had taken my mother's view of things.

"Eve. You cannot cook. At all."

"Not the point," I say.

The new kid on the bus followed Natalie and I into our homeroom. Perfect. The new guy, who had a very good idea of just how very strange I was, had my same schedule. I hoped he was not one of those guys who enjoyed getting laughs at the expense of others because the ammunition he had against me would ruin me at Ad Prima. Not that I had not done a decent job already of creating my very own ruin, but I wasn't trying to add fuel to the fire. Magic, myths, solving arctic mysteries. It wouldn't sound good. Kids filed in and we all took our seats. Natalie insisted on being right up front, even in home room, every day, because she did not want to miss anything. Ever. I sat with her, right up front, every day, because she was my best friend, and it was a solid show of support. Plus, she took scrupulous notes in every class that she always later shared with me. So even though I would much rather have placed myself in the very back row where the new kid tried to disappear to, I parked myself next to Nat in row one. She shared notes, I provided moral support. It was a reciprocal relationship.

Ms. Snow made her way to the front of the classroom. Her red hair was swept into a French twist with a few bright curls escaping to frame her tiny, rather elf-like face. She wore vintage cat eye glasses attached to a chain that swooped across her brown cheeks. She was dressed in the grey uniform all the teachers wore, a suit jacket with the Ad Prima Academy logo on the left sleeve, a grey button up, and grey trousers. The teachers wore all grey all the time and most did not add anything to their uniform, but Ms. Snow often added a pop of color that earned her strange looks from the other staff. A swipe of lipstick, a bright ring, that day she wore round green earrings that made me think of tiny Christmas ornaments. She looked like a vintage librarian from Grams the Great's days, which was perfect because, in addition to being our advisory professor, she was the school librarian. She was very strict in the classroom, just as all our professors were required to be, but it was in the library that I came to know and love Ms. Snow.

The head librarian at Ad Prima Academy had cultivated a collection in this school that no other schools had. She was an absolute legend. She knew I loved to read and research, and I had gotten more beautifully bound books, all adventure stories, lore, mythology and art, than I ever would have gotten at any other school. Point for Mom, who had researched every school in the city before settling on the highly acclaimed Ad Prima Academy. It literally meant 'most excellent', and I know Mom just imagined Nat and I would excel beyond her wildest dreams, be the very first, the tops of our class, and be set for life. Nat had not disappointed her, but I was far from the most excellent. However, I thanked Mom frequently when I walked into the library and Ms. Snow was there, with no judgement about my math skills or my lackluster grades in science or even the mediocre grade I had in history despite loving it because Mr. Michaels had surprised us with a pop quiz, and I had not gotten around to the reading quite yet. I would get that grade back up. Science was another story. Ms. Snow, as my advisory professor would often talk to me about a plan to keep my grades strong, but in the library, she would never say a word about my grades. In fact, I think her green eyes actually twinkled a bit when I walked into the library. Sometimes she had a book already picked out for me. Fairytales, biographies on artists from the past with bright pictures of their famous works, or adventure stories for me to get lost in. I adored her for that.

Ms. Snow cleared her throat to call the classroom to order. Her voice was soft, barely above a whisper, another reason she belonged in the library, but somehow, she managed to command the respect of every unruly sixth grader in the room. I was never sure how she accomplished this.

"Good morning students," she began. "I trust you have all had a restful weekend and are ready to learn?" She peered at us over the rims of her glasses with a strict, no-nonsense look, and we all nodded our obedience. "Excellent. Well, before we go over the announcements, I would like to introduce you to our newest student."

I could hear him sliding down in his chair without even looking at him. Poor, tall kid, he had nowhere to hide, and I did not envy him as every head swiveled to look towards the back of the classroom to see the new student they had already earlier tried to assess on the sly. Ms. Snow's introduction had given them permission to blatantly stare. I remained facing forward. One less set of eyes on the poor guy. Hopefully he would remember my kindness later and choose not to share what he had surely overheard on the transport on the way to school when I thought only my cousin was listening.

"Students, this is Desmond Carter. He has just moved here from out of the country. I hope you will all make him feel welcome at Ad Prima Academy," she said and quickly moved on. Ms. Snow was like that. No reason to go on and on. She would let Desmond share what he wanted to share, with who he wanted to share it, when he wanted to share it. We knew his name, he had been recognized and not ignored, and now she would attend to business. Ms. Snow went over school announcements, and I quit paying attention and began to think about how I was going to rope Nat into helping me bring back Christmas.

I imagined trying to take on this adventure without Natalie. We had been born just three months apart. I was older, but it had never really felt that way, her always acting more grown than me. Mom and Uncle P.J., who were polar opposites, bickered and swiped at each other with sarcastic comments, but they were also close. Which meant Nat and I were close. We were more like sisters than cousins. I never did anything without her, and that was going to have to include saving Christmas and Santa Claus. But the fact that she could not even begin to grasp what I was talking about when I mentioned the lost holiday was making it all extraordinarily difficult.

The school day crawled by as I struggled to focus on anything school related, my mind on Christmas and getting through to Nat. The math test went horribly, like, really horribly. I dreaded what Mom was going to say. I was pretty sure I had at least not failed, but Dr. Ramos seemed to have figured out that I might be

29

looking at Nat's answers on test days as he had moved us several desks away from each other. I glared at the back of his balding head in frustration, wishing him coal in his non-existent stocking with all my might, but there was nothing I could do but plow forward and try to focus on the numbers that swam on the screen in front of me. I smiled sweetly at Dr. Ramos when the exam was over, hoping to inspire some kind of sympathy in the man, but he was a numbers guy. Almost zero emotion from him ever. And so, inwardly, I continued to wish coal for him.

I walked out of math class crossing my fingers and hoping for at least a pass and made my way to science, another class I was barely making it through. I slumped down in my seat, front row, right next to Nat. She gave me an encouraging smile as she asked after the math test, even though I'm sure she already knew the answer. I just shook my head, and her face was full of sympathy, but no judgement. That's why I loved her. She read my stories and adored them. She had my sketches and paintings hanging on the wall of her room. She was not the least bit worried about my lack of prospects for the future. She was good at everything math and science, but the arts were mine and she made me feel good about it, even sometimes like she was jealous of my abilities. She knew my mom would be furious with me, though, and the look on her face now was just one of love and support. I was dead when this grade loaded into the school data base and Mom got the update. Dead. But at least I had the world's best best friend.

Dr. Osman, the science professor was rambling on and on and I was not really paying attention, obviously thinking about Santa Claus, when suddenly she said something that brought me back into the classroom. I was on high alert.

"You will be working in groups for this project. Each group will choose a region of the world to report on. Your reports should include the geography, climate, biodiversity, and human life and its impact on the region. You are, of course, free to add other items of interest to the region you choose for extra credit on this project."

I was sitting straight as a board now. Nat and I had already looked at each other and whispered 'partners.' We were always partners for group projects. Before she could say anything else, I threw my hand in the air and waved it wildly just to be sure Dr. Osman would notice me.

Dr. Osman gave me strange look. I was not the type of student to shoot a hand in the air in excitement, at least not in science class. "Yes, Eve," she said with some measure of curiosity and maybe trepidation in her voice. She likely assumed I was raising my hand to voice some complaint about the project, but I was about to prove her wrong. This was the most perfect coincidence in the history of coincidences, and I was going to capitalize on it.

"Nat and I will take the Arctic Circle," I said hurriedly. Though I was fairly certain it was not a region anyone else would be salivating over, I was not going to take any chances. This opportunity had just dropped itself in my lap and today I was going to follow the advice of my mother and seize it. I added a quick 'please' because at Ad Prima Academy, manners were a must, and I avoided looking directly at Nat so she would have no chance to argue. I heard her sigh next to me, but she voiced no complaint.

Dr. Osman's dark eyebrows shot up in surprise at my excitement and enthusiasm. "An interesting choice, Eve," she said. "And since you so rarely show any enthusiasm in this class, I'll approve your request." She looked at Nat for confirmation and my cousin shrugged her shoulders and nodded, looking resigned to her fate. "I would like you all to work in groups of three, however. Is there another student who would like to join Eve and Natalie on the Arctic Circle?" Oh no. Dr. Osman had completely burst my excited bubble with that offer to my classmates, and I crossed my fingers and hoped there would be no takers.

I inwardly cursed Nat and her insistence on the front row because there was no way for me to see what kind of trouble was stirring behind me. I stubbornly refused to let these other students know I cared, and I did not turn around to see who may be volunteering to work with us. I saw Dr. Osman's eyes look towards the back of the room and smile. I did not have time to deal with a third wheel on this project and I dreaded who might be trying to join our group. There were plenty of morons at our school who would jump at the chance to be in a group with Natalie. They may not realize the level of her genius, they may think I was odd, but everyone knew Nat always got top marks and there were always kids who would be willing to deal with us if it meant doing little work and still getting that good grade. It was all I could do to remain facing forward, maintaining my attitude of nonchalance.

"Excellent, Desmond," Dr. Osman said. "Girls, I trust you will do a good job of acquainting Desmond with our research library as he is new to the school."

I groaned quietly to myself. The new kid was a wild card. I had no idea what we were getting into with him, and all I could do was hope for the best. Maybe I could pawn enough work off on him that I could focus on what was most important – finding Santa Claus. Maybe he had not heard how crazy I had sounded on the transport after all. Maybe he had a genuine interest in the Arctic Circle. Or maybe he had just already heard that Nat would most definitely guarantee him top marks on his first assigned project at Ad Prima Academy. Either way, a third person in our group was a complication I did not want to deal with.

Desmond Carter

We had claimed a quiet corner of the science classroom to collaborate and 'brainstorm' as Dr. Osman called it. Other groups of three were gathered around the room as well and there was the low rumble of chatter as students began planning for this newly assigned project that would ultimately be a huge part of our grade. I was feeling hopeful that this assignment could accomplish multiple things for me, the first being to help me solve the mystery of a certain missing magical saint, but I certainly would not complain if it also helped boost my rather sorry science grade. I was also excited that this project would earn us extra time in the library. I loved being in the library more than any other place in this school and while I was never the best at compiling it all at the end, my research skills were top notch. I would not even need to count on Nat entirely to make this project a good one.

However, as we both stared at this possibly unwelcome presence in our midst, I began to grow nervous. Desmond Carter. While the other groups had started planning, the three of us were sitting there awkwardly. I eyed him suspiciously. He was very tall, athletic looking, and, I noticed, rather handsome now that I allowed myself to actually look at him. I could tell in a few short weeks he would be a part of the cool kid group. He had that air about him. I eyed him suspiciously trying to figure out his angle. Why on earth had he volunteered to work with Nat and me? I mean, she was a nerdy kid with her nose always in a book, whose gorgeous features no one had bothered yet to notice, and I was......well......me. And being me had not done me any favors at Ad Prima Academy. I supposed he would figure all of that out soon enough and this would be the last group project where he'd throw his hat in with us. I just wished he had figured all of that out before the most important project of my life had been assigned.

I was silently attempting to measure this stranger, figure him out, when Natalie, who was not about to let her grade go up in smoke because we had to work with the new kid, broke the tension.

"So......the Arctic Circle.....should we start with what we already know? The Arctic Circle is located approximately 66.5 degrees north of the equator," she began, and I settled myself in for a solid geography lesson. "The exact degrees do vary depending on the Earth's axial tilt. It covers roughly 5.5 million square miles, which is a little less than 3% of the Earth's surface area. At the center of the Arctic Circle lies the North Pole. Unlike the South Pole, located on land, the North Pole sits in the middle of the ocean. It was once a solid mass of floating ice, which hosted life such as polar bears, arctic foxes, and reindeer, all now extinct. The ice disappeared mysteriously overnight in the year 2025. Scientists hypothesize that the ice melted due to global warming, though there has been some who argue against this as it happened really rather quickly." Nat had my full attention. The North Pole, home to Santa Claus and extinct reindeer, and some rogue scientists who questioned the global warming theory were exactly where I wanted to focus this report. She was already diving into the mystery of it all.

Nat went on. "Within the Arctic Circle are the Arctic Ocean basin and the northern parts of Scandinavia, Russia, Canada, and Alaska, which, as I hope you know," she eyed me as she said this, "is a part of the United States." Thanks Nat. I narrowed my eyes at her. Just because I was forever mixing up numerators and denominators didn't mean I didn't know my fifty states. "I'm thinking," she said, "that for the extra credit piece we can look into the disappearance of the ice masses at the North Pole and cover some of the extinct species." Perfect, Nat. I would not even have to convince her to work on exactly what I needed her to be working on! And she was helping me get that science grade up! "For the rest, I say we each research a different land region that the circle encompasses, I can take on two if needed, and then bring it together by comparing similarities and differences. Thoughts?"

"Wow," Desmond said, looking, to his credit, very impressed with my cousin. "You already knew all of that?"

The color rose to Nat's dusky cheeks, and I wanted to shout that I was sure there was more she already knew but was just holding back, but I knew it would only embarrass her more. So instead, I volunteered to research Scandinavia, thinking it might have the most information on Santa Claus, based off previous research and reading I had done. But our third wheel foiled my plans.

"Can I?" he almost whispered. I had not expected shyness from him. "It's just that…. well…….I just………" he was stuttering and clearly uncomfortable. "I would love to take Scandinavia," he then stated clearly. "But we could break up the Scandinavian countries a bit if you wanted. There's Greenland, Finland, Denmark, Norway, Sweden, Iceland……. I mean, I'll do them all if you want, but I just…." he trailed off, his confidence wavering again.

I looked hard at him. Why did he know so much about Scandinavia? If I had not been researching it for years, trying to find information on Santa Claus, reading all the books Ms. Snow had helped me find in the library, I would not have known any of those things. Was Desmond another super genius like Natalie, or just another kid like me with an unnatural interest in the Arctic Circle?

I thought about if for a moment. I had been researching this area for years and turned up nothing. Maybe he would find something I had not. But I had overlooked other countries like Russia and Canada, and the state of Alaska. Maybe it was time for me to see if I had missed something. "It's fine," I said. You can take Scandinavia. I'll work on Russia. Nat, you good with Canada and Alaska?" Nat nodded and Desmond looked relieved.

"Also, for the extra credit part," Desmond began tentatively. "Well, there have been other mysteries in addition to the sudden disappearance of the polar ice. People disappearing, for example. I would like to research that as well. I mean, I'll do all the other research first, but if there's time, I would like to add that, if the two of you don't mind?" His English was accented, but just barely so and I remembered Ms. Snow had said he had moved here from out of the country. But the accent was so imperceptible, I could not even begin to place it, and I was still feeling too stubborn to show any interest in this person and ask where he had moved from.

Also, in the face of what he had just said, his slight accent was the last thing I cared about. I was blown away. He knew about the Arctic Circle disappearances? Or had he just been spying on Nat and me, and was now trying to impress us? I could not figure this kid out, and I just hoped he would not ruin this project for me. Either way, things had worked out for me today, and since I was now working on 'believing' as Grams the Great had instructed me to do, I was going to chalk this all up to Christmas magic. I could call it a coincidence, but, and I even whispered the words out loud to myself, I believed.

I would leave my judgement for Desmond Carter's character to another time. I had a holiday to save and as long as he did not get in my way, it would all be fine.

Ms. Snow

Ad Prima Academy valued its library and thought each and every student should be encouraged to make full use of its vast collection. Therefore, each grade had a dedicated hour to spend in the library every day for study and research purposes. Of course, access to these resource materials had been a key selling point for my mother, even though she had found the use of archaic bound books and bright décor frivolous. Luckily for me, Ms. Snow's digital collections were also extensive. Sixth grade's library hour was seventh period, the last of the day. I made it through English and history with some measure of attention paid to the lectures, and then I made my way to Ms. Snow's haven. Desmond, Nat and I agreed we would use our library hour today to begin our research process and I wondered if Desmond had toured the whole school yet, or if I was going to get to see his first reaction to the wonder our librarian had created within our otherwise drab school. The school was grey and dark like most other buildings in the city of Spokane, like most of the world had become since Santa Claus left us. Dark hallways, drab classrooms, furnishings and décor were sparse and utilitarian, it was as though they wanted to stomp any happiness out of every child when they designed this dungeon of a school. Yet, somehow, Ms. Snow had gotten away with creating a brightly lit and beautifully decorated oasis amid the drab.

And when we walked into the library, it was very clear Desmond had not had the full tour. I had led the way to the library, and I turned to watch his face as he entered.

"Welcome to Ad Prima Academy's renowned library," I said, and I watched happily as his eyes widened. His appreciation for the library was a good sign. Maybe he would turn out to be an okay guy.

The first thing I noticed every time I walked into Ms. Snow's library was the smell. A book has a certain smell, especially an old book. Most people store all their books in their net accounts, digital copies of everything, and most of their books were works of non-fiction. But the amazing Ms. Snow had shelves full of old bound books. We could use the Ad Prima Academy Library's net account to borrow any number of books and other proprietary material not found for free on the net, but there was something special about those old bound books. I liked to feel the weight of them in my hands, I liked the feel of dusty paper between my fingers, the rustle as pages turned. Mostly though, I loved the smell, like trees salted with dust and time and that smell washed warmly over you the moment you crossed the threshold into Ms. Snow's domain. I really believed the students of Ad Prima Academy had a taste of Christmas joy, for just an hour, when they were in that library.

Desmond, I don't think, noticed the smell, so much as he noticed the colors. Old books from floor to ceiling in every color you could imagine. Ms. Snow said once she had considered organizing them by color but that was not how Dewey Decimal, whoever he was, would have wanted it and so they were properly organized by genres and authors' last names and the effect was a color splash of patterns and words that felt even brighter after leaving the drudgery of Ad Prima's hallways. I watched Desmond's eyes sweep across the room taking it all in. The tables with data ports to sync with were tucked neatly into a corner and Ms. Snow had added live potted plants to make them feel less out of place in this ode to the vintage and the whimsical. The walls were painted a rich, deep green, though I have no idea how she managed to convince anyone to let her do that. Rich leather chairs and couches filled the space giving students comfortable places to enjoy their books. There was even a fireplace on the far wall, though we were never allowed a real fire. But it was my favorite spot to be. I would sit with a book in the oversized leather chair that sat next to it and imagine a crackling fire with chestnuts roasting and read away my whole library hour. Fiction. Adventure. Folklore. Art. Mythology. As much as I could get my hands on. Today, though, we had business to attend to and I turned my gaze wistfully away from the picturesque fireplace and cozy chairs. I needed to find as much information on the Arctic Circle as I could in that hour.

"This is wild," Desmond whispered.

"Isn't it," Nat said, and she looked proud of our little school.

"I don't know how Ms. Snow gets away with half the things she gets away with in here," I said, "but it is my absolute favorite place in this entire school. In fact, it is my favorite place period," I added a bit dreamily. Then I felt my face get a little warm as I realized I was being very sappy and dramatic. "Let's start researching," I said switching to my most serious voice and hoping Desmond had not noticed my show of whimsical abandon.

Desmond went straight to the data ports. Go figure. But oh well. There would be plenty of solid information on Scandinavia there and probably on the rapid melting of the polar ice as well. Natalie followed him, which, I was not surprised by. It's where she, and most of the kids in the school, always went to first.

It was always the younger kids that liked the physical books. Ms. Snow had a collection of beautiful children's books with glossy, colorful pictures that the younger grades would flock to. She had a special section of the library with carpets and cushions and cute stuffed animals, and I could remember loving that corner when I first started at Ad Prima Academy. In fact, it was my first introduction to a vintage book and that is where the love affair began, I guess.

When we got older, kids started to laugh at the younger kids with their picture books and stuffed animals, but I never did. I hoped at least a few would be inspired like I was by Ms. Snow. It made me sad to think that all the books she had collected would sit on lonely shelves, unloved, unread, and forgotten. I had six more years after sixth grade before I graduated from Ad Prima Academy, and I promised myself I would read as many of her books as I could in that time. To read them all would take a lifetime, and I wondered if Ms. Snow herself had even read them all. One would have to be an immortal saint like Santa Claus to have the time for that.

While my project partners went to the data ports, I went to Ms. Snow. At the ports you could plug in and simply speak your search terms, but Ms. Snow had a sense for her books. Search terms were narrow, search terms missed nuances, search terms were literal, and of course search terms would never help you find what you weren't exactly sure you were looking for. I heard Nat explaining to Desmond as I walked away from the two of them that Ms. Snow and I had a special relationship, and he shouldn't worry about my research capabilities. I smiled when she told him I knew my way around our library better than anyone. That's what you call a best friend.

Ms. Snow had her nose in a beautiful leatherbound book looking lost to the world. I knew she would look up over the tops of the pages to see who needed her before it would even become necessary to clear my throat so she would know I was there. She, just like I would have done, would read as many words as she could squeeze in before she was interrupted. I only felt a little bit bad taking her away from her story. Helping students in the library was her job, after all, and this was of the utmost importance. I also knew she spent at least an hour every day after school alone in the library and I can only assume she was reading. I wondered if her life at home was too chaotic for reading, like mine sometimes was, or if she just appreciated the ambience she had created in the library so much that it kept her longer at what was supposed to be her workplace.

"Eve," she said peering over the top of her spectacles and her book to look at me with a bright smile on her face. "What is it we are looking for today?"

As she slid an old worn bookmark into her book and closed its pages, I told her about our science project, explaining that I needed to research the part of Russia that fell within the Arctic Circle and the extinct animals that had once lived on the North Pole's ice and within the cold regions of the Arctic Circle. She was rattling off sections to visit and pointing me in the right direction without even looking anything up and I was paying attention, ready to head to those sections of the library, but then a new thought struck me. The net had been wiped clean of everything Christmas, but Ms. Snow's library was full of old, like really old, some older even than Grams the Great, printed books. Then a second thing occurred to me, and I wondered how I had not thought of it before. Ms. Snow was a walking book catalog.

"Also, I would like to know where to find your books about Christmas," I blurted out, fingers crossed and breath held, waiting anxiously for the disappointment I was sure would come.

"Check the children's section first. Then try the author Charles Dickens," she immediately said and then she looked at me strangely and her eyes got that glazed look. The enchantment. But somehow, briefly, Ms. Snow had remembered. Goosebumps. For years I had been searching the net and all that time what I needed was right here in my favorite spot in the whole world. I wanted to smack myself for my own stupidity and short sightedness.

"I'm sorry, Eve," Ms. Snow said in a dreamy voice I had never heard her use before. She looked distressed, confused, and she shook her head as though to clear her thoughts. She put down her book, which I saw was entitled *The Unnaturally Long Life*. She put her hands to her temples as though her head hurt and I heard her mumble, "I must be coming down with something," before she straightened her slender back and clasped her small hands in front of her. "Also, Eve, you will find excellent books on reindeer, which were native to the areas in the Arctic Circle you are studying, in the children's non-fiction section, in addition to polar bears and arctic foxes."

I wanted to hug her. I wanted to hug her because I felt bad for confusing her, but mostly because I had just asked her about Christmas, and she had answered. I thanked her quickly, more quickly than was probably polite, like I shouted 'thanks' over my shoulder as I hurried away, practically running like a kindergartener to the children's section. It was completely empty as all my sixth-grade classmates were sitting in front of data ports staring at holograms of different regions around the world.

I went first to the non-fiction section. Reindeer. Arctic foxes. Polar bears. Nothing about Christmas, at least not on the covers of these books, but I grabbed them anyway. If anyone questioned what I was doing here, these extinct animals of the Arctic Circle would be my explanation. Then I moved to fiction. Stories. I had been through these shelves when I was younger, before Grams the Great lost her mind, moved into my home to be looked after, and began telling me tales of Santa Claus. Is it possible I had already read about Santa Claus here and had just forgotten, enchanted as I had once been? Or maybe the enchantment kept me from ever picking up a book about Santa Claus? Or, and I really hoped I was wrong about this, maybe Ms. Snow had no books on Christmas because the enchantment had wiped them out too and she just had not heard me properly?

I was shaking all over with excitement and nervousness, but as I perused the picture book corner, stepping over cushions and nearly tripping over a stuffed giraffe, my excitement ebbed. Nothing. I slowed down. I had been overeager, that was all. I took a deep breath and I BELIEVED. I believed in Santa Claus, my eyes tightly shut, doing all I could to draw magic and adventure towards me, just as Grams the Great has said must happen. And then I tripped. Over a stuffed penguin. Thanks to the cushions it was not a loud fall, but I knew at least a few classmates had to have seen it and I refused to look up to meet anyone's eyes. Let them talk about me later, but I would not let anyone see my shame. I could hear the snickering, but I acted as though I could not. I just lay there, like I had meant to go down.

I left my face buried in a floor cushion for a moment so that I could compose myself. Believing had left me sprawled face first on the library floor of the children's picture book section with half my class staring at me in disbelief. Why had it not worked? I knew I could not lay there forever. That would only make it worse. I had to face the music, so I lifted my head and looked straight at the bookshelf in front of me, pretending for any gawkers that I had done it all on purpose to see the bottom shelves. Red, gold, and the word I had been looking for anywhere other than from Grams the Great's mouth for years now was there, in print, right in front of me on Ms. Snow's perfect library shelf. Christmas. My heart began to race. *Twas the*

Night Before Christmas. I reached for it. Next to that, *The Grinch Who Stole Christmas.* I pulled that one down as well. *The Polar Express. The Christmas Mouse. Rudolph the Red Nosed Reindeer.* How had I missed these? Christmas had been under my nose this whole time. My hands were shaking with excitement as I pulled book after book off the shelf. And then I felt someone looming over me.

"Are you serious?" Desmond hissed. "We have been researching Scandinavia, Canada, the melting of the polar ice! And you are over here playing around with picture books and stuffed animals?" I was shocked by the rage I heard in his voice. Why was he so upset? And how dare he speak to me like that when we had only just met that day?

I held up the picture book with the reindeer on the cover, but he just shook his head. I felt ridiculous sitting there on the floor, my baby hairs standing on end thanks to the static in the floor cushions, with a stack of picture books piled next to me. I didn't really know what to say and people were staring. My cheeks felt hot, but, at the same time, why was I going to let this new kid make me feel foolish? Why was I going to let him ruin my moment? I had found Christmas books. It was real. Grams the Great was right. I now had definitive proof that Christmas and Santa Claus were not something my batty Grams had made up, and I WAS going to bring it back and no new kid or school project was going to stop me.

"Why are you smiling like that?" Desmond practically shouted in the library. "I asked to work with you two because I heard you on the transport. I thought you would take this seriously. Clearly, I was wrong!"

Saved by the bell. I looked over at Nat, who had joined just in time to hear Desmond's last words, and she didn't look any less annoyed than he had. As the bell signaling the end of our school day rang, Desmond turned his back on me and stormed out of the library without looking back. Nat sighed. She turned and walked away from me too, which stung. Why was she siding with the new kid? Nat would forgive me though, she always did, and for now I needed to get these books checked out.

I made my way to Ms. Snow's desk. You just needed the library's code for digital information, but Ms. Snow liked to check out her physical books the old-fashioned way. It's the one thing about her I thought was rather silly. Filling out an old card and filing it with her felt like a waste of time. I vaguely remembered Grams the Great talking about libraries switching over to digital filing systems when she was in her teenage years, but no one else I knew understood why Ms. Snow insisted on paper forms. My stack was rather large and probably over the limit and though she raised a finely arched red eyebrow at me, she did not argue. Perks of being her favorite student, I guess. Then she surprised me by handing me a book with a beautiful blue and white linen cover. Charles Dickens' *A Christmas Carol*. I could hardly believe what I was seeing.

"Ms. Snow," I said tentatively, "What is this?"

"Hmm, oh……. Charles Dickens," she said absentmindedly. Ms. Snow was not absentminded. She frequently had books for me, and they always came with explanations about the author, why she thought I may like it, and which parts were her favorite. What was going on?

I filled out the card tucked into a pocket on the back cover of the book and handed it back to her with the rest of the cards from my pile of children's books. She had not commented on the books and did not seem to be able to even focus her eyes on them. I felt a little bad checking out more than was allowed when I realized it was because she was enchanted and not because I was her favorite student.

"Ms. Snow," I said experimentally. "Thank you for the all the Christmas books."

"You are most welcome Eve," she responded and for a moment I thought I saw recognition in her bright, twinkling eyes. Then it was gone, and she muttered something about the Victorian era, what a prolific writer, greatest characters in literary history, and I nodded and rushed away because even though I could listen to Ms. Snow talk about books all day I really did want to catch up with Nat and try to explain myself. I hoped Ms. Snow, in her state of enchantment, would not remember how rude I had been.

Desmond's Secret

Nat's locker was right next to mine, but when I arrived, she was not waiting for me like she almost always was. I sighed and decided not to dwell on it. Nat was mine, and she would always be mine, and even if she was currently annoyed with me, we were going to be fine. No new kid could change that. I grabbed my jacket out of my locker, shoved the books the best I could into my satchel, carrying the few that wouldn't fit, and I rushed off to catch my transport home. I made it to the launch attached to the 10th floor of the school just in time, and I knew I was disheveled and a little sweaty when I sank down next to Nat. I did a quick scan of the transport for Desmond who was all the way in the back and ignoring me as hard as he could. Good. Nat looked at my bulging satchel and the extra pile in the seat next to me. I had grabbed every book on Christmas on the shelf in the children's section, plus the animal books, and then Ms. Snow's addition of *A Christmas Carol*. My cousin rolled her eyes skyward, and I sighed. I think she had rolled her eyes at me more that day than she had in our entire lives as cousins. Not that I was not always giving her reasons to be exasperated, but today I could tell I was wearing her patience thin, and that was not normal for her. I decided not to even try to tally Nat's eyerolls, however, because I had more important things to focus on.

I handed her *Twas the Night Before Christmas* without comment. I just wanted to see what would happen if she saw it in print. It was a red, hardbacked book with embossed gold writing. The front cover bore holly leaves in the corners and across the front of it flew reindeer pulling a sleigh with a smiling Santa Claus dressed in a plush red suit trimmed in white fur at the reins. I needed to know if Nat's eyes would glaze over. I hoped they would not. I hoped she would start reading and something would click. The enchantment would break. Weren't books magical? She picked up the book and threw it right back down and none too gently. I took it up from the seat and put it back into my satchel.

"Eve, what were you doing in the library?" she asked me in an exasperated voice. "You looked crazy! And now our science project partner doesn't even want to work with us anymore! What is that going to do to our grade?! You know you need to get your science grade up." This was not the Natalie I knew, other than the part where she worried about her grades, and I could not figure it out.

"Sorry Nat," I said.

How could I explain to her what treasure I had just uncovered at the library or my weird behavior if her eyes were only going to glaze over and her mind was going to blank? And she seemed to be truly angry with me and not just exasperated with my antics. Nat did not get angry with me. I slid the book on arctic foxes into her hands. This explanation would have to do for now. I would find a way to get through to her. I had to believe I would, but right now, I just needed her to not be furious with me.

"Is a children's picture book on the arctic fox really the start we need to get going on this project? You just wasted an entire library hour. There's better information on the net! You should see what Desmond was able to do in that hour!"

I noticed her cheeks go a little pink when she said his name. Great. Natalie was crushing on this third wheel now. I felt a twinge of jealousy. We were a pair. We had each other's back and always had. Now this extra shows up ruining everything just when I needed her the most. I ran my hands over my really messy curls which had come loose from the quick ponytail I had thrown in that morning. Mom was going to kill me. A failed math test and here I was walking around looking wild, and I was supposed to be a reflection of her.

"Let's go to your house," I said thinking if I pulled myself together a bit before I saw Mom maybe the math grade would go over a little better. "You can help me fix my hair before I see Mom, and I'll lock in and do some work on Russia, ok?"

Nat's face softened. "Ok. You can stay for dinner. Dad took the day off, so you know it's gonna be good. BUT you have to PROMISE you'll work!" Now she was starting to sound more like my best friend.

I promised, crossed my heart, all the good stuff to convince her, and I did plan to work on the project. But

I hoped to get some Christmas reading in as well. And maybe, if I tried hard enough, I could get Nat to focus on the Christmas books. I sent a message to Mom and Dad letting them know I was headed to Nat's to work on a project and Uncle P.J. would be providing dinner. Dad replied that he had been looking for an excuse to take Mom out for a date and they would pick me up on their way home. I wondered if maybe Dad had seen my math grade and was hoping to soften Mom up a bit, but I did not check the log. Sometimes ignorance is bliss. Mom would be in a better mood after being wined and dined and maybe this math test would just fly under the radar.

Whatever Uncle P.J. had roasting in the oven smelled just exactly like what I imagined a Christmas feast would smell like and my mouth started watering before we were even all the way inside. There were a lot of mouthwatering moments around Uncle P.J. Dinner was hours out though and it was going to be difficult to smell that food roasting and focus on Russia. Luckily, my superbly amazing uncle handed us a plate of still warm cookies, rattling off something about whole grains and antioxidants in the chocolate. I didn't care as long as they tasted good, and with Uncle P.J. things always tasted good. We both hugged him, gave him the cursory answer of 'good' when asked about our days, thanked him for the snacks, and disappeared into Nat's room. Barely had we settled in though, when Nat's doorbell rang and Uncle P.J. was yelling for us. We raised our eyebrows in question at each other, but neither of us had any idea who could be at the door looking for us. I hoped my parents had not decided to come early for me. I was not about to miss that dinner my uncle was cooking up and Nat and I had legitimate work to do.

"Your science partner is here," Uncle P.J. said opening the front door wide enough to let Desmond enter.

Didn't that dummy know you didn't just show up at people's houses? How did he even know where Natalie lived? I narrowed my eyes at him, and it was not the subconscious kind of narrowing that you don't realize you're doing. I openly glared at that kid. But my stupid cousin was grinning widely, like he had not just rudely shown up unannounced at her front door.

"Nat, you didn't tell me you had another partner coming over to help you work," Uncle P.J. said, but he didn't seem bothered, which annoyed me. Did he seriously not care about this act of rudeness? Was he not worried about his daughter and niece's safety?

"Sorry, Dad," she said. "Do you mind?" and when he shook his head, his longish curls getting in his eyes as he did so, she grabbed Desmond by the arm and dragged him upstairs telling him the cookies were still warm if he was hungry. Sheesh, Nat. This kid just showed up at her house unannounced and she invited him into her room and offered him cookies. I was too stunned to speak.

There was nothing for it but to follow the two of them up the stairs and back into Nat's room. Desmond sat in the chair by Nat's desk, tentatively taking a cookie from the plate she offered him. To his credit, he at least had the good sense to look nervous. It was just like in the classroom when we all had to push our desks together. Silent. Nat and I were always talking, and when things did go quiet it was never a nervous silence like this. I really did not like having to deal with an extra person, this strange new kid who we knew nothing about. I just wanted it to be me and Nat, so I could keep trying to break this enchantment and get her to remember Christmas.

"How did you find where Natalie lives?" I finally demanded of him, and my tone must have sounded a little harsher than I meant it to because Nat gave me the side eye like I had done something wrong. Well, you can't just show up at someone's door and expect not to get the third degree. I should have made my tone harsher.

"Sorry," Desmond mumbled. "I know just showing up at your house looks a little crazy. I sort of, well, I followed you home." He slapped his hand across his forehead. "Oh man, that sounds a lot worse out loud then it felt when I slipped off the transport behind you. It was a last-minute decision and once I was off the school transport, I had no choice but to follow through. Not exactly sure how I am going to get home now." He looked at us sheepishly, waiting for our responses.

We were both a little speechless as we looked at the lunatic and I wondered if I should start yelling now for Uncle P.J. Desmond looked right at me though, with dark, sad eyes, and shrugged his shoulders and held up his hands innocently.

"Please don't think I'm crazy, Eve," he said. "I just felt like I needed to apologize to you. Moving here to Spokane has been rough, and I wasn't thinking clearly. Not when I yelled at you in the library, not when I followed the two of you here. I'm a mess. I know it. But I wanted to tell you I was sorry, and I hope we can still work together because this project is really, really important to me."

"Why?" I said reserving my forgiveness. But then I noticed the genuinely deep sadness in his eyes. Maybe I had misjudged. Grams the Great always said you could tell a lot about a person through their eyes, the windows to the soul. I had not noticed before that Desmond had kind eyes. I hadn't been paying attention. I had been preoccupied with my adventure. But Grams the Great is batty, so for now I kept my guard up. He was going to have to do more than have sad eyes.

He looked from me to Nat and back to me again, then sighed. "I used to live in Helsinki. That's in Finland," he said looking at me. Of course, he knew Nat would already know. "My parents were scientists there, studying the weather patterns in the Arctic Circle. They went out on an expedition one day and left me to stay with friends. They were supposed to be gone a month. They never returned. This was nearly two years ago. I continued living in Helsinki with my friend and his family, but once my parents were officially declared dead their will went into effect. I had to come live with my new legal guardian here in Spokane, a cousin of my father's and his only living relative. Our friends, the Salo's, tried to keep me as I had never met this cousin, but I think there was money involved for the cousin and they had to abide by the law. My friend, Esa, and I were trying to solve the mystery of my parents' disappearance but now I'm here and it's hard to keep looking for them from so far away. I have been feeling so helpless, I miss my parents and my friends so much, and then I heard you talking on the transport, Eve. I heard you trying to convince Natalie to look into the mystery surrounding all the tragedies that have occurred in that area. When the project came up, I had to jump in. I thought, if we were researching the area, and since you were already interested in the area, well......you see."

Stunned silence. So, Desmond and I both had ulterior motives when it came to this science project. Guilt washed over me. I had been so cold toward him, and hearing his story, well, he didn't deserve that. My sweet, soft-hearted cousin had real tears in her eyes and ran over to hug him. The surprised look on his face would probably have made me laugh if we weren't in the middle of such a serious moment. Desmond had followed us home like a creeper, but he had also laid himself bare. Okay, Desmond Carter. I let my guard down and I figured I would probably have to forgive him for sneak attacking us at Natalie's own home. I even decided I would throw myself into helping him solve the mystery of his missing parents. The only question left for me, was how to get Desmond and Natalie on board with helping me bring back Christmas. Because ultimately, I thought, it was likely all a part of the same wild mystery.

The Letter

D esmond," I said, because I wanted to test his mettle. "How do you feel about bound books?" and I laid out my treasure trove from the library across the floor of Natalie's room.

We had spent the last hour researching for the project. It was a collaborative effort, and we had gotten quite far. I knew Nat would make sure we got an A, but for my part, I worked hard on the research efforts. I didn't want to be a slouch. The information had flown between us, we had a good start on the project requirements and had even delved a little into the part we would do for extra credit – the mysterious tragedies and the rapid disappearance of the polar ice. I was feeling good about our group now. Desmond turned out to be very smart, nowhere near the genius my cousin was, but he was sharp. He was also excellent with research. Nat had been right about that part. I wanted his help with my Christmas project as much as he wanted our help with finding his parents, and the more research we did, the more I thought about it, the more I became convinced the mystery of the arctic tragedies was somehow tied to the disappearance of Santa Claus and the world's enchantment.

Desmond eyed my books but seemed to be having trouble focusing on them, so I slid a book about polar bears into his lap, starting slowly.

"My parents had a collection of bound books," he said. "We moved a lot for their work, so it was a small collection, but my father loved poetry and my mother loved the mystery novels of Agatha Christie." He was smiling but his face held so much sadness still. "On their anniversary every year they would hunt down a new book together. It would be their adventure. That was their gift to each other. A book and an adventure. So, Eve, I love physical books, bound books. I love them very much."

He picked up the Charles Dickens book and ran his hand over the textured linen cover. His eyes were not glazing over. Yet. I watched as he opened the book. I watched him hold the pages to his nose and breath in. "It reminds me of Mom and Dad," he said. "The smell, the feel of books." If there had been any doubt left in my mind about Desmond, it vanished in that moment, when he breathed in the pages of my library book.

"Can you read the title," I said slowly, my heart hammering. He looked at me strangely, but I suppose it was strange question.

"*A Christmas Carol* by Charles Dickens," he said, and he turned to the first page scanning it. "Marley is dead, to begin with. There is no doubt whatever about that. The register of his burial was signed by the clergyman, the clerk, the undertaker and the chief mourner," he read. "A strange book, Eve. Why did you take this one?"

I didn't know how to answer him. I looked over at Nat whose eyes had glazed over. She was swiping through maps of the Arctic Circle and largely ignoring us. I could not believe Desmond was still focused, still with me, and I could not believe he was casually reading to me from a book about Christmas. And, what I was struggling with the most, was that the book he was reading about Christmas was a dark, gloomy story about death. What? I picked up one of the children's picture books and handed it to him hoping for something better. "Read this one," I said.

"Eve," he said glancing at Nat. "Shouldn't we be working on our project?"

"Read it," I said forcefully.

He opened the book. "It's a poem," he said his face softening and I knew he was thinking of his father's love of poetry and had forgotten I had just strongly ordered him to ignore our school project and read children's literature instead.

"Twas the night before Christmas when all through the house, not a creature was stirring, not even a mouse, the stockings were hung by the chimney with care in hopes that Saint Nicholas soon would be there, the children were........who is? What?" and he looked up at me in confusion and I knew I was losing him.

"Focus Desmond," I said desperately. "I think these books, Christmas, I think it might help us figure out what happened to your parents!" Natalie's head had snapped up at the sharpness of my voice and Desmond looked like he was trying to fight off a headache. I was desperately trying to keep his attention, to get Natalie to wake up, to somehow break the enchantment that held them both.

Then there was a rapping at Nat's door and Uncle P.J. was there and my books, the moment, it was all forgotten. Dinner. As excited as I had been for dinner an hour ago, I wanted to scream at Uncle P.J. to go stuff his dinner. I had almost had them, or at least, Desmond.

"Desmond, will you be joining us as well?" he asked cheerfully, and Desmond looked dreadfully uncomfortable.

"Yes!" Nat and I both said in unison and Desmond looked at us gratefully. "Don't worry," Nat said. "Dad cooks enough for an army every night even though it's usually just the two of us. You'll be doing us a favor. Fewer leftovers to throw away."

"If we are lucky," I whispered to Desmond on our way down the stairs, "Uncle P.J. will send us both home with some of the leftovers."

The food was insanely good. Delicious. Uncle P.J., in his affable way, inquired after our science project, asked Desmond a million questions about life in Helsinki and how he was warming up to Spokane, and told way too many silly and embarrassing stories about Natalie and me as babies. And I was right. Uncle P.J. wrapped up to-go boxes for both Desmond and I to take with us. I knew Desmond had no way home, so I had messaged Mom and Dad before they arrived, and we took him home. His house was small and not in the best neighborhood. It looked empty too, but he let himself in and when lights came on in the windows Dad pulled away and we were headed home. It bothered me, sending Desmond into that empty, dark house, knowing he would be missing his parents and there would be no one for him to talk to, no one to take his mind off things. It felt wrong to pull away and leave him there, but there was nothing else we could do. I was glad, at least, that he had a pile of food, including dessert, from Uncle P.J. to keep him company.

I was wondering if I should tell my parents about Desmond's life to see if they could help in some way, but before I could bring it up my math test caught up with me. Mom had clearly been holding it in while in the presence of others, but she yelled the whole way home, while Dad looked uncomfortable and disappointed. I had known all day it was coming, and I endured the misery with the bravest face I could muster, nodding at Mom, answering when necessary and doing my best to convince her that I was going to work harder. Then Mom eyed my bulging satchel and the few loose books on the seat next to me.

"Seriously Eve? Maybe you should spend your library hour studying math instead of wasting your time on picture books!" She was irate. I tried to explain to her that it was for the research project Nat, Desmond and I were working on, but that went over with her about as well as it had with my project partners.

Mom kept going as we walked into our house and only stopped when we found Grams the Great snoring loudly in her ugly, reclining chair.

"I'll wake her and help her to bed," I offered.

"Thanks Eve," Dad said. I did not tell them I had a selfish ulterior motive. After the tongue lashing I had just received, any credit I could get in their eyes, was needed.

"Grams," I whispered as they carried the leftovers from Uncle P.J. out into the kitchen. "Wake up Grams. Time to go to bed."

She had fallen asleep to some show or other and I switched it off for her and held out my hand to help her up. She flicked the lever on her chair, and it slowly lifted her up and out as she grabbed my hand for support. She looped her arm through mine, and we made our way to her room. I could not wait to tell her all that had transpired that day.

I gave her a second to wake up before I started talking about the Christmas books I had found on the shelves of Ms. Snow's library, and about how Desmond had briefly been able to listen to me about Christmas. Her eyes sparkled as I talked, her cheeks flushed, and for a minute I could see her as a young person, unruly and wild, waiting up all night for Santa Claus.

"Will you read them to me," she said like a child begging her mother for a bedtime story. I laughed. I was hoping she would want to read them. That would mean I could ask her a million questions about what they all meant.

I tucked right into her bed with her and pulled out the first book about a family picking out their Christmas tree. The watercolor illustrations of the family in the story reminded me of my own, especially the white-haired laughing granny and lots of food piled on the table. It looked like a family reunion at Uncle P.J.'s with all the children, grandchildren and great grandchildren of Grams the Great gathered together. Except these people were laughing and dancing and joyful. I wanted so badly to experience that joy. I imagined a Christmas tree in Uncle P.J.'s living room and his dining table laden with food and hoped I could make that daydream come true one day. For all my family. For all the world.

After that we read *Twas the Night Before Christmas*. This poem, with its old-fashioned words, confused me a bit but it gave names to all Santa's reindeer, and it saddened me to think they were all gone now. Extinct. I looked up at Grams as I finished the poem and there were tears in her eyes as she begged me to keep reading to her. The next book was about a little girl who had written Santa Claus a letter asking for a special doll for Christmas. Grams told me she used to write Santa Claus a letter every year.

"How did the children get the letters to Santa Claus," I asked, curious because she had not mentioned letter writing before, and I had always been under the impression that no one really knew the location of Santa Claus's workshop in the North Pole.

Grams giggled like a little girl. "Oh, Eve, we just wrote *Santa Claus, The North Pole*, on the envelope and dropped them in a mailbox. They got there. They just did. No one knows how. But it didn't matter. He brought a gift whether you wrote a letter or not. I just always thought Santa Claus appreciated the letters. Certainly, he deserved some thanks for all the joy he was bringing."

I kept reading to Grams until she fell asleep. She was so old and tiny and wonderful, and I hoped she would be proud when I brought the world the joy of Christmas once more. I made sure to pull her extra blanket up around her so she wouldn't get cold in the night and then I tiptoed out of the room. As I brushed my teeth, changed out of my grey school uniform and into my grey pajamas and crawled under my grey covers, a very colorful idea was forming in my head. I could not stop thinking about bright, shining letters to Santa Claus.

I looked back through my books and found it was a theme in many of the stories, sending letters to the North Pole. The North Pole was gone though, and I did not really think it was going to work, not with this enchantment lying over the world. I could try though, couldn't I? I could write a letter to Santa Claus, not to ask for toys, but to ask where he was. I had read nothing tonight that said anything about Santa Claus writing a letter back to any child, but that didn't mean he wouldn't. And since Christmas was coming up, could I not just ask for his whereabouts as my gift? It was a longshot, I knew it, but it was another opportunity for me to believe.

I threw my blankets off and dug in my satchel for my sketchbook and pencils. If I was going to do this right, my letter would have to be hand-written. I could not send an email to the North Pole. It just felt like the wrong way to go about this plan I was still forming in my head. And it occurred to me that there was a certain kind of magic in pencil to paper. My hand would form these letters, my breath would fall on this paper, the scent of my home might linger so that when Santa Claus opened it he would have to know it came from me. I picked up my favorite pencil, a drawing pencil and I stared at the paper. I had no idea, really, what to say so I began to doodle. A portrait of Santa Claus, just as he looked in the books, standing next to a tall pine tree under a starry sky. I'm good at drawing, at least, better than I am at math. But I needed the right words. Taking time to sketch the portrait calmed me, gathered my thoughts, and I remembered what Grams had said. It shouldn't matter what I wrote, that was not the point, I simply needed to write. So, I told myself to stop overthinking and I put my pencil to the paper.

Dear Santa Claus,

My name is Eve Farrington. I am twelve years old, but if Grams the Great is right about you, then you may already know that. You disappeared from the world eighty-two years ago. You probably don't need me to tell you that either. Grams the Great says the people don't miss you and they don't miss Christmas because you can't miss what you can't remember. At first, I thought that because you had been gone for eighty-two years the world had just slowly forgotten you, but now I think the world is under an enchantment. Strange things happen to people at the mention of anything having to do with Christmas.

My great grandmother, Ms. Carol Blackwood, remembers you though. She is 127 years old, but when you disappeared, she was only forty-five. She is losing her mind a bit in her old age, and she says that is why she can remember Christmas and no one else can. Everything I know about Christmas I learned from her, and I have no idea why I remember her stories, but I do. All of them. And today in the library, my teacher, Ms. Snow, told me to check the children's book section when I asked for books on Santa Claus before she got funny and couldn't focus. My new friend, Desmond, could almost focus on Christmas too. His parents, like you, are no longer a part of this world. I want very badly to help him solve the mystery of his missing parents. They were scientists who never came home from an expedition to study the Arctic Circle. I hope I can help him, and I hope he and my cousin,

Natalie, can help me bring you, and Christmas, back to the world. It is a gloomy, grey, place without you.

From what I can tell, children once wrote you letters to ask for specific toys, to tell you what they wanted. I don't know if this letter will get to you, I don't know if the enchantment will stop it, or if Grams was being batty again and you always had to do more than write Santa Claus on an envelope and drop it any mailbox. But I believe in you, I believe in Christmas, and I want to give it back to the world. So, I am going to try this, but I am not going to ask for a toy.

Santa Claus, I have never had a Christmas present. In fact, no one in the world has received a Christmas present for 82 years. I think it makes us gloomy. I think we are not so very kind to one another. If I could ask you for a gift this year, Santa Claus, I would simply like for you to write me back and let me know where you are. If you do that, I will try to rescue you so you can return Christmas to the world.

And if you just decided to retire, that's okay. We don't need gifts. But could you please tell me how to help the people remember the holiday and be festive again? This sadness has been here so long most of us don't know any different. Santa Claus, I just want you to write me back and tell me how to bring joy back to the world.

Signing off with all the belief in the world,

Eve Farrington

There. Grams the Great said I had to be a winter storm to bring Christmas back. I did not feel like I was there yet. My letter did not feel brave, adventurous, or stormy. In fact, I felt a little silly after I read it over. But I was going to believe in Santa Claus, I was going to write his name on the letter I had folded up into a small, neat square, and I was going to send it out into the world to magically find its way to the rightful recipient. I would not change it no matter how silly it sounded, because I was afraid to ruin the magic of what just came from my heart.

In Grams's day mail was picked up and delivered daily she had told me, but technology had eliminated the need for all that wasted paper, plus we were still trying to grow back our forests after decimating them. But thanks to Christmas magic, there was a package, probably the shoes Mom ordered and hated and vowed to send back, ready and waiting to be shipped. I taped my letter to the underside of Mom's shoe box and hoped she would not notice. My backup plan was that if she did see it her eyes would go all glazed when she read Santa Claus on the letter and the whole package and my letter to Santa Claus would go out in the mail together. There was nothing to do now but wait. And believe.

Candy Canes

E ve, you have too many books checked out
already," Ms. Snow told me sternly. "I am not
really sure how you got away with taking so
many!"

She sounded annoyed with herself for not paying
closer attention and I did feel a twinge of guilt because
I had taken advantage of her enchanted state. But I had
to have these books. I had wandered over to the Agatha
Christie novels thinking of Desmond. I had hoped
maybe he could take one home and when he was lonely
a book to remind him of his mother might cheer him
up, but what I found was crazy. Agatha Christie had a
book entitled *Murder for Christmas*. It did not sound
very joyful, but I read the synopsis on the inside cover,
and it was about a detective who solved a murder that
occurred while a family was gathered for the Christmas
holiday. I had wondered while I was leafing through the
pages, what would happen if I could get Desmond to
understand Christmas with this book. I had wondered

if that might break the enchantment on him. I could not remember the moment when the enchantment on me was broken. I just remembered Grams and her stories as though they had always been there. Thinking about using this book to break the enchantment on Desmond led me to start thinking about breaking enchantments in general. And all of that led me to be standing at Ms. Snow's desk with an Agatha Christie novel and a stack of books on witches, magic, lore, and enchantments.

Denied. And none of this, I was certain, would be on the net. The book on Christmas would absolutely be unsearchable. The rest of the books were ancient. I was not sure where Ms. Snow even found them, but it would have been shocking to find any of them in digital format. I could search for information on breaking enchantments, but for some reason I thought those old books would give me the better information. The title of one book was *Ancient Enchantments and How to Break Them*. I had to have it. I considered briefly sitting down and photographing all the pages, but it was very much against all Ms. Snow's rules and while I was not against taking slight advantage of her being possibly enchanted, I did want to show some measure of respect to her library. Plus, I did not have the time.

I decided to throw caution to the wind. "Ms. Snow, I must have these books. I believe the entire world is under an enchantment that has made them forget all about Christmas and Santa Claus and I want to use them to find out how to end the enchantment. Well, except for this mystery novel," I said, holding up a book with a purple and black geometrically designed dust jacket. "*Murder for Christmas* is for Desmond. His mother was a fan, and I am trying to cheer him up and break the enchantment on him at the same time." She was either going to go vacant on me, let me have the books and forget the whole conversation, or she was going to remember Christmas and either scenario would be a win for me. I watched her face. "Santa Claus," I said slowly, "is real, Ms. Snow, and I am trying to bring him back. These books will help. Please may I check them out today."

"Eve," and for a second, I thought Christmas had gotten through to her. Were there tears in her eyes? She reached for the stack of yellowed cards I had already filled out and added them to her filing system. There were not many there. Most were from me. I slowly picked up my stack of books. "Eve," she said my name again slowly as I had started to back away from the desk. "Good luck.........with your.......... research." She put a hand to her temple as though her head hurt, and I felt the guilt weigh on me. I had tricked Ms. Snow again and she had only ever been kind to me. But it wasn't as though I wasn't hoping even harder that I would break through to her. Like Desmond, somehow, she had almost been able to hear me. I told myself that the joy I would be bringing her in the end would make up for my treachery, but I was not so sure I believed myself.

I had spent some of the library hour going over our science project with Natalie and Desmond, but we were making really good progress so at the end of the hour we decided on a little free time. I had no idea what Nat decided to study up on. Probably some high-level math I'd never understand. I was pretty sure Desmond was working on the Arctic Circle mysteries, and I didn't blame him. If I were in his shoes and my family was missing, I would exhaust myself trying to solve the mystery too.

The bell had already rung, and as usual, I had pulled books off shelves up until the last minute. Desmond and Natalie had cleared out. It was okay, though, because we were all heading to my house after school to finish our project. Nat's house was bigger, and the food was definitely better, but she had not seen Grams for a while so the Farrington house it was.

"More bound books?" Desmond asked, smiling, as I plopped down across the aisle from him and Natalie just as our transport began to pull away from the dock.

"Absolutely," I said. "Don't worry. I'll share."

"Ugh, you are so weird," came a voice from behind me that I knew only too well. Ava Russell. "Why do you insist on hauling those dusty things around. They are making me sneeze," and she let loose with the most obviously fake sneeze I had ever heard.

"Poor Ava," her friend said handing her a tissue.

"*Magical Spells and their Counterspells*," Ava read out loud and a peal of giggles rang out around her. I slunk down in my seat. "Desmond, someone should have told you on the first day not to team up with these two weirdos for the science project."

Poor Desmond. He was finding out now why Nat and I kept mostly to ourselves. She was too shy to make friends, and Ava was right about me. Weirdo. Grams the Great said that outcasts made the best heroes. It was always the underdog, the unsung hero, the nerdy kids, who ended up having the magic that saved the day in the end, I reminded myself. Either way, even if I was not a weirdo, I would never want to spend any time with Ava Russell or her cronies.

Ava was pretty. Somehow the grey of our school uniforms set off her blue eyes and nearly white hair perfectly. She knew how to play the game, had the teachers fooled, was nice to enough kids to have friends but used kids like me and Natalie to keep herself and her friends entertained. She was the worst thing about Ad Prima Academy. I pictured the name Ava Russell as the very first one on the naughty list, a list whose existence I had recently learned of from one of my library books. Santa Claus used to keep track of the children who would not receive gifts from him due to poor behavior. I hoped it was a short list. I really did. I was trying to spread Christmas cheer, not make some kids feel worse because they got nothing. But I also hoped Ava Russell was on that short list.

Nat looked uncomfortable and was doing what she always did when Ava came to call, and that was pretending not to see or hear her. I got it, but it left me to deal with her alone. I suppose if we both pretended not to see or hear her maybe she would leave us alone, but it just wasn't in me. What she had said to Desmond though, I was not sure how to respond to. What if he was regretting teaming up with us? I could not speak for him. I could not tell her that he was happy to have met us. I hoped he was, I had let me guard down, let him into the circle, he'd eaten dinner at Uncle P.J.'s, and I was not sure what it would feel like if he ditched us for Ava, ditched us to be one of the cool kids.

"What was your name again?" Desmond said as though he only half noticed her sitting there.

Oh Desmond, you wonderful, amazing, human. He had just hit Ava harder than any snarky retort I could have come up with. EVERYONE knew her name at Ad Prima Academy.

"It's Ava," one of her friends said in surprise and Ava glared at the poor girl.

"Oh. Well, Ava. I would love it if you would sit down, be quiet, and leave my friends alone. Thank you."

Desmond had not let us down. In one week, he had shown up at Ad Prima Academy, inserted himself into our science project and our lives, and he had just put Ava Russell in her place for us, knowing it would seal his doom at this school. Desmond had just become a friend for life.

Nat looked up at him with wide, surprised eyes and broke into a radiant smile. She looked like she was about to hug him. Ava looked shocked. I do not think she had ever been spoken to like that. It was silent in the transport as her friends stared at her, waiting to see how she would respond to this insult. Desmond picked up one of my books and opened to the first page, nonchalantly reading it as though he didn't have a care in the world. I winked at Ava. Couldn't help myself. Then I grabbed *Magical Spells and their Counter Spells,* attempted to pull off Desmond's same air of nonchalance and dove in. We would be to my house in twenty minutes and that was valuable research time that I was not going to let Ava steal from me. The school bully flipped her blond hair over her shoulder and sat back down with a pout on her face, and I glowed in triumph.

Grams the Great was up and about when we walked in the door. "Coffee, Eve," she said. "I need some coffee." She must have been opening cupboards for more than a minute before we arrived because half of them were still wide open. Nat began softly closing the cabinets behind her, waiting for our wrinkled great grandmother to notice she was there.

I knew she wanted hot, brewed coffee and all Mom ever had was the stuff that came in cans with pull tabs. I pulled one out of the fridge when her back was turned, poured it into her favorite coffee mug and popped it in the microwave. If she did not see it came from a can, and if I served it to her hot with a splash of cream and a sprinkle of cinnamon, she would be okay. I fixed her coffee and when she wrinkled her nose at me, not at all fooled, I promised I would have Uncle P.J. get her some real coffee soon. Grams sat down at the kitchen table where I had set her mug down and took a slow slip. Then she noticed Natalie and Desmond.

"My little mathematician! Come give your Grams a hug my beautiful girl," she crooned to Nat. Mostly I was not jealous of how proud Grams was of Natalie's genius. Mostly. I had Grams to myself a lot of the time and we had Christmas. She patted the coils of braids on top of Nat's head. "So beautiful," she said. "And finally, someone besides me has noticed." She was eyeing Desmond and Nat's cheeks turned absolutely crimson. Desmond pretended not to have heard. "Well, girls. Don't be rude. Who is this handsome young man with the dark eyes. Your great grandfather had dark, dark eyes just like that, you know. Handsomest man in town, he was."

Goodness. "Grams, this is our friend Desmond Carter. He just moved to Spokane. Desmond, this is Grams the Great," I introduced her by her title because I know she loved it. But I could not expect poor Desmond to call my Grams by that name, so I added, "Ms. Carol." Grams would be furious with me if I had used her last name. She preferred things to be a bit less formal than that.

Desmond took her hand up in a firm handshake. "I have heard a lot about you Ms. Carol. I am glad to finally meet you."

"Call me Grams, please," she said looking absolutely overjoyed to have his company.

Nat was poking around in the cabinets looking for something to snack on. "You aren't going to find anything yummy. Told you we should have gone to your house," I told her. Our cabinets were always fully stocked, but it was never anything worth eating.

"Not true," Nat said happily as she held up a bag of popcorn. "Heat and serve!" she said happily. Mom's favorite. She could probably survive off popcorn alone, and Nat knew she would always find some in our house but never in her own. Uncle P.J. did not stock food that could be microwaved.

The popcorn popped and we sat down around the table with Grams. I pulled out the Agatha Christie mystery novel and set it on the cold concrete surface of our table. "I checked this out from Ms. Snow for you," I said sliding it over to Desmond and watching his face.

"Agatha Christie," he said, and a smile spread across his face and almost, almost reached his dark eyes. "You remembered. *A Murder for Christmas,*" he read. "If I promise to return this to the library, may I take it home with me tonight?" he asked eagerly.

"Of course! That's why I got it." I decided not to push the Christmas part. Yet.

"Why all the spell books, Eve?" Nat asked. "What are you plotting now?"

"I am fairly certain you are all enchanted. The whole world I mean. There is a man called Santa Claus and I think he has been kidnapped and the world has been enchanted to forget him." Never mind. The words just came out. I guess I was pushing Christmas. Now. I have never been known for my patience.

"It is all true! And my Eve is going to bring Christmas back!" Grams shouted proudly and clapped her hands together. "Won't that be fantastic!"

Nat was staring at us. "That silly old myth again," she said and then walked away with glazed eyes to retrieve the popcorn. She brought it back in a bowl and set it in the middle of the table, then went to our fridge and pulled out three cans of juice. She drank fresh squeezed fruit juice at her house. My house, well, I was not entirely certain what was in those cans, but it was all we had to wash our popcorn down.

Desmond was staring at his book. I don't think he had heard much of what I said, or at least he had not retained any of it. But he was reading the book. He was reading about a family gathering for Christmas and he had not closed the book yet. I figured I would let him read and I kept flipping through the book on counter spells. I decided that Ava may have been right about that one though. It was silly and I could find nothing on how to break an enchantment. I found an herbal recipe in one book. Lemon balm, dried bones of hummingbirds, locust wings. I figured I could get lemon balm from Uncle P.J., but humming birds and locusts only showed up during the summer and we were living out the cold winter months. I tried to picture capturing a hummingbird and drying its bones and I moved on. I needed another option.

Desmond was reading and Natalie was shoving popcorn into her mouth while working up lines of latitude and longitude for the North Pole. Thank goodness for our science project. She was helping me right now and did not even realize it. I was glad the two of them were engrossed, but I was getting nowhere.

I looked at Grams the Great. She was lifting her mug to her lips with a shaking hand, wisps of white hair falling all around her face. "Grams, I know you remember Christmas because you lived through it and now you've gotten too old to remember to be enchanted, but why can I remember all your old stories when no one else can?"

"Oh, that's easy darling. Candy Canes."

"I've never had a peppermint, Grams," I said. "They don't even make candy canes anymore. Gone. With Christmas. That can't be the reason."

"Oh Evie Pie, but you have! It was a very old peppermint candy cane. Found em in an old dresser when I was moving," she said casually. I sat up straighter. Was she being serious? Or was this crazy Grams.

"Eve, I've lost my glasses again and this coffee is terrible," she complained, wrinkling her old nose at the brown liquid in the cup.

"Grams. The peppermints. Focus." I could not care less about her glasses or how terrible her coffee was. Fake cream and coffee from a can were the best I could do for her. Right now, I needed to know about the candy canes.

"Hmm. They're under my bed. Had to hide them from your mother so she wouldn't throw them away. That woman is just like your great grandfather! Telling me I can't have any sugar. Eve, I'm practically dead already! Who cares about my health!" she shouted. "Maybe that's where I put my glasses too. Check for me, will you?"

"You have peppermint candy canes under your bed?" I asked incredulously.

"Hopefully my glasses too!"

"Grams, are you serious? That is how my enchantment was broken?"

"Well, they are probably ninety years old, so I wouldn't eat any more if I were you. Might upset your stomach. Especially if you mix it with that strange juice you're drinking. But if you are going to go check for them, see if my glasses aren't under there too."

Natalie was still working with her map. It glowed above her head as she plotted data points and munched on popcorn. But Desmond was staring at Grams and me.

"This book," he said. "It's a family gathering, Christmas, but I don't know what..." He was trying to puzzle it out, but I could see the enchantment taking him away from the Agatha Christie novel. He began to watch what Natalie was doing and pushed the book aside. Forgotten already. I had worked so hard to find Agatha Christie for him, to bring him some comfort, and this stupid enchantment was taking it all away.

"I am going to get Grams her glasses," I said and left them sitting there. I was only cautiously hopeful as I made my way down the hall. Could it really be this simple?

As I entered her room the same thought kept running through my head. It could not be this simple. But I had to try. I had to believe. I lay flat on my stomach and looked under her bed. It was a disaster. Candy canes clearly were not the only thing she had hidden from Mom under her bed. I pulled out socks, books, food, things I could not even name. Dust was flying. I was about to give up when, in the back corner,

I spotted a box of green and red with gold writing. I had to slide all the way under the bed to reach it and I hit my head on the way back out. Rubbing the lump that was forming, I sat up, opened the box and there they were. Red striped canes, shaped just like the cane Grams used to walk, but tiny and perfect. They were wrapped tightly in plastic. The box was crumbling, falling apart in my hands, but the peppermint candy canes held their shape. And two were missing from the box.

"One for me, one for you." The memory came back to me now. "Don't tell Celine I gave you all this sugar."

I had been looking through her piles of pictures, listening to her stories of the past. She had been muttering some word I could not understand and then we had eaten the candy canes. I could not remember the candy because as I ate it, I was still enchanted. Candy canes. It was that night that I first remember her telling me about Christmas. It was all coming back to me now. I took two out of the box and ran back into the kitchen, grabbing the pair of glasses resting on the nightstand beside Grams' bed on my way.

Grams was sitting at the table humming softly to herself, a Christmas carol I think. She made a face of disgust between each sip of coffee she took as though she had forgotten between drinks that it tasted terrible. I paused in the doorway to the kitchen taking in the scene. Nat and Desmond engrossed in our project. Grams in her own world. I took a deep breath. I was almost afraid to hope.

"Merry Christmas!" Grams shouted when she saw what I was carrying. I held her missing glasses in one hand and the beautiful striped peppermint cane candies in the other.

"Candy?" I said to Desmond and Nat holding the arched red and white striped sticks out to them and largely ignoring Grams who held all the excitement of a child and was not helping.

They both declined. The enchantment. How had Grams gotten me to eat the peppermints? I looked over to her. "Grams, when you gave me these peppermints how did you convince me to eat them?" I whispered to her.

Nat and Desmond were both looking at the map now and seemed excited about something, but I was having as much trouble focusing on what they had going on as they were having trouble focusing on Christmas. I had one goal at that moment and that was to break the enchantment on my cousin and my new friend so we could all work together to save Santa Claus, bring back Christmas, and solve the mystery of Desmond's lost parents.

"Ahhhhh, Christmas Eve, you are an anomaly my dear. None quite like you. Didn't even have to try," and as Grams spoke, I saw she was centered, there for me, a rare moment of absolute lucidity. "You have Christmas magic in you so when you saw those dusty old pieces of candy the first thing you did was pop one into your mouth. You and I have been carrying on about Christmas ever since." She smiled proudly at me, laughter dancing in her eyes, that Christmas joy I'd been longing for just below the surface. "I'd been trying for years with you. I almost had you so many times. Remember when we went to look at Christmas trees? Your poor mother was so worried about sasquatches we couldn't stay long. But you....... that day Eve...... if Celine hadn't started screaming about a sasquatch when a chipmunk scurried by and rushed us all out of there.....that pine tree smell would have gotten you. I know it. It was one of those ninety-year-old candy canes that finally did it, though. Complete accident. You were in my room, sketching my portrait...... still have that portrait in my nightstand drawer, by the way. Youngest I've looked in decades!" She laughed heartily at that. "Well, you were sitting on the floor using my old photos to draw me, and you saw them peeking out from beneath my bed. I figured trying them out couldn't hurt. You ate yours without hesitation and the next thing I knew there was a lovely portrait of a young, spry Carol Blackwood standing next to a lovely Christmas tree complete with a star on top."

"Grams," I breathed. "You've never told me this story before."

Grams shrugged and laughed at me. "Didn't know you didn't remember it silly billy. Of course, I should have it hanging on the wall, but that would just get Celine going on about how you need to stop being so whimsical and start focusing. So, it's in my drawer. She's seen it a few times, snooping around in there, 'just tidying up' but she always closes the drawer and forgets about it. Enchantments, Eve, are strange things, aren't they?"

"So, if I can convince Desmond and Nat to eat these really old pieces of peppermint, the enchantment should break," I muttered, sort of speaking to Grams but more to myself. "But if I'm wrong, I could make my friends sick from eating candy nearly a century old......."

"Nobody ever got sick from eating old candy," laughed Grams.

I was fairly certain she was wrong about that. A lot of people have gotten sick from eating old food. Yet, I had eaten the candy canes, and I was fine. Maybe they had a bit of magic of their own. If only there were more of them! If I had enough candy canes, I could wake up the whole world! But there were just a few left. What if I could wake up my whole family and maybe Ms. Snow? Christmas for just us? But that felt wrong too, keeping all the joy to ourselves. For now, I needed to focus on Natalie and Desmond. With them, I was certain I could bring back Christmas for everyone without resorting to feeding old candy to the world.

"You two should really try these candies," I said waving the canes in front of their faces, trying desperately to convince them. "They are soooo good," I emphasized. I thought about eating one myself to convince them, but it felt like a waste of magic since I was no longer enchanted. Who knew when I might need another magic candy cane?

"Eve, we are working on something!" Natalie said. "You could help." There was annoyance in her voice, but I ignored it. I had an agenda.

What were those two so engrossed in? I looked more closely at the map shimmering above their heads. Nat's fingers worked wildly. She was putting in data points while Desmond mostly watched, but occasionally weighed in. Their shoulders were touching as they worked together, and that twinge of jealousy hit me again, but I ignored it. I needed to focus on my agenda.

"You know Eve, my favorite holiday drink was always a white chocolate peppermint mocha with whip cream on top and real pieces of candy cane peppermints crushed and sprinkled right on top of the whip cream," Grams said pulling my attention away from my science partners who were now intensely focused on our science project and working very much without my help.

"Grams, I promise, I will call Uncle P.J. and get you some good coffee, and when I save Christmas you will have peppermint mochas to your heart's content, but right now I need to figure out how to get these two to eat these candy canes and you are not helping!"

Oh. Wait. Grams was rolling her eyes at how dense I was. I guess Natalie had come by that habit honestly. But if she could just be straightforward even once!

"Grams! You are brilliant," I cried as rushed to the cabinets digging for something that I could make cocoa with. Surely Mom had some of those packets. It took me a minute to find what I was looking for but, sure enough, Mom had instant hot chocolate in little bags made for microwaving. Poor Uncle P.J. I vowed never to tell him that I broke a magical enchantment on his daughter with instant hot chocolate. It would break his heart. I also vowed that if I brought back Christmas the first thing I would do would be to get Uncle P.J. some candy canes. His homemade cocoa was legendary, and a splash of peppermint could only take it up a notch. To honor my uncle, I did make the cocoa in a pot on the stove and used milk instead of water. Well, the milk substitute my mom had in the fridge, but still better than water. I dropped two candy canes into the pot and let them dissolve completely. I thought about crushing one on top like Grams had said, but I did not want to risk the enchantment taking over if they saw the red and white bits floating on top. My deception complete I poured two steaming mugs. Then, so they would not be suspicious, I quickly made myself one of the instant packets and walked back to the kitchen table.

I placed the warm grey mugs in front of my friends, and I promise, those boring mugs somehow looked cheerful as the steam rose from the top. My own mug just looked like a dull, grey coffee mug, being full of instant hot chocolate minus the magical candy canes. They did not look down. I had to be casual about this or it may not work. I needed those two to drink that cocoa because I was tired of deceiving them. I was tired of pretending I cared about science. It was lonely being the only one in the world besides your batty great grandmother to know about Christmas. Unlike the rest of the world, I did know what I was missing, or at least in a way I did. I needed to share all of this with my friends.

"Can you two take a break for a second. I made us some cocoa. Sounded good on a cold day. I was hoping you could bring me up to speed on what you're working on over here. Grams had me a bit distracted." I was sorry to throw Grams under the bus, but I knew she would understand.

They pulled their eyes away from the complicated lines and data points they had worked up and sat down in their chairs each taking up a mug. Natalie, at least, understood that Grams could sometimes be a huge distraction.

"Thanks Eve," Nat said. It seemed that since I was not talking about Christmas and instead asking about the science project, her annoyance with me had dissipated.

They were drinking and I was elated. I stared at their faces waiting to see if they would change any. Grams was holding her breath. Nat was talking about data points. They had moved on from the main part of the science project and were fully focused on the extra credit, or rather, on solving the mystery of the disappearances in the Arctic Circle. They had been looking at where explorers in the Arctic Circle had disappeared over the last eighty-two years, since the ice had melted into the sea. They had plotted data points into the map. How Nat figured that out I was not sure but, there were quite a few, more than I had realized, covering the map. Only, they were not jumbled and random as I would have thought they would look. They were concentrated. It looked like a small area to me, but Nat would have to explain the distances. I looked back at Nat and Desmond waiting for them to explain what I was looking at, Christmas briefly forgotten, but their mugs were empty, and their faces were shining. It had worked and I had not even been paying attention.

"Well now," said Grams the Great. "Who wants to hear about Christmas?"

An Unexpected Response

I had been longing for so long for someone other than Grams the Great to share Christmas with and everything I had been wishing for was coming true. Grams had shared everything she remembered about Christmas, from being a little girl waking up on Christmas morning to being an adult who trimmed the tree, hung the lights, and cooked the turkey. She talked about snow people, sledding, caroling, Christmas parties, bits of tinsel found all over your house months after the holiday was over. Grams was so delighted to see Nat and Desmond following her every word that I thought she would never stop. Reindeer and elves, lights strung up all over the city, parades, parties, ice skating, my great grandmother left nothing out. Most of her stories I had heard before, some were new, but all her stories were beautiful, nostalgic, full of a magic we had never known in the grey world left behind after the disappearance of Santa Claus and the enchantment. Natalie and Desmond drank in her words, just as I had been doing for years, and I felt so happy, so relieved, I was nearly crying as I listened to all her stories again.

But eventually Grams the Great, in all her 127 years of age, grew tired, and I helped her to her room so she could rest a while. She promised us when she awoke we would all make gingerbread houses and prepare for Christmas, which was coming up quickly. I did not tell her that finding the supplies to make gingerbread houses would likely prove difficult in a world where gumdrops were a memory hidden deep in the recesses of time and no one knew what gingerbread was. I hoped, maybe, she had a recipe tucked away in her head somewhere, but I also knew I'd have to catch her on a good day for that.

When I came back to the kitchen Natalie and Desmond were poring over the children's Christmas books I had brought home from the library and speaking in low hushed voices. Their eyes met mine when I came into the kitchen and I thought I would find joy, but they looked apprehensive, even scared. It confused me. I remembered feeling nothing but excitement and promise thinking about Christmas, but I had been younger when my enchantment broke. I had not realized there was an enchantment. Maybe finding out you had been enchanted, that the world had been enchanted for eighty-two years, and learning about Christmas and Santa Claus all at once was too much. The process had happened more gradually for me.

"I have been trying to get you to hear these stories for years now, Nat! You don't know how difficult it has been, talking to you about Santa Claus all this time, and you would forget or go all loopy every time I tried! And Desmond! For a moment in Nat's room the other night looking through these books, you were so close," I was gushing. I was so excited, so overjoyed, I neglected to read the room.

"Eve, this science project, solving the Arctic Circle mysteries, helping Desmond find his parents.........you were just trying to find out more about an old holiday they used to have when Grams the Great was a child?" Natalie questioned, her voice full of skepticism and frustration.

"Yes! I want to find Santa Claus and bring Christmas back! I want to end this enchantment on the world so the people can feel joy again!" I was failing to see why Natalie and Desmond looked upset.

Desmond shook his head in disbelief. "I thought you wanted to help me. I thought you were my friend, Eve. How could you deceive us like this? You used me and my desire to find out how my parents died to help you solve the mystery of a forgotten myth?"

"No, Desmond, no, it's not like that," I said, looking to Natalie for support. But she was shaking her head at me. "I tried to tell you! I told you both all of it, but you could never hear or even remember my words. You were enchanted."

"This book?" he questioned, holding up the Agatha Christie novel. "You got this to force me to remember a forgotten holiday, didn't you? It had nothing to do with remembering my mother!" There was fury in his voice, but worse than that there was pain.

What had I done? I could not respond. He was not wrong. I did look for Agatha Christie because his mother had loved the mystery novelist, but I had chosen that particular title because I'd had another angle. It did feel sort of heartless when I looked at it from his perspective. I didn't know how to respond.

"I don't believe you, Eve!" he shouted. "Nothing to say for yourself?" He had tears in his eyes, and he kept blinking, wiping them away, turning his face so we would not see him cry. I wanted to tell him tears were no weakness. I wanted to tell him with all that pain and loss he was carrying there was no shame in crying. Through my own tears, I wanted to say all this to him, but the words would not form, and my lips stayed silent. I had been so reluctant to let him in, but he was the one who should have kept his guard up around me. And Natalie just sat there, looking at me as though I had betrayed her as well. That stung.

"Please, you don't understand," I began. I had to say something. "I think your parents' disappearance and the disappearance of Santa Claus might be linked. I was trying to help you and help Santa Claus both. I've been trying since we met you to solve both mysteries, together. That's why I snuck the magic candy canes into your cocoa and broke the curse! So you could have the full story, so we could all work together on this, full knowledge, full disclosure on everything."

This was not how I had imagined finally breaking this curse would look and my heart was breaking inside my chest. I was frustrated, I was angry, but with my friends or with the unfairness of life I was not sure. Why was this going all wrong?

"You fed us magic candy canes? What?! Where did you get them? How did you know they would work? How did you know they were magic? You could have poisoned us? Did you think about that?" Desmond was shaking now he was so upset, and all the while Natalie just sat silently staring at her map.

"Desmond, please, don't be angry. Please. We are so close," I said softly. "We can find out what happened to your parents and find Santa Claus."

Desmond slammed his fist down on the table and stood up from his chair so fast it tipped over backwards and crashed to the floor. "Santa Claus is a myth! And my parents are dead, Eve! And I thought you might be able to help me find answers, but you were wasting my time chasing some children's story. There is no 'we' any longer. I'll figure this out on my own."

As he fled my kitchen and made his way toward my front door, Nat and I both chased after him, begging him to wait but he did not turn around to look at us. He slammed the door behind him. I turned to look at Nat who had tears streaming down her cheeks.

"Can you believe him?" I said. "He just doesn't understand!"

Nat shook her head at me. "I don't understand, Eve," she said quietly. "I don't understand at all. You have been distracted, not helpful, and you barely did your fair share of the science project because you were spending all your time reading Christmas stories in the library. While Desmond and I have been working tirelessly trying to figure out the Arctic Circle mysteries that you brought to my attention in the first place, you were mixing up cocoa out of magic candy canes that you tricked us into drinking without knowing what they might do."

I could not even comment on the candy canes. She was right. I had rushed to feed them to Desmond and Natalie disguised as hot chocolate with little care for what the consequences might be. Grams the Great said I had eaten them first, but her mind was gone, and could my memories be trusted? I could have killed them with ninety-year-old candy, but I fed it to them anyway because I had a single agenda.

"Nat, please. I have been trying to talk to you about Santa Claus for years! Don't you remember any of that? Now I think that the Arctic Circle mysteries, including the fate of Desmond's parents, might just be tied to the disappearance of Santa Claus. I was not trying to deceive either of you, or even slack on the science project. That's why I fed you the candy canes! I needed you two to really KNOW what was happening!"

Natalie shook her head at me and one of her golden braids fell loose from the pile on top of her head as she did. She looked so disappointed in me, a look I had never seen on her face before. We were best friends, a team, I needed her to understand. "Please," I begged her. "Show me your map, tell me what you two were working on. Now that you have all the pieces to this puzzle, I know you'll crack it faster than ever."

But Natalie, my best friend since before we could walk, saved her work carefully and switched off her gamma. Then, shaking her head at me, and tucking her braid back into the pile on her head, she too turned and walked out my front door. Nat had never walked away from me like that. We rarely argued but when we did, it was never anything we didn't work out then and there.

I sat down at my table. I had no idea what to do. I was trying to hold back my tears. I drafted and deleted multiple messages to Nat, to Desmond, to both. I didn't know what to say. I did not know if I wanted to beg for their forgiveness or if I felt like they should be asking for mine. Deceit is a funny thing. When you are doing the deceiving, you justify it to yourself, you feel like you have your reasons, and you often convince yourself you have done nothing wrong. But when you have been deceived, it hurts, no matter what. And it hurts especially when it comes from a friend, someone you have placed your trust in. Nat and Desmond were hurt and rightfully so. But so was I. And they could not understand that I had tried to be honest with them, and the only way I could really be honest with them was to deceive them into eating those candy canes. This enchantment, even broken, was wreaking havoc.

I put Desmond's toppled chair upright, gathered my Christmas books from the table, including the Agatha Christie that Desmond had not taken with him and wiped tears from my eyes. I wondered if Ms. Snow was still in her library. She was another person I had deceived, and I decided I was going to at least do right by my librarian. I set aside a few of the Christmas books to keep for a while longer, my favorite ones. I also kept a few of the books on enchantments, the ones that had not been full of recipes that included eye of newt and bat's wings. The rest I put in my satchel. Then I caught a transport back to Ad Prima Academy, a place I would normally never have dreamed of returning to after school hours, but now I hoped desperately that Ms. Snow would still be there, quietly reading in her beautiful, bright, otherworldly escape from the heavy, sad world.

Ms. Snow was there, her red hair swept up in a bun, with a few soft curls escaping. In the soft light of the library her skin had taken on a purplish hue. She looked up at me in surprise. I must have looked a mess because her face instantly softened, and a look of worry came over her. "Eve, is everything ok? What are you doing here at this hour?"

"I realized I had way too many books checked out, Ms. Snow. I did not want to take advantage of you. I love your library and your books so much. I brought these ones back. I kept only the allowed limit," I told her.

"Eve, this could have waited until tomorrow, but thank you." She was quietly waiting for me to say more, and I realized I had not just come to return her books. I needed to talk to somebody.

I set the books on her desk. It was an embarrassingly large pile and I felt that pang of guilt again. I hoped she would one day understand that I had only wanted to save Christmas. I hoped they all would one day understand that.

"Thank you, Ms. Snow," I said turning to leave, even though I really wanted to tell her everything.

"Eve, wait. Please. Tell me what's bothering you. You've been crying. I'm sure you did not come all this way to return a few extra books." Her voice was soft and comforting, as comforting as the room she had created. I turned back towards her.

"I've just had a huge fight with Nat and Desmond," I cried to her. It was impossible to tell her everything because she was enchanted and would not understand. But I told her it was a misunderstanding. I told her a lot of it was probably my fault. I told her they were both furious with me and I was afraid they would never forgive me.

Ms. Snow smiled gently at me. "Eve, I have been working in this library now for twenty years," she said softly. She certainly did not look old enough to have worked anywhere for twenty years, I thought, searching her face for a wrinkle and noticing again that her skin looked purplish in the soft light of the library. "I have

94

never seen two girls who were closer friends than you and Natalie. It may take her some time, but she will forgive you. You apologized to her, yes?"

"I did. I think." I could not remember if I had actually said I was sorry to my cousin or if I had just been frantically trying to explain myself.

"Well, maybe you should make certain you have apologized to her. And to Desmond. It seems he fits in well with the two of you," my librarian told me.

She was right. Ms. Snow and I talked books after that. I told her I wanted nothing more than to create beautiful stories of my own when I grew up but that no one read stories anymore. They read reports, blurbs, sound bites, and Mom had reminded me many times that there was no way to support oneself as an adult writing stories. Ms. Snow looked sympathetic to my plight.

"We all have to eat, Eve," she said, "but you will find a way, I am sure, to do what you love and feed yourself as well."

I hoped she was right. Either way it had been good to talk to her. It had been calming to sit, surrounded by books, in that warm, lovely room and be listened to. I knew I had my work cut out for me. I had to earn the forgiveness of my friends still, and then, of course save Christmas, but at least Ms. Snow had forgiven my deception and brought a little peace into my chaotic heart.

I returned home only minutes before my mother. I was sitting on the couch, trying to sort out the apology I needed to make to Nat and Desmond when I heard the door opening. I had left empty cocoa mugs and a half-eaten bowl of popcorn on the table, and other than my grades, there was nothing that upset

Mom more than coming home to her house in a disarray. I met her in the kitchen and before she could get upset with me, I jumped on the mess I had left behind. "Sorry, Mom," I said. "Just got distracted. I'll have this cleaned up in no time."

"Evie Pie, are you okay?" she asked with soft worry in her usually edgy voice. "You look like you've been crying." Lines of worry creased her brown face. My Mom was strict, and grouchy, but I never doubted she loved me.

"I'm fine. Just had a little argument with Nat. But it will be okay."

She had a box under her arm, probably new shoes, Mom really loved shoes, and she set it down on the table. I must have looked a mess because Mom softened her tone and put a hand on my cheek. "Eve, my love, are you sure that's all?"

"Mom," I asked her hesitatingly. "What if I don't feel like I did anything wrong, but neither did they, and it's all just a big misunderstanding. What if I tried to explain and they just don't understand? What do I do? Nat can't stay mad forever over a misunderstanding, can she?"

Mom smiled and her face relaxed. "Baby, sometimes you just need to give people time to cool off. When people are hurt or angry, they don't always want to hear explanations. Give Nat some time. I'm sure by the time you get to school tomorrow, whatever it is you two fought about, she'll be ready to move on."

I nodded and took a deep breath. "Dad will be late tonight," she said. "Shall we just have some cereal for dinner and not have to worry about clean up?"

Anytime Dad was going to miss dinner Mom used it as an excuse to eat cereal. One of her favorite meals.

I don't think she really minded preparing a real dinner as much as she hated cleaning up the mess.

"Sounds good to me," I said, because staring mindlessly at a television screen and not having to do dishes was just what I needed.

"Oh, and Eve, one more thing. Just because you don't think you did anything wrong, doesn't mean you didn't. Don't be too stubborn and hard-headed to apologize if it's what Nat needs to move on."

That struck a chord. I suppose sometimes I was hard-headed. I would apologize to Nat and Desmond both tomorrow. It was going to be ok. For the rest of the night, I took advantage of my mother's unusually calm mood and I leaned against her on the couch while we watched a documentary on the discovery of the sasquatch. It wasn't the way to get my mother back out into those woods, but it was still a good show. When Dad came home, Mom had dozed off. He scooped up our cereal bowls and loaded them into the dishwasher for us.

"How was your day kiddo?" Dad asked as he kissed the top of my head.

"Fine. How was yours?"

"Long," he said. He picked Mom's box up off the table and shook it around tipping it from side to side. "More shoes, do you think?"

I laughed and nodded my head, but then something caught my attention that made my heart skip a beat. Something was stuck to the underside of Mom's shoe box. Something that looked suspiciously like a handwritten letter. How had I not noticed it before? Dad set the box down. "You look tired hon. I'm going to go wake your mother and take her to bed. Why don't you do the same?"

I agreed, but as soon as he left the kitchen, I flipped Mom's shoe box over and grabbed the shabby paper stuck to the underside of the box. Eve Farrington was sprawled across the center of the paper. The swirling cursive letters had been printed with a thick charcoal pencil and in the upper left-hand corner in the same swirling letters was written - Santa Claus. That was it. Santa Claus and nothing more. I heard Mom and Dad coming and shoved the letter into my back pocket. As they came into the kitchen, I mustered up a fake yawn that I hoped was not too overly dramatic, said my goodnights and practically ran to my room.

Santa Claus had written me back. As nervous and excited as I was, I was still careful not to damage the envelope or my name written across the front as I tore into the letter. I could not believe the words I found written on that soft piece of parchment, paper that felt like it was a century old.

Dearest Eve,

I awoke, after what I now perceive to have been an eighty-two-year sleep, to the sound of the arrival of mail. Of course, mail delivered to Santa Claus does not arrive by means of ordinary post and is often noisy, but it is extra so when the letter breaks magical barriers. It would seem that in writing me a letter you have awakened me from an enchanted sleep. I only wish I could say that the letter also freed me from this accursed prison I have awoken in.

The last thing I remember is my nemesis, the Yeti, arriving in the North Pole on Christmas Eve just as I was readying my reindeer for departure. You may have heard him referred to as the abominable snowman, or he too may have been forgotten to this enchantment, but he has been my enemy for thousands of years. Yet, he has mostly avoided me, preferring to live alone on the coldest and most unforgiving peaks and mountains he could find. He is a recluse and the last of his kind in this world. He has magic of his own and has never used it for good, but he also mostly remained hidden in the high Himalayas and left humankind alone. He has always known if he went too far, he would have to answer to me. It was only the unlucky few who explored too deeply and stumbled upon him who suffered his magical wrath.

As humans began to explore further and further into the wilder places, I knew he was growing even more restless and angry. I was prepared for him to attack the humans, watching, and waiting. I thought to come to your rescue. What I was not prepared for was a direct attack upon myself. I was a fool and for eighty-two years now your world has paid the price for my mistake. I can only imagine the sadness the weight of this curse has caused you all.

The enchantment the Yeti cast wiped my name and any memory of Christmas from the world. It would seem there was something the Yeti did not count on, however, and that was the existence of magic in humans. It is rare, but it does happen. I believe that your very own Grams the Great must carry some magic in her blood for she, and she alone, remembered my name and taught it to you. Christmas magic is the strongest magic there is and after eighty-two years it has found its way back into the world.

Eve, I believe I may still have friends who escaped the clutches of the Yeti. My wife, the elves, the reindeer, and others lay asleep around me in this cave we are in. However, there are some I do not see. Eylif, the captain of my guard may have not been captured. She is a polar bear. If you can get word to her that I am alive, she may be able to come to my rescue. You may also find some help from the sasquatches in the Alaskan wilderness. They were no friend to the Yeti and have strong forest magic. Finally, my daughter, Holiday Claus, is not here. I choose to believe she and Eylif, my dear family, are out in the world somewhere. I choose to believe this because to believe otherwise would destroy me entirely. Find any of them and you will find help.

If I could grant you your Christmas wish and tell you where I was, I would do it. Sadly, I cannot tell you the exact location of this dark prison the Yeti has left us in. I can only tell you this, Eve. We are in a cave somewhere very cold and very far from civilization. I can hear the crash of the Arctic Ocean waves. I would know those waves anywhere. The cry of the albatross and the howl of the wolf surround me. I know the trees outside this cave to be larch, pine, and white spruce. These clues all lead me to believe that the Yeti has kept us close to our northern home, far from any humans that may lend us aid. These are the only clues I can give you, and I am afraid they are not much.

Eve, you are only a child, and I know the weight of what I am about to ask of you. You must find a way to free me and break this enchantment cast by the Yeti, for on the eve of the eighty-third year, Christmas Eve, it will become a permanent and unbreakable curse. Not only that, but I will cease to exist, and the world will sink into an unimaginable sadness, a chaos of wars, a tumult of catastrophic events, a cacophony of

devilry the likes of which the world may not survive.
The Yeti will finally have his solitude as the rest of the
world dies around him.

    You are the hope of the world, Eve Farrington.
You must stop this enchantment from becoming a
curse before the arrival of Christmas day! Believe in
the magic of Christmas. Believe in yourself. Bring
back Christmas and help me to defeat the Yeti.

    Sincerely,
    Santa Claus

    P.S. In the spirit of Christmas I would be remiss if
I did not thank you for the lovely portrait. I will
treasure it for all my days, whether the time I have left
comes down to days or years, it will be special to me
always.

    Santa Claus was alive. He had written me back. I
held my letter in shaking hands, staring in disbelief at
the beautifully old-fashioned handwriting and wishing
it bore better news, happy news, that matched the
scrolling brightness of the words that rolled across the
paper. I read it twice more. What was I to do? I had set
my mind to bring back Christmas, but the
disappearance of Santa Claus had been an abstract
idea, his kidnapping a speculation. This made it real.
This letter made it real and frightening. An evil,
magical Yeti, cousin to the sasquatch, had cast a curse
on the land. How was I supposed to deal with a Yeti? I
thought of Desmond's parents. Had they crossed paths
with the Yeti? I wanted to rip the letter to shreds and
pretend I had never heard of Santa Claus, had never
met Desmond and promised to help him find out what

happened to his parents, had never, ever vowed to bring back Christmas. I was not brave. I was not adventurous. I wanted to read stories, tell stories, not be in stories. I wanted to sit in a soft warm place, sipping cocoa, safely reading the adventures of others while snow fell outside my window.

While snow fell. But snow would never fall again if I did nothing. Not only would the snow never fall again, but Santa Claus had said on the eve of the eighty-third year, on Christmas Eve, the curse would become unbreakable, and the world would be cast into chaos.

I tore my eyes away from the paper I held in my hands with its words that swirled like snow and looked at my face in the mirror. Dark eyes stared back at me. The tracks of the tears I had shed this afternoon were still faintly noticeable on my brown cheeks. My disheveled curls, skinny arms and legs, and unassuming height did not give the appearance of one who could battle a yeti, but Grams the Great had always said mirrors could only reflect our outward selves. It was the strength we held inside that counted. I held my head high and told myself that I WAS going to be a storm. I was a winter blizzard, and I was coming for the Yeti because I was Santa Claus's only hope, I was the world's only hope. I folded my letter and tucked it into my back pocket. There was just one person I needed to talk to before I left.

The Flight

I knocked softly before entering my great grandmother's room. The tiny old woman was tucked warmly into her bed holding my library copy of *A Christmas Carol*. She looked up at me as I entered.

"I used to love this story," she said softly.

I had only read the first bit, or rather Desmond had read it aloud to me, but it was about a dead man. I had been too busy to read any more after that. I raised my eyebrows quizzically at my great grandmother, forgetting for a moment why I had come.

Grams laughed. "Old Scrooge and his ghosts! You must read it Eve. When you get back of course! There is so much more to the story than a dead business partner."

"How did you know I was leaving?"

"You have no poker face, kid." I was not even sure what that meant. Grams sighed. "Been expecting it, snowflake. You can't bring back Christmas without some kind of adventure. Now, tell me your plans, Evie

Pie," she said conspiratorially and patted the bed beside her.

I snuggled in next to her. Time was not something I had a lot of. Christmas Eve was a week away. Just a week to find Santa Claus before the world as I knew it was over. I had only wanted to bring joy to the world, but now I was being tasked with saving the world from so much more than grey sadness. But, despite lack of time, I needed to confer with Grams. I needed her knowledge. I needed her approval. I needed just a bit more time with her......just in case. I wanted more time with Mom and Dad, Nat and Uncle P.J. and even Desmond, but they would try to stop me. I leaned my head against Grams the Great's shoulder, read my letter from Santa Claus to her, and told her my plan. Steal Dad's auto and get to Alaska because it was the closest and try to find the sasquatches. From there I would head to the Arctic Circle and try to find Eylif, the polar bear captain of the guard. Not much of a plan. But the biggest part of my plan was simply to believe in Christmas magic, believe that a kid like me could pull this off.

Grams wrapped her frail arms around me and pulled me close. "Ok. It's a good start. I see only one flaw. You are planning to do this alone?"

"Grams, you're too old to go with me."

"I am. Old women don't adventure. But, and it is very important you listen to me Eve, no matter how batty you think I am, old women are wise, even once we've lost our minds. Old women have years and years of life behind them. I cannot go off riding reindeer. I'd freeze. But I can give you all my wisdom." I looked up into my grandmother's soft green eyes. "We are going to go get Natalie and that handsome young man you've just met. I will not allow you to leave on this adventure alone!"

I shook my head. "They're mad, Grams. They don't want to talk to me. And I shouldn't put them in this kind danger. At first, I thought we would just be searching for a lost magical saint. I thought it would be toys and reindeer and candy canes. Now, I have to fight a magical yeti who cast a diabolical enchantment over the world! I cannot ask them to come with me for that!"

"Eve Farrington! Did you not listen?! I can only offer you wisdom. Your friends may be upset now, but they will be even angrier if you leave without them! We'll take your dad's auto, get your cousin and your friend and set off on this adventure!"

"Grams, I thought you weren't going."

"Only far enough to make sure no adult stops you from getting where you need to go. Been trying to think of a way to put this retirement money to good use. I'll fund your adventure! Now, help me find my slipper socks and a coat. There is no time to waste!"

I shook my head at her. She was the best. Really. And she was right. With her, an adult, we could actually board a plane or a boat. I was doubtful that Nat and Desmond were ready to forgive me, but at least I would have Grams to help me take those first steps out the door. I tried to think of the right message to send my friends. I drafted a million different explanations, but in the end, there was nothing that could be typed into a message that could explain anything that was happening.

Grams and I tiptoed out of the house dressed in the warmest clothes we owned, quietly slipped into Dad's auto, and flew off into the dark, foggy sky. I had a backpack full of food sitting in the back seat, but I had not wasted the time to pack anything more than that. Grams assured me that even though she had not driven in quite some time she had kept her license current.

"You never know what adventures may lie before you, even when you are 127 years old," she had said with a wave of her arm and wink of her green eyes.

I watched her pen a note to my father. 'Be back soon. Nothing to worry about. Just helping your daughter save the world. Cheers, James!' I had to laugh a little when I read it despite the nerves that tickled every little piece of my body, and despite knowing how worried Mom and Dad would be when they found us gone and only that note for an explanation.

Natalie's house came into view, and I tried to swallow the ball of nervousness in my throat. She had to forgive me. She didn't have to come with me, but I needed her to forgive me. Grams pulled the auto right up to her bedroom window, a bit jerkily being out of practice. We grazed the side of Uncle P.J.'s house and I hoped the damage to the house and auto would not be too noticeable. I rolled down the window and tapped gently, hoping to get only Nat's attention and not Uncle P.J.'s. I had finally sent her a message on the drive that I was about to tap on her window because I didn't want to scare her. She had not responded, and I began to worry as, my knocking went unanswered, that I was going to die on this adventure without mending fences.

Finally, Grams rolled up her shirt sleeve and called Nat herself. Grams hated her 'gadget' but would still use it in emergencies and, while half the time she could not figure out how to make it work, tonight she miraculously found Nat's number and had her dialed up in only seconds.

"Young lady, stop being a dummy and open your window this instant!" she demanded of her other great granddaughter. I gave her a look of thanks as Nat mumbled she was coming and waited for her window to open.

Nat's eyes were wide as she opened her bedroom window and saw Grams the Great behind the wheel of my dad's auto.

"I'm sorry, Nat," I said to her, the apology bursting out of me. "I was caught up in Christmas and careless with everyone's feelings," I began.

"It's Desmond you need to apologize to," she said with narrowed green eyes.

"We will get him next."

"We? I'm not going anywhere tonight! Dad would kill me, even if it is with Grams!" She thought about it for a second then added, "Especially if it's with Grams! Are you supposed to be driving??"

"My license is current," Grams said solemnly. "Now, Eve can explain better while we drive, but the world needs saving, and my granddaughters are the only ones who can do it. Natalie, stop whining, dress warmly enough for the Arctic Circle and get in this auto."

Nat tried to argue, tried to question, but Grams and I both urged her to hurry, promising to explain on the way. Strangely, my cousin did as we asked, and I wondered if I had been in her position, if I would have done the same. I knew that if Grams the Great had not been there, she likely would have never opened her window to me. I wondered if she realized just how real all of this was, or if she just thought she was going on a silly night drive with her batty Grandmother. Either way, I was happy she was with me now. I was also very happy that somehow Uncle P.J. had slept through all the noise.

"Desmond is ignoring me," Nat said once she was settled in. "I've been messaging him all night, but he has not responded. That is the only reason I got in this auto with you two lunatics. We need to make sure he is ok. I was about to wake Dad and make him take me over there. I think there's something wrong."

"I'm sure he's fine, Nat," I said though I was not exactly sure. I had seen his dark house and worry began to gnaw at my chest.

I handed Nat my letter from Santa Claus, thinking it would be best way to begin to explain to her why I had shown up at her window in the middle of the night demanding she join me on a wild adventure. Nat read it. She was silent. I watched her eyes go back to the top of the paper and read it again. I think she read it at least four times before she looked up at me with shocked eyes.

"Is this real? Where did you get this?" Natalie demanded.

"It came in the mail. I read about children writing letters to Santa Claus in the library books I found. I thought I would try it. Just to see what would happen. Grams told me you did not even need a real address, that all letters addressed to Santa Claus would make it to him. After you and Desmond left, Mom came home with a package and there it was."

"Shoes?" Nat said and I nodded, smiling a bit despite the seriousness of the situation. She knew my mom. "Eve, how do you know this is real, like actually from Santa Claus? What if it's a prank? Some kind of joke?"

"It's no prank, Natalie!" Grams the Great shouted. "I would know that handwriting anywhere!"

"Nat, no one I have ever talked to knows who Santa Claus is. No one in this world would be able to read this letter from Santa Claus and walk away with any memory of it, let alone be able to draft a fake response with this much detail. Trust me! I have been trying to get you to hear about Christmas for years. Desmond, Ms. Snow, they got close, but then their eyes glazed over, and they went all weird. The only explanation for this letter is that Santa Claus, himself, wrote it."

Nat was shaking her head. "So, you get this letter in the mail and now you want to run off to the Arctic Circle with only Grams the Great to help you?"

"No, you silly thing. She is going to the Arctic Circle with you and Desmond. I'm just gonna sneak you onto the right plane or boat. I'm far too old for adventuring."

"No."

"It's ok, Nat. You don't have to go. I didn't really expect you to. I wanted to apologize to you and Desmond before I left, but I won't ask the two of you to put yourselves into the kind of danger I'm sure will be waiting for me on this adventure."

Nat sighed. "Eve, I was really angry with you when I left your house. Then, when I got home, I couldn't figure out why. I think it was part of the enchantment, maybe, trying to hold on, making us angrier than we should have been. Between sending messages to Desmond, I've been trying to research Christmas, Santa Claus.... there's nothing. And the more I thought about it, the more I remembered you trying to talk to me and Desmond about it. Desmond is hurting. His parents are dead. Maybe it was wrong of you to agree to help him figure out the mystery of the Arctic Circle when you only wanted to solve the mystery of Christmas, but I know if you could have told us, you would have. I guess what I'm trying to say is.........I believe you......about this whole Christmas and Santa Claus thing...........it's all too weird not to believe. And I forgive you. And I know you were not trying to hurt Desmond on purpose, but he's still hurt. I'm not sure how he is going to process all of this....... that the world is in this much danger. Also, I'm really worried about him. So, let's just get to his house, make sure he's ok, and the rest of this.......... well....... I need to think about it. What you are proposing is insane!"

That was good enough for me. Grams the Great was grinning as she pulled away from Nat's house. The branches of the tree in Nat's yard scraped against the outside of Dad's auto and I flinched, thinking of the scratches it likely left. "Oops," Grams said, then she winked at me and whispered, "Don't worry, Evie Pie. She'll come."

I had a million things I wanted to run by Nat, all these thoughts and plans whirling around in my head, I was sure if I could talk them over with her, she could help me solidify all of it into something that made sense. She always did. Her mind was so perfectly organized, I knew she could take my jumbled thoughts and straighten them out for me. But I also knew she needed time to think, time to process, and so I kept my mouth shut as we made our way to Desmond's house. The ride was not smooth with Grams behind the wheel and after we nearly collided with a second auto Nat shouted for Grams to pull over.

"I'll drive!" she screeched. "It will help me think and help us all stay alive!" Grams did not even question her, but I looked at her in astonishment. She must have noticed the incredulous look on my face. "Dad taught me two years ago," she explained, and I must admit, I was a little bothered she had kept that secret from me for so long. "Don't be upset, Eve. He's planning on teaching you soon as well. He said every young woman needs to be able to make a fast getaway. He also said if Auntie Celine can take over the planning of his daughter's education, he can certainly give you early driving lessons."

She was too worried about Desmond to laugh at this, but she did smile at me as she said it. Nat took over the wheel, expertly steering us into the night sky. She did not even look nervous. Dad's auto acquired no more scratches, and we were soon parked in front of Desmond's dark house.

"Should we just knock on his door?" I asked as we all stared at the strange, dark place. It made me shiver, looking at that dark, unlit house. The world was grey and somber, but Desmond's house was more than somber. It was eerie and lonely. It made you want to run.

Natalie never answered me. She just opened the door of Dad's auto and stalked to the front door. I admired her bravery and resolve. Something about that strange house scared me. But I was not about to let my cousin take on that fright alone, so I pushed my fear aside and followed her. Grams the Great appeared to have fallen asleep. Nat was already banging on the door when I caught up to her.

"No one is answering. I don't think he's in there," I said to her as we both stood awkwardly on the porch, waiting, hoping that Desmond was just being slow to answer the door.

"Where else could he be?" Nat said as she tried his number again, hoping he would pick up the call. "We are his only friends here. He has no one else. Maybe he's just sleeping?" she wondered hopefully.

"Hello," came a muffled voice. On Nat's second attempt, Desmond had answered his phone.

"Where are you?" Nat said in a panic, her tone demanding.

"I left. My cousin lost it. We've never been close, but something is wrong with him. Tonight, he was mean, screaming and yelling, tried to hit me. I don't know what came over him, but I had to get out. I'm running away. Back to Helsinki. My friend, Esa, he said he would hide me if he had to, but to just come. I'm going to figure out what happened to my parents."

"Desmond, I am at your house right now. With Eve. Where are you? We will come get you."

"I don't want to talk to Eve. And I don't want you to come get me. Nat, I need to get out of here. I'm sorry. You've been such a good friend. I won't lose touch, but please don't try to stop me. I have to go!"

"Of course you do," Natalie said to him. "But we're coming with you. Now tell me where you are? The airport?"

"Nat, you can't come with me to Helsinki! You have a family, a life here! What are you talking about?"

"We were already leaving, already coming to take you away. I can explain more once we have you, but Desmond, don't leave this city without us," she said. Her voice was gentle, full of empathy for our friend, but firm.

"I bought a plane ticket with my cousin's credit card. The flight was supposed to leave an hour ago, but there has been some kind of delay. A problem with the plane. I have no idea when we will be able to leave. Nat, I don't know what to do. I need to know what happened to my parents, and I can't do that here with my crazy cousin. But if this plane does not take off soon, he'll figure out where I am, and it will all be over. He doesn't care about me. He just wants the money he gets if I'm living with him. I can't let him find me."

It was, to me, nothing short of Christmas magic that his plane had been delayed and he was still in the city. Desmond was meant to be with us, and Natalie and I both knew it. Now we just had to convince him of that and get him safely out of this city before his cousin could stop us. I opened my mouth to speak, but Nat shook her head at me, and I knew she was right. Hearing my voice would only convince him to hang up on Natalie. So, I shut my mouth and left it to her to convince him.

"I can be there in twenty minutes, Desmond," she said softly, but urgently. "I will get you to Helsinki, I promise. Once there, if you want us to leave you with Esa and never speak to us again, we will respect that. But, Des, please, just let us come get you. We will get you away from your cousin."

There was a long silence while Desmond sat on Natalie's words. In the background I could hear the airport noises, but not a sound from my friend, not even his breathing, could be heard. My heart was hammering. I did not want Desmond out there in the world alone. I wanted him with us. Something in my heart told me we needed him to succeed on this adventure and he needed us to find out what had happened to his parents. But more than that, he was my friend, and I wanted him to know we had his back, that we would always be there for him.

"Ok. I'll be outside. Pick me up in front of baggage claim."

I pictured how hard it probably was for him to walk away from the ticket he had purchased that would grant him freedom from his cousin. I knew how badly he wanted to be back in Helsinki, where he had a friend, connections to his parents, but he was trusting Natalie and I to come get him. He had chosen us. I promised myself I would be a better friend to him going forward, assuming we all lived through this disaster. And that thought hit hard. Nat had convinced him to come with us instead of boarding a safe flight to Finland where he had people. What had we done? She did not let me think about it for even a second though, as she ran back to Dad's auto and barely waited for me to climb in beside her before she took off at a breakneck speed to get our friend. Grams the Great was still asleep, one fuzzy slipper sock pulled up over the top of her sweatpants while the other had drooped down around her ankle and over the top of her sneaker.

When Desmond hopped into the auto, I could tell Nat wanted to hug him and punch him at the same time but could do neither because she was behind the wheel. Instead, she shouted at him. "You had me worried sick!"

"I'm sorry, Nat. My cousin. I don't know what came over him, but I thought he might kill me. I just fled. Grabbed his wallet off the table on my way out the door and bought a plane ticket. I figured he owes me, all the money he gets for housing me. I did turn his wallet in to airport security though. Told them I'd found it on the ground. Hopefully, he gets it back, but I really did think he was going to kill me. I did not return your calls because I was afraid you would try to stop me."

I could tell he was feeling guilty about his theft, about not calling Nat back, but I did not blame him in the least. I had been there, keeping secrets and doing things you would not normally do because you felt you had no other choice. I had added to my guilt fleeing without a word to my parents.

I wondered if his cousin's sudden rage had anything to do with the curse. Santa Claus had said the world would sink into sadness, chaos, and wars in his letter. Was it already beginning? Would it hit the people who were already bad even harder? But I did not share this guess with Desmond. It would do no good. There was so much to tell him, so much to catch him up on. And we still needed to devise a plan. I had thought to go to Alaska first, but maybe Helsinki now? Nat had promised we would get him there, but I had no idea how. There was so much planning we needed to do, but I let Natalie just talk. She told Desmond everything. I let him read my letter. She told him we thought his parents' disappearance was tied to the Yeti, something we had not even fully discussed, but a conclusion I definitely agreed with. Desmond took it all in as Nat drove. I was paying no attention to where she was going, just listening to her talk. And Grams the Great continued to sleep.

Nat was going full speed now, and it occurred to me that we were far from Spokane and headed west, but I still did not know what she had in mind. When there was finally a lull in the tale she was spinning for

Desmond, I started to ask her, but Desmond spoke first.

"Eve, I'm sorry. I'm sorry I got so angry. It was weird...waking up from this enchantment. Something just came over me." He looked abashed and I felt not more than a little guilty. None of it was his fault.

"You had every right to be upset," I said. "I'm sorry too. Desmond, I never meant to hurt you or trick you. I just didn't know how to navigate this enchantment, the project, finding your parents, any of it. I'm sorry."

"Ok," Nat interjected. "I think we can all agree, especially with the strange behavior of your cousin, and our strange reaction to waking up from the enchantment, that Santa Claus is right, and the world is in danger. We are already seeing the effects, a deepening of the sadness into anger, rage, all of that. Dad was grouchy tonight. The teachers at school have been meaner than usual. Ava Russell is even bullying her own friends now. Let's not dwell on who did what because I think none of us could help it. Can we agree that we are all sorry and go back to being best friends? There is a world that needs saving, and we need to focus."

"Agreed." Desmond and I said in unison.

"Aw, Natalie, I see you are taking us to Bellingham?" Grams suddenly chimed in. "Your plan, then, is to take the ferry to Alaska? Perfect." She was fully awake now and somehow had figured out Natalie's plan before I had.

Hemlock

I think this is where we part ways, my dears," Grams the Great said. She had purchased us passage on the ferry, and now it was time to say our goodbyes. "I'll find my way home from here and fill your parents in, so they won't worry too much. They'll be so proud!" She clapped her hands together like a child as she said this, and I did not have the heart to tell her how wrong she was. I also worried how my childlike grandmother was going to find her own way home.

I had nothing to worry about, however, because Natalie had taken care of it already. She had called a transport to take Grams straight to the airport and home to Spokane. She then told Grams she would message her father to pick her up once we were safely on the ferry and out of reach. It was a good plan.

Grams the Great pulled all three of us into a group hug, kissing the tops of our heads. Then, shouting 'go get em kiddos!' she walked away muttering about how proud everyone was going to be and was driven off by a stranger in a transport. She was wrong, of course. Mom, Dad, and Uncle P.J. would not be proud. They would be furious. But it could not be helped.

"Let me see all your gamma's," Natalie said once Grams had left us.

I'm not sure what she did, but somehow she knew how to disable the tracking in our devices so our parents would not be able to use them to locate us. Natalie also disabled the tracking in Dad's auto before flying it onto the ferry and parking it expertly. Desmond was so impressed with her his mouth was hanging open, but Nat did not seem to notice. She was all business. I was so relieved I had listened to the wisdom of Grams the Great. Without her I would be floundering. Completely. I had no idea you could catch a ferry to Alaska from Bellingham, which Nat had managed to drive us to in just two short hours. We could have taken Dad's auto all the way, but it would have meant flying through Canada, which would mean a check at the border with a twelve-year-old behind the wheel. I was worried Desmond would be upset we were heading to Alaska first, but he was not. Natalie had explained that it made more sense geographically to go to Alaska first and see if we could find any sasquatches. While she drove, she had Desmond and me search for frequent sasquatch sightings in the Alaskan wilderness and now that we were on the ferry, and she was no longer behind the wheel she was already working out which forests we needed to go to first.

None of us knew what kind of help the sasquatch might be able to offer and all of us were terrified of trying to find them. They were unpredictable animals, sometimes violent, always mischievous, and since they had been discovered, people avoided the wilder parts of the forest. I did not know how much of the lore of the sasquatch was real and how much was exaggeration from scared humans, but Santa Claus had said they were his friends. I was not sure what kind of help forest apes would be to us, but I thought about Eylif, the talking polar bear, and decided, as unbelievable as all of this was, to simply believe in Christmas magic. The Alaskan sasquatch, according to Santa Claus, had some kind of forest magic, and all we could do was hope that in some way it would help us locate the missing saint. Santa Claus had given us so little to go on in his letter, so we could not afford to ignore any of it, no matter how terrifying it sounded.

"We need to focus on the Alaska triangle. Its coordinates lay between Juneau, Anchorage, and Utqiagvik. There have been strange disappearances and tragedies there for hundreds of years, well before the disappearance of Santa Claus. A lot of paranormal activity, vortexes, UFO sightings, strange lights in the sky.........." I trailed off. I had read a bit about it while researching our project and I was not particularly excited that we needed to head right to the center of all this strangeness and mystery, but when a world needs saving, you have to put on your big kid pants and get things done.

We were tucked into a corner table in the cafeteria of the ferry scarfing down cheeseburgers and fries. Mom's prepackaged, ready to eat approach to meals was finally working to my advantage as I had been able to pack non-perishable provisions quickly and easily for a weeklong adventure, but Grams had given us access to her credit account and said to spend what we needed. We had decided to purchase meals when and where we could and save our packed food provisions for times where we may have no other option. Also, I was not the kind of kid to pass up cheeseburgers and french fries when I could get them. We washed it all down with soda pop too, which was a rare treat for both Nat and me. Now we just had to hope no one figured out we were using our grandmother's credit account and either use it to track us, or worse, shut it down. We were definitely going to need to use it again to buy warmer winter clothing once we arrived in Alaska. The curse had left us in a world with no snow, but the temperature in the Arctic Circle was still well below freezing this time of year and none of us had the right gear for that.

Natalie let the research she had been doing spread out across our table. "These are where the most recent sasquatch sightings have been in the area you are talking about, Eve. The Alaska Triangle." She indicated a place on the map where there was a strong concentration of data points. "There are several places that might be worth trying based on the data, but I think the heaviest concentration is right here," she said pointing to a spot on the map that showed it was a boreal forest, remote and heavily treed.

"So, we start there," said Desmond, licking the ketchup off his fingers.

Desmond was skin and bones and every time I watched him eat a meal, the way he scarfed it down like it was his first in ages and left not a single crumb behind, I wondered how well his cousin fed him at home. True, boys his age were unusually hungry, but I was still glad we had gotten him away from his cousin. I don't think he was any safer with us considering we were headed straight for a place known for strange disappearances and unexplainable events, but at least he was loved. And fed. For now.

"But promise me we will not spend too much time searching for sasquatches in Alaska. I can't imagine some animals will be able to do much to help and Esa is expecting us in Helsinki soon."

"Promise, Des," I said, and I meant it. We had no idea what we were getting into with these animals and Helsinki was a good starting place to look for both his parents and Santa Claus if the sasquatch thing did not pan out. Deep down though, I believed we would find help, if for no other reason than because Santa Claus, himself, had pointed us in this direction.

"Nat, we still haven't shown her what we were looking at when she slipped us the magic peppermint hot chocolates," Desmond said. I remembered now their excitement over some discovery that I had completely forgotten about in all the ensuing drama after I broke their enchantment.

Natalie nodded her head and switched the display to another view on her gamma. I looked excitedly at the map that popped up revealing lines of latitude and longitude and more data points. Of course, Natalie had approached this mystery scientifically. Desmond too. I was the only one drawing pictures of Christmas trees and thinking I would be the hero of the story for it. But I guess that is why we have always made a good team. I would cook up messy schemes and she would turn them into an organized reality. This was the scheme of a lifetime though. The stakes were much higher than our attempts to pilfer cookies from Uncle P.J.'s pantry when we were four. I needed to get my head out of the clouds and focus.

"These are the disappearances that have occurred in the Arctic Circle for as far back as we can find," Desmond said. "We started with my parents and then we looked at locations of other scientists and adventurers who have disappeared. Of course, they are approximate locations. We don't have exact coordinates for where any of these people disappeared, just data for where they were known to be headed. But Eve, look at this!" He pointed excitedly to a heavy concentration of data points. "My parents last known location falls into this area. We think there may be something going on here."

"I looked at it again, Des, after we left. After reading Eve's letter from Santa Claus, I began to think. We found this smaller circle within the Arctic Circle, but we didn't know why everything was concentrated here. So, I rechecked some of the dates. They all fall within the last eighty-two years. What if this area is the home of the Yeti?" Natalie pondered. "If it's not his home, it has to be tied to this enchantment in some way."

I was not sure when she had found time to cross reference data points with dates, but I was excited. I had always known if I could just get Nat on this project she would solve it, even if she didn't know what she was solving. She had the answer before I awakened her and Desmond. They had found it together. All it took was breaking the enchantment and she had already begun unraveling the mystery. But poor Desmond, now thinking how gruesome his parents' deaths likely were at the hands of an evil Yeti. I suppose he had to have been prepared for bad news, since his parents had already been presumed dead. Still, no one is prepared to hear that it may have been a violent end at the hands of a mythical Yeti, and I hated that creature in that moment. Strange, but the enchantment he had cast on the entire world hurt me less than the pain I now saw in my friend's eyes as he thought of his parents. It was less abstract. Desmond's sadness was right there in front of me. It felt heavy on us all as we sat around a plastic table on a ferry to Alaska looking down at Nat's data display.

That heaviness, that realness, made me realize that, in fact, none of it was abstract. Real people were suffering. I needed to remember that. It was all real. Real and very heavy. Christmas had started as a playful idea, something to make everyone feel more joyful and happy in a sad, grey world. I had obsessed over it for so many years with Grams the Great, but I had never imagined that I would one day end up on the adventure I was on now. The pain Desmond was feeling, a pain so contagious Nat and I could not help but feel it, would spread across the world if we did not stop it. There would be millions of Desmonds out there hurting. So, I let the realness of my friend's pain sink in, I let it wash over me, I felt it, and all of that gave me the strength to be brave. I could not return Desmond's parents, but I could stop this evil from spreading across the world and I could bring as much joy as possible to the rest of my friend's life.

"So, we go there after Alaska? As close to that spot as we can get?" I asked nervously, but I felt like I already knew the answer. What other option did we have?

"Do we?" Desmond said, which surprised me. "I mean, there is likely a murderous Yeti who wants to destroy all of humankind living there. What are we going to do about that? And honestly, I am beginning to think, now that we know about the Yeti, that I know what happened to my parents. I think we need to find the polar bear, reinforcements, or at least come up with a plan to defeat the Yeti before we just show up in his territory, show up to the spot where he has been murdering every other person who has visited."

Nat put her arm around Desmond's slumped shoulders. "What if we figure out how to free Santa Claus first? Wouldn't our job be done? Couldn't he deal with the Yeti then for us? And get justice for Desmond's parents and all the others?"

"Any ideas on how to find Santa Claus?" I asked, hoping my genius cousin had also solved that problem on the short drive to the ferry.

Unfortunately, she had not pulled off the impossible. Yet. None of us had a single good idea. As the ferry sliced through cold, dark water we put our heads together. Nat plotted data points and read through some book she had packed with her. Desmond and I searched for possible geographical hiding places near the water, caves mostly, but there were not a lot of well documented caves so far away from civilization. We were trying to find out as much as we could about an area that humans avoided. It was difficult terrain with unforgiving weather, and the people who had ventured in, had mysteriously not returned. As the sky darkened, and we prepared to sleep for the night, the feeling that we had very little to go on weighed heavily.

It was a thirty-six-hour ferry ride in which we slept little, researched as much as we could, and ate heartily to keep our energy up, but as the ferry pulled into harbor at Ketchika, we realized we had used up three days of the short week we had to save Christmas, and we had accomplished almost nothing. We pulled away from the ferry in my dad's auto, fully charged from the plugins on the boat, and prepared to fly deep into the Alaskan wilderness, with Natalie plugging coordinates into the GPS and taking off at full speed. We had no plan, but we had bravery, Christmas spirit, and we believed in ourselves, we believed in our purpose.

We stopped in Anchorage for supplies, using Grams the Great's gifted credit account to suit up. Grams had told me to spare no expense, so we were outfitted with the best gear you could get for an arctic adventure. We shoved our lighter coats into the trunk of our stolen auto in case we needed an extra layer later. I would have found it hilarious to look at my prim cousin, hood up with just her green eyes visible, looking like a fat marshmallow in the all-white suit she had picked out, but our mood was too somber to laugh at our snow suits. In Anchorage we also ate a large, hot meal in a quiet diner. From there Nat, following coordinates she had punched into the GPS system, guided us into the Alaskan wilderness.

We drove for hours. There were moments of wild chatter and theorizing, but many more moments of thoughtful silence. I don't know where Nat and Desmond's minds were wandering to in those moments, but I spent them simply trying to believe in what we were doing. It was all I had. When Nat finally set the auto down in a small clearing she had sighted amid thick, towering trees, I felt resolved and ready to face anything that might come our way. This was going to work, and the sasquatches could not possibly be as frightening as they appeared in the documentaries.

"This was not exactly where I wanted to land," she said, "but I'm afraid I urgently need to relieve myself."

"That's okay," I said. "Let's just see what turns up here while we're landed. It's as good a place to start as any and I really need to stretch my legs."

I stepped out, taking a deep breath of the cold air and the piney scent of forest. It smelled so good, the tang of pine, the wet earthy ground, the clean freshness of unspoiled air. The feeling of being there, I nearly dropped to my knees it was so overwhelming. Desmond did drop on one knee in awe of our surroundings. We were city kids from a grey world, and so very few of us ever left the city for fear of what we would find in the wilds. I had only been to the outer edges of a forest and only once. This was something else. Something better. I felt joyful in a way, like I was home. All I wanted to do was breathe, just breathe it all in, and with every breath that filled my lungs I felt happier. Our cheeks were rosy now, our eyes glistened and I saw the same happiness on Nat and Desmond's faces that I felt filling my own soul.

But we still had no plan and once the shock of all the wildness and beauty wore off, we stared stupidly at each other. "What now?" Natalie asked as she returned from the other side of the auto where she had gone for privacy. She had gotten us here with her brilliance and her maps, but now that we were standing amid the trees she had gotten us to, she had no idea what the next steps were. My turn.

"We believe," I said, and I was surprised by the confidence I not only felt but heard in my own voice. It was dark. It was the time of year in the Alaskan wilderness where the darkness never let up. Perpetual nighttime. It's said people can get sad and depressed, but in that moment I could not understand how. The stars, the rays of moonlight that gently brightened our little clearing, the crisp night air, it was all so peaceful and calming. But, I suppose, darkness has a way of leaving you unsure, if for no other reason than you cannot see what is surrounding you. Looking out into the trees and not knowing what was there, not even knowing what time it was, day or night, was disconcerting if nothing else.

Desmond reached out and ran his fingers along the needles of the tree closest to him. "White spruce," he said. "They smell so good." He had clearly paid attention to the vegetation portion of the report we had been working on for school. "Eve, what exactly are we supposed to believe?"

"We believe in the magic of Christmas, in Santa Claus, in ourselves!" I exclaimed. "We are here looking for sasquatches friendly to Santa Claus. I say we walk into the trees, make as much noise as possible and believe they will come to us."

"Can't we stay right here in this clearing?" Natalie argued. "Since we are just believing they will come to us. As soon as we walk into the trees, we lose the moonlight. We'll just be sitting ducks for whatever animal might want to eat us! There are more things out here than sasquatches, you know!'

"Grizzly bears!" Desmond added.

"At least if the bears or the sasquatches come at us, Uncle James's auto is here, and we can hop in and make a quick getaway. We can't save the world if a bear eats us, Eve," my cousin implored. "Also, the minute we walk into those trees we are lost! My gamma has no reception out here and I don't want to try to find our way back to this clearing and our auto in the darkness. Actually, now that we have lost reception, I am not entirely sure I can even fly us back to any city. We may already be lost, but I'd rather be lost flying around in a warm auto than lost in the dark and freezing woods."

"So, we make noise here, then. I read if you bang on rocks and trees, you can call a sasquatch to you," I said. I did not bother to argue with her because I knew she was right, and I did not want to cause her further panic. We were three city kids who had no business traipsing off into a dark forest. I picked up a heavy fallen branch and began to knock it against a tree. Then I looked up at the stars and began to shout.

"WE ARE HERE SASQUATCHES. SANTA CLAUS SENT US. WE NEED YOUR HELP!"

Natalie and Desmond began to do the same. We hollered, we banged sticks on rocks, we yelled, we begged them to show themselves but other than a startled bird or two we heard nothing.

"Doesn't making noise scare wildlife off?" Desmond finally asked. "Maybe we should have stayed silent?"

"Oh." I said feeling a bit deflated. I had heard that before as well. If you go into the forest and you don't want a cougar to eat you, you should make a lot of noise. Animals are supposed to be more scared of us than we are of them. I felt a little foolish. But I had read you could make knocking noises to call sasquatches. I was sure of that. Now I didn't know what to do.

Nat pulled out one of the thermal blankets we had purchased and spread it out on the ground just next to Dad's grey auto. She did not seem to want to move too far away from our getaway. She sat on the ground and leaned her back against the cold door of the auto, then patted the ground next to her. "Let's try silence for a bit then?" she said. "We will give it a little time and then move on."

But after a while of sitting quietly, saying very little to each other, nothing happened. I have never been known for my patience and fifteen minutes of stillness was all I could take before I got up and began to pace. I hummed Jingle Bells to myself as I paced and believed. Paced and believed. Paced and believed. Nat looked like she was about to doze off with her head on Desmond's shoulder, and Desmond looked like he was trying to hold as still as possible so as not to disturb her. He even gently moved a braid that had fallen across her face. The cold air had begun to bite more than it had when it was new and fresh to us and I spread another blanket over the top of Natalie and Desmond, thinking she should get some sleep before she did any more driving. Then, I pulled my hat down lower over my ears and continued to pace and believe.

"I used to camp with Mom and Dad," Desmond said quietly after I had paced in silence for some time. "This reminds me a bit of that. They were never as frightened of sasquatches as other people were. They thought the woods were for us all. I think they thought if we spent enough time in the trees, we could erase some of the sadness that weighed us down, not knowing we were just an enchanted people. But, you know, even enchanted, we had enough happy moments. Especially on those trips, with a campfire and marshmallows, and the peace of the woods."

"Dad and I had happy moments too," said Nat, lifting her head from Desmond's shoulder. So much for her getting some rest. "Maybe that's what the curse only becoming unbreakable on the 83rd year means," she pondered. "Happy moments kept us sane, but when it fully sets in, becomes unbreakable, we'll lose those moments and that is when the chaos will sink in?"

I figured she was right. She usually was. "I had happy moments too. With you two, with Grams and Mom and Dad and Uncle P.J. Even with Ms. Snow in the library," I told them. "I think you're right Nat. Our connections, the little moments.........what will happen to the world when we lose those?"

That image left all three of us thoughtful and quiet. It made me feel even more determined to win, to beat the Yeti. Desmond and Natalie sunk into the stillness of the night and huddled deeper under their camping blankets. It was strange how quiet the forest had become. There had been rustling and bird calls when we landed, but now it was eerily quiet. I ignored the eerie feeling. I needed to pace. I needed to think. I needed to work things out in my head.

I have no idea how long I paced. Another hour, maybe two? Desmond and Nat had both nodded off, but I stubbornly refused to stop believing. Pace and believe. Stay awake or we all get eaten by grizzly bears. Pace. Believe. Then a rock crashed into the tree just above my head with a loud crack and pine needles and bark flew all about us. Nat and Desmond jumped to their feet just as an eight-foot-tall creature jumped from a perch in the trees, landing in the middle of our clearing just between me and my friends who were still huddled close to the auto. This creature let loose a roar with a timber so deep I could feel it reverberate throughout my body. I was frozen where I stood. I wanted to yell at Nat and Desmond to get in the car and get away, but my lips would not move, and my voice was stuck in my throat. I had seen pictures of a sasquatch, but nothing prepares you for how large they loom in real life. This thing could have torn me apart with his bare hands and all I could do was stand there stupidly. He roared again. He uprooted a dead tree and threw it. He threw more rocks. Then he leaned down towards me bringing his amber eyes level with mine and he roared again, in my face, teeth bared and when he was done my ears were ringing and I was paralyzed with fright.

Tears were leaking from my eyes. I had never been so terrified. Still frozen where I stood, I looked into this creature's eyes. I would not wilt.

"Please," I managed to croak, though my legs and arms were still frozen. "Santa Claus sent us. Please don't eat us."

I tried to meet the gaze of this animal through my fear and when I did it became clear to me that he was no animal. His eyes held as much intelligence, as much life as any human eyes I had ever looked into. But he only leaned back and grunted, his eyes narrowing. He waved his arm toward my dad's auto, a soft growl now rumbling in his throat. Then he stalked back off into the forest.

I am not sure what came over me in that moment, but I forced my legs to work again and tore off after him. Natalie and Desmond were yelling for me to come back, but I had seen something in those eyes. He knew Santa Claus and I knew it, and we needed his help.

"Come back," I screamed as I ran into the dark trees. "We need your help! Please! The Yeti has Santa Claus, and we need to help him. He called you his friends! Please!" I think I was crying. I know I had no clear thoughts in my head. I was operating solely on belief. And maybe adrenaline.

Then, in the pitch black of the forest I ran straight into reddish fur and muscle and bounced off, landing hard on my backside. Before I could catch my breath, I was lifted into the air by my ankles and the creature who had tried so hard to terrify me carried me back to the clearing where Nat and Desmond were frantically calling my name and flung me to the ground. He grunted and growled some more at me and disappeared back into the forest, a blur of red fur and long limbs. Undeterred, I chased after him again, ignoring my bruised backside, and again he put me back. But this time before he walked back into the trees he spoke.

"Leave." It was just one word, but he had clearly spoken it. Then he was gone again, and I dropped my head into my lap and cried.

"Did that thing just speak?" Desmond asked as he and Nat came to my side.

"What were you thinking?!" Natalie cried.

"We have to go after him," I said rising to my feet and preparing to take off into the trees again.

"I think it wants us to leave," Nat said to me gently as Desmond held me back so I would not run into the woods again. "We knew they may not help," she said. "I think it's time we figure out how to get to Helsinki. That creature seems like he wants us gone, like gone in a way that we may not live through if we do not leave. Now."

"We don't even know how we are going to get to Helsinki! Only Desmond has a passport," I said sullenly. But I was supposed to believe. I screamed again into the trees. "Santa Claus has been held against his will in an enchanted sleep for the last eighty-two years by your cousin, the Yeti. On Christmas Eve the enchantment will become an unbreakable curse, Santa Claus will cease to exist, and humanity will sink into war and chaos. No one, not even the creatures in the wild are safe from war and chaos! Santa Claus was your friend! Please! Help us."

Then, because I had lost faith, not in Christmas, never in Christmas, but in the stupid sasquatches, because that screaming, howling beast had felt so intelligent to me, but not kind, I turned and began to walk toward the auto, mud spattered, bruised and bedraggled.

"Let's go. We will figure out Helsinki and try to find Eylif. And if we don't find Eylif, we will save Santa Claus ourselves." I was determined. I had known getting help from the sasquatches was a long shot, but I had thought the problem would be finding them. It had never occurred to me that we would actually find sasquatches in the vast Alaskan wilderness only to be denied their help. I was angry and frustrated with the creatures. But I was determined not to let it ruin my Christmas spirit, my belief that we were going to beat this Yeti. So, I strode towards the auto, and I threw open the door and I was about to climb in when a face popped up on the other side of the auto and I screamed and jumped backwards, falling flat on my already sore behind.

Nat screamed behind me as well, but once the shock faded, we realized we were staring into the face of a different sasquatch. This one, even in the darkness of night, we could tell was younger. Smaller. His fur was shiny and black and his golden eyes, which shone in the moonlight, looked even brighter against his blackness than the other sasquatch's had. I was breathing heavily now. I just wanted to get into the auto and leave. This creature was less hulking, but still huge, and he was staring nervously at us. Was he going to eat us? Destroy the auto? Or did he just come to get a look at the strange humans who had been screaming into the trees. But then, I saw what I had not seen in the other sasquatch's intelligent eyes. Concern. Kindness.

Tentatively, quietly, I asked, "Are you here to help us?"

"I don't know," the sasquatch replied, and I was shocked by the gentleness of his voice.

"Did you know Santa Claus?" Desmond asked as he came to my side, dragging a speechless Natalie with him.

"I was very young when he disappeared, but I remember the friendship. He would bring food, cookies, he called them, to the children on Christmas day after he delivered gifts to the human children. He spent much time in our forest with us. Santa Claus loved the trees here, some of the oldest in the world. They were his friends too."

Despite the fear I was feeling, I laughed a little. I had wondered how he had eaten all those cookies children left waiting for him. He had been sharing them with the forest dwelling sasquatch children who had probably never tasted human food before. How strange and probably delightful to taste a Christmas cookie when you had only eaten the food of the forest before. I could only hope one day to taste a one myself.

"Santa Claus thought the sasquatches of the Alaskan wilderness may be able to help us rescue him. Can you?" I asked shaking the thought of gingerbread boys and sugar cookies from my head.

"Maybe."

"Either you can, or you cannot," Natalie said, ever practical, and finally coming out of her shock.

"I can. But I do not know if I will, or if I should. Tell me more about the enchantment." His voice rumbled, deep, but soft, in the icy cold air.

I told him everything. About the sadness that covered humanity, about how the world had forgotten Christmas, about my letter to Santa Claus. I pulled it out of my pocket and offered to let him read it. He took the paper in his hand and briefly looked at the scrolling words, but he did not linger over the paper as others had. It occurred to me that maybe sasquatches could not read. I told him we had only a short amount of time before the enchantment cast by the Yeti would become a permanent curse and the world would be swallowed by chaos.

"You won't escape it. Humans are capable of such destruction." It made me sad to say that, but it was true. We were a violent, aggressive animal, humans, and I could only imagine how we would behave under a curse that made us even more so.

"We have our magic. We may survive it."

"Many of you would die first. And your friend? Santa Claus? You would abandon him to the Yeti? And all the other animals of the forest that would suffer or perish?"

His eyes were so gentle, so full of kindness. I had to believe he would not do this, let Santa Claus remain imprisoned by the Yeti, and let the forests suffer, if he could help it.

The giant sasquatch shook his head sadly. "The Yeti's enchantment is of the enemy. He should not have done this. He is supposed to care for the trees, for the wild creatures of the earth. That is why he was given magic, why all our kind were given magic. Instead, he has bowed to the powers of evil and many creatures have died to serve his fell purposes."

"Then help us!" I begged.

"I had to hear your story first. I had to know that you were honest and true. Many humans have come to our forest, searching for us. They have not always been true. You do not seem interested in finding where we are hidden or exposing our ways to the world. I know also from your story that you are true friends to each other. You are brave and determined to embark on this quest. Your reasons for rescuing my friend, Santa Claus are pure. I think I will help you."

"You can tell all those things from one short tale?" Nat asked with skepticism in her voice. I shot her a look that I hoped said 'please don't anger the sasquatch!' We needed his help and she wanted to be skeptical.

"I can. I am magic. Is that not why you came seeking our aid?"

"We came because Santa Claus said you were his friends and may help," Desmond said. "We know nothing of your magic. All we know of the sasquatch is what the world of humans has taught us, which is that you would likely eat us. We did not even know you could speak. We just......" and Desmond shrugged, looking for the right word. "Hoped."

"Believed," I added.

"Even braver than I thought," said the sasquatch.

"I'm Eve," I said deciding it was time for introductions. "This is my cousin, Natalie, and our friend Desmond."

The sasquatch nodded to each of us in turn. "I am Hemlock."

Hemlock, the giant sasquatch sat down on the stump of a tree and his amber eyes watched us closely.

He broke a bit of the yellowish fungus growing in layers up the side of the decaying stump and began to munch. He offered a chunk to us, but we hesitated.

"Eat. This fungus has roots deep within this tree and down into the very earth surrounding it. It will lend you both nourishment and the protection of our magical forest as we seek to confront the Yeti."

"It won't poison us?" Desmond asked skeptically.

"Poison?" said Hemlock.

"Of course not," Nat chimed in. "It's Laetiporus Sulphureus, also known as sulphur polypore, or chicken of the woods. It's known to have a meaty texture and tastes similar to chicken, at least when cooked. It's likely safer to eat than the candy canes Eve fed us. I am not sure we should eat it raw, however. Those mushrooms can cause gastrointestinal problems or allergic reactions in some people. But no, it will not poison us."

"If I am to accompany you, then you need to learn to trust me. Eat," Hemlock said. "This forest is tended to by the sasquatch, every plant here has magical properties. Let my forest strengthen and sustain you for I believe our journey will be long and full of peril. You will find that you can last far longer without sleep or nourishment once you have tasted the food of my forest."

I reminded myself that my role was to be the believer, to trust in Christmas magic. So far it had not let me down, so I pulled a solid hunk of the mushroom from the base of the rotting tree, brushed a bit of dirt off it with my gloved fingers, and I bit into it. It was chewy and tasted like earth, not chicken, but it was not an unpleasant taste. And Hemlock was right, I could feel the magic in the raw fungi from this forest strengthening and nourishing me, filling me but not leaving me heavy like the diner food we had been surviving on had done. I felt energized and full of life. Desmond and Natalie followed my lead and Hemlock nodded his head in approval.

"Now then," he said. "I think we should be on our way."

Esa Salo

O n our way to where?" Desmond asked with
skeptically raised brows. I was wondering the
same thing. Did the sasquatch know something
about where Santa Claus was that we did not.

"Mmmmm, that is the question," rumbled the
sasquatch. "I suppose we need to make our way closer
to the North Pole or the Yeti's territory."

"Assuming you know where that is, because we do
not," Nat said, "do you really think it's wise for us to
just go strolling in there? People are disappearing,
assumed to be dead, and we think it may be the Yeti's
doing!"

"Your assumptions are likely correct," agreed
Hemlock. "But how else are we to save him?"

"Hemlock, in his letter Santa Claus told me to seek
the aid of his captain of the guard, a polar bear named
Eylif. Do you know her?" I asked, thinking finding her
might be a better first step.

"I know of her. I am surprised to hear she escaped the Yeti, while others at the North Pole did not. What else did your letter say?"

"Santa Claus was not sure she escaped," I told him. "He said his wife, the elves, and reindeer were with him, but Eylif and his daughter were missing."

"His daughter is missing? Holiday Claus was my friend," Hemlock said sadly then he shook himself. "All the more reason to make haste. If there is a way to save Santa Claus and his daughter, then we must do it."

Desmond looked tentatively at the sasquatch. "We have also been searching for answers as to what happened to my parents. They disappeared on an expedition to study the arctic, and we think it has something to do with the Yeti. I know rescuing Santa Claus is more important than discovering how my parents died, since they are already gone and saving Santa Claus means saving the world, but we had planned to go to Helsinki where my parents and I once lived. I have a friend there and he may have information on my parents. It's possible this knowledge could be linked, maybe give us some clues."

"Sasquatches do not take lives," Hemlock said, looking troubled. "Though the Yeti is, well, he has lost his way. It may or may not have been him who took the lives of your parents."

Natalie then explained to Hemlock the maps they had plotted. With no service in the wilderness, she was unable to show him the actual map, but I do not think he would have needed it.

"The area you speak of is certainly within the Yeti's territory. Even the sasquatches now avoid that area. But it is also possible there is something else important about that location," Hemlock said thoughtfully. I had the feeling he was keeping something back from us. "Helsinki!" he said succinctly. "Friends, I cannot go into the city with you. My presence there would be catastrophic. But I can take us to the closest forest. You will have to make your way from there. I will search the forest, talk to the trees and animals, and find out what they know while you meet with your friend and see what information he can share with us."

"Wait! Talk to the trees?" Natalie said. "I mean, science has proven that trees do communicate in a way through mycorrhizal networks, but how can they give you information? They're plants!"

Hemlock laughed and it was a throaty rumble that sounded like the earth quaking. "Science! What does science know? The understanding you humans have of the forest and the way the trees, plants, and animals communicate with each other is very limited. I am a sasquatch. I speak all languages, from the language of the trees to the tiniest insect. Even your language, little humans."

"An hour ago, I did not know sasquatches could speak at all," I said. "I suppose it's not too farfetched to believe you can communicate with the trees. The bigger problem here, is how we are going to fit you into our small auto and get ourselves through customs at the border and into Helsinki!"

Hemlock laughed again and I felt the rumble vibrate my bones. "Little humans, again, I am a sasquatch. This auto of yours will not be necessary for me to travel. However, since you are insisting on going into the city, I suppose we should bring it with us."

Hemlock then did something I do not have words to describe. He disappeared. He took two steps and was gone. He did it in the brightest patch of moonlight in

141

our little clearing so there could be no doubt that it was not a trick of the shadows. And then he was behind me.

"I am a sasquatch," he said again. "The dimensional laws of the earth hold no sway over me. I go where I will, and I need to take no more than a step or two to get there." I was so startled at his voice behind me I nearly screamed, but I managed to stay calm.

"Can the Yeti do that too?" Nat asked. Hemlock nodded his head, and I felt a chill creep up my spine. Hemlock's magic felt, well, magical, but to think that a creature with so much malice had the same abilities frightened me. I looked at my scientific cousin and I could tell she was having a much more difficult time than I was believing all she was seeing, but I could also see she was pondering some kind of big idea

I remembered reading somewhere that sasquatch footprints would suddenly stop. I had read stories of hunters who would have a sasquatch in their sights, and then suddenly their quarry would vanish into thin air. There had been theories the sasquatch was an interdimensional being, either alien or paranormal, but most of those were considered fringe theories. When the sasquatch was finally proven to exist those theories just faded, and people only saw them as a kind of ape, a primate who had managed to stay hidden in the wilder parts of the woods, but nothing more than a cousin to the gorilla. Yet, there was Hemlock showing us that there was some truth to some of those fringe theories. Clearly, he was no ghost, nor was he a man from mars, but he did have magic that I do not think any human theory could ever explain.

"How do you think Santa Claus was able to deliver all those gifts in one night?" Hemlock asked as the three of us continued to gape at him in disbelief. "We taught him our magic. Not only could he travel the world at a brilliant speed, but he could also evade detection." The sasquatch looked amused at our bewilderment, but then he took on a more serious tone. "Children, I must ask that all you see while you travel with me, you keep to yourselves. If the human world were to view us as anything other than a creature with no more intelligence than a monkey it would be catastrophic to the sasquatch. That is why my brother did not want to help you. The risk is too high. You must give me your solemn promise to keep our secret."

We were quite dumbfounded at this point, but we managed to all nod our promise to Hemlock. Our new friend then motioned for us to get into Dad's auto, and we obeyed. Before we could even strap ourselves in, we felt the sasquatch lift the auto from the ground and then set it gently down seconds later. When we got out, we were in an entirely different forest.

"The beauty of Helsinki," Hemlock said as we stepped out of the car and looked all around us, "is that the old growth forests are very near the city. Welcome to Haltiala, as they call this forest here in Finland. You should be able to find your friend from here. I intend to disappear into deeper wilds than this, but these trees will be kind and keep me from the eyes of humans long enough to see you safely off."

If we were, in fact, in a forest in Finland, very near to the city of Helsinki, Hemlock had brought us in two steps what it likely would have taken us a full day or more to travel. Not only that, but no passports had been needed. Natalie was beside herself. My poor aspiring scientist cousin had just broken all the laws of the natural world and she was spluttering and wide-eyed.

Desmond was looking around and grinning from ear to ear. I could see the recognition in his eyes. He was home. That was all the confirmation I needed, and I threw my arms as far around the gigantic sasquatch as I could get them, knowing that even though I was putting all the strength I had into this hug, I was a kitten hugging a lion. Still, Hemlock was startled by the embrace. In the daylight I could see just how shiny his black fur was. I had read that sasquatches had a terrible, filthy smell, but Hemlock smelled of earth and loam and rainy skies, and it was comforting. He hugged me back with one arm and gave my head a pat with his other huge hand.

"I am happy, little human, that you are so grateful for my help. Maybe you are all not so terrible as we thought."

"You think we're all terrible?" I asked with sadness but not surprise.

"Yes," Hemlock said simply.

"Then why help?" Desmond asked.

"The sasquatch are here to look after the earth and all her inhabitants. Are you humans not inhabitants of the earth? Part of nature itself? You have done much harm to the earth and those who you share your home with, but that does not mean I wish death and destruction upon you. My brother, who you met first in the forest, does not see things exactly the way I do. Not that he would have eaten you. It is just that it is his job to frighten away the humans. But he did not want to help you, either. He, like many others of my kind, believe that we should patiently wait for you to destroy yourselves. There are those among the sasquatch who believe that you humans have set yourselves apart from nature and so you must be treated as such. But, for Santa Claus, I am breaking our rules about interacting with humans. Also, I was curious. I have never spoken to a human other than Santa Claus and his family. I know as little about you as you seem to know about me."

"I don't care why you're helping us, Hemlock," I said. "I'm just grateful you are." And I could say no more because the sasquatch was not wrong about humans. We were a disaster.

"We should waste no more time," said the sasquatch. "Go into the city. See what you can learn." He then dropped a soft, white pebble into my hands. "Take this. It is how I will find you again. When you have learned what you can from your friend in the city come back to this place or any place heavy with trees and rub the stone. I will come to you. God speed." Hemlock then turned and took several large steps deeper into the tall trees and disappeared.

"Christmas magic!" I said turning to Nat and Desmond with a wide smile. They were smiling back. "Five minutes ago, we were in a forest in Alaska. Now look at us!"

"Desmond, what is Esa's address?" Natalie asked, ignoring my exclamations of Christmas magic. I left her alone, letting her pull up the navigation to the address Desmond recited, while she processed all the non-scientific magic that was going on around her.

"I sent Esa a message as soon as I recognized where we had landed. He's expecting us. Let's go!" Desmond said. I smiled at his excitement to see his old friend and Nat and I hurried to the auto. I hoped Esa was as amazing as Desmond made him out to be.

145

We parked Dad's muddied vehicle in front of Esa's house less than an hour later and a smiling, freckled boy with the brightest red hair I have ever seen came flying from the house. He crashed into Desmond, and they threw their arms around each other, hugging and laughing. Then Desmond introduced Natalie and I and the four of us went into Esa's house.

We sat around a glass table with polished wooden legs and Esa set a plate of some kind of cheesy bread down in front of us and steaming mugs of hot chocolate, per the request of Desmond before we arrived. Desmond looked at me questioningly and I nodded. While he distracted his friend, I dropped an entire pre-crushed magic candy cane into his cup. Esa took a sip and peered down into his mug, surprised by the bite of peppermint. Desmond was quick to distract him with a story from their past involving bikes and outrunning bullies and Esa continued to drink from the mug of altered cocoa.

We had been out in the cold woods all night and the hot food Esa had set in front of us did not last long on the table. Though the sustenance from the forest food we had eaten had still not worn off, in fact I was not sure I would ever feel hungry again, the warmth of the food going down was what we really needed. The hot chocolate was delicious, creamy and thick with just a hint of saltiness to it. Esa and Desmond were talking a million miles a minute, reminiscing about all their old hijinks, and Nat and I quietly ate and listened. I was so delighted to hear about Desmond's life growing up in Helsinki, that I almost forgot why we had come to see Esa in the first place. As the boy took the last sips from his mug of cocoa, Desmond began to weave the tale of our own adventure, from the day he overheard us on the transport up to meeting Hemlock and magically arriving in Helsinki through a fold in the dimensions of the world.

Esa stared, wide-eyed with disbelief and looking like he was trying to decide whether or not to laugh. "You're joking," he said in his accented English. "Christmas? You've made friends with a magical sasquatch? This is your best prank yet, Des!"

"This is no prank," Desmond said and all the mirth and laughter that had been in his voice only moments before upon being reunited with Esa was gone. He looked at his friend with such sincerity I wondered how anyone could possibly disbelieve him.

"Well, let's talk about that polar bear, then," Esa said matching Desmond's serious tone. I instantly knew why Desmond loved him. He did not argue, he had only barely questioned, and then he had jumped right in to help. "Are you sure she's one of the good guys?"

"Santa Claus said she was the captain of his guard and a friend in his letter," I told him and handed him the folded-up letter I had taken to leaving in my jacket pocket, ready to show as proof that what we were doing was real and necessary. Esa read it, and then read it a second time, just as everyone else I had shared it with had done. It was too unbelievable not to give it a second read.

"I ask because there have been polar bear sightings," he said as he finished reading. "It's why I reached out to you. It's said the polar bear is vicious, rumored to have attacked some folks. They are even saying this polar bear could be linked to some of the disappearances that have happened on these arctic expeditions. I thought maybe your parents......." Esa

147

trailed off and I could tell by the look in his eye that he had been dreading sharing that with Desmond. Death by vicious polar bear attack even though polar bears had been extinct for several decades, was not a pleasant image. Certainly not news you would want to deliver to your best friend.

"Do you suppose Eylif has been enchanted?" Nat asked.

"Maybe she betrayed Santa Claus and that's why she isn't with him, wherever he is," Desmond said somberly. I could tell he was trying not to think of how painful it may have been to be mauled by a polar bear.

Esa shrugged. "Or she could be a perfectly friendly polar bear and what we've got going on here is nothing but the rumor mill." We all looked at him and he shrugged again. "Just thinking about your sasquatch friend is all. Before their existence was proven, there were all kinds of wild rumors about how savage and vicious they were. Even now, people are terrified of them. Sounds like they were wrong. Could be the same for this polar bear."

"Let's hope so," Desmond said.

"So, where have the polar bear sightings occurred?" Nat asked, ready to jump in and find Eylif.

"Funny, but before polar bears went extinct, there were none living in Finland. Now, it seems, there is one roaming around the Arctic Circle, including here in Finland. It was the Finland sighting that got me looking into things. I started following the story. It, or I guess if it's your Eylif, she, seems to be making the rounds through the Arctic Circle. She's been seen in Alaska, Canada, Denmark, and Sweden. There are even rumors of a white bear in Russia. I think someone in Norway called it an albino bear. Most of these stories are being treated as a hoax. People saying they saw this mysterious white bear, or a polar bear for attention, or it was some other type of animal, and they just imagined it to be a polar bear."

"It sounds to me like she's searching," said Natalie. "If she is traveling the Arctic Circle and she's been seen outside places that would have been her natural habitat, she must be looking for something. But this is all assuming it is the same bear."

"And," I added excitedly, "if it is the same bear she clearly has some magic to be able to travel across oceans like that!"

"The Arctic Circle is huge. Roughly 9,900 miles in circumference. How will we ever find her?" Natalie said.

"Or 16,000 km," Esa said, easily converting to the metric system.

I figured Nat and Esa were about to be the best of friends with his miles to kilometers conversion. But I was not interested in their facts or hearing how daunting our task was going to be. There was no way we could cover 9,900 miles, and I did not really even understand how the whole circumference thing factored in. What I did know was that some of those miles were ocean and Eylif was not going to be in the middle of the ocean, and so far, Christmas magic had not failed us. Esa was the only one who looked at me strangely when I told them this, but he had not seen our Christmas magic in action.

"Well, I will tell you this," Esa said. "The most recent sighting was nowhere near here. If you had told me all of this before you came, I could have sent you to the right country at least!"

"You wouldn't have been able to help. The enchantment. You would have heard Santa Claus, Christmas, and polar bears and probably just hung up on me," Desmond told him.

"But......oh yeah, the enchantment. Wait.... I'm hearing you now! Am I going to forget all this after you leave? Am I about to go all fuzzy and blank?" Esa shook his red hair and looked a bit nervous. Oops. We had forgotten to tell him about candy canes!

"The peppermint in your cocoa! I slipped a magic candy cane in while you weren't looking," I told him, laughing just a bit at the look of fear on his face that he might forget our whole conversation. "Desmond gave me permission!" I threw in. I didn't need anyone else mad at me for sneaking candy canes into their drink. But Esa thought it was hilarious.

"I thought it tasted wrong," he said roaring with laughter. "But it was still delicious, so I drank it."

Esa told us the last polar bear sighting had been in Russia two weeks ago. Which meant we had no idea where Eylif was now. We were looking at maps, talking strategies, trying to figure out how far Eylif could have gotten based on time between sightings and distance traveled (a math equation I was leaving entirely to Nat), when Esa looked up at us with worry.

"It's Mom, Des," the red-haired boy said after glancing at his messages. "Natalie and Eve's parents somehow tracked her down and she is asking me if I know where you all are! What do I say?!"

"My cousin!" Desmond groaned. "He must have given them your mom's contact info. Don't tell her we're here!"

I felt a knot of guilt in my stomach. Mom, Dad, and Uncle P.J. had been calling non-stop. And sending messages. I had ignored all of them. They had to be worried sick. And with the enchantment strengthening and people's moods growing angrier, I had to think they were not doing so well. I looked at Nat and she looked as guilty as I was feeling.

"Have you responded to any of their messages?" I asked her and she shook her head no. "Esa, tell them we were here and safe," I said throwing caution to the wind. I did not want them to suffer more than they needed to. "They should at least know we're alive. We're leaving anyway. I'm afraid if I call, if I send a message, I'll lose my nerve. This way, they'll know we are ok. But tell them we left! Tell them we're coming home soon! I do not want them to try coming to Helsinki looking for us!" Esa nodded and began to draft the message to his mother.

"I just remembered something!" I shouted as I felt the round white stone Hemlock had given me in my pocket. "We're friends with a sasquatch! We have to get back to the forest. We can reach Hemlock there and he can take us to any forest we want to go within seconds. Forget maps and prioritizing, Nat. We can check them all."

"This I have to see," said Esa. "I'm going with you!"

What the Trees told Hemlock

Bringing Esa with us was putting another child in danger, but there was no talking him out of it. I figured if the world was going to sink into chaos and death if we failed, we could not afford to pass up any help. With all the people under an enchantment, and my magic candy canes now depleted, we were on our own. If I had access to the president or someone more powerful, I may have saved the last magic candy cane, but I was just a kid who had stumbled upon a mystery. Now it was up to me to save the world, but I was pretty sure with Natalie, Desmond, Hemlock and now Esa by my side, we were going to stick it to this horrible Yeti and the world would be joyful once more.

We wasted no time waiting around for Esa's parents or ours to stop us. We piled into Dad's auto and headed right back to Haltiala, stepping into the cover of the thickest trees we could find once we had parked. Nat tried to get as close as she could to the same place we had left Hemlock. We had no idea if that was necessary or not, but we figured it couldn't hurt. Esa was nervous, hopping from one foot to the other and I reminded myself how anxious we ourselves had been waiting in the woods trying to draw the attention of the sasquatches we had hoped would be there. At least Esa would not have to contend with Hemlock's terrifying and much larger brother. I still did not like to think about the way his thunderous roar had paralyzed me where I stood.

The woods were cold, and a heavy fog had swirled through the trees cloaking everything in secrecy. I was glad for it. The people were all at home, staying cozy and dry, while we did our best to save them in secret. If our parents were to find us, it was over for the world and Hemlock could definitely not be seen in the presence of four children. Not only would that terrify everyone in Finland, but it might also alert the Yeti that we were coming, and we had help. The fog was a gift today and as it swirled about my legs, giving the world a mysterious and magical feeling, I smiled and took joy in its wonder.

I was thinking again about the time Mom and I had taken Grams the Great to the edge of the forest so she could smell the pine trees and breathe in the fresh air. It had always been one of my favorite memories, but now that I knew Grams had been trying to wake me up to Christmas, it was even more so. Mom had not wanted to go into the trees, but Grams and I had talked her into walking a little ways in. I will never forget that air, the first breath of wild I had ever taken. No smog, no city noise to choke the air from your lungs, just fresh clean trees, cool and calming to your soul. In Haltiala, in the wilds of Alaska, the air was even more delicious, and I wanted to never leave. I held Hemlock's stone tightly, as smooth and cool in my hand as the air felt in my lungs. Briefly, I imagined just hiding there forever, away from the chaos and danger, but only briefly. The peace of the woods can fool you like that. Make you feel safe and warm even on the coldest days, but humans are weak creatures and once hungry and cold, we cannot survive out there. It would not be long before that place that felt so like an embrace to me in the moment would turn on us, remembering how unkind we had always been to it. We would not last, and we would be dooming the rest of humankind to even try.

I rubbed the stone with my thumb and felt it grow warm at my touch. Hemlock arrived within seconds, though if I had not been expecting him, I may not have noticed his inky form appear in the trees and mist. I realized now how sasquatches had remained hidden from the world for so long. It occurred to me that possibly we 'proved' their existence because they finally let us. If humans knew that sasquatches existed and were frightened of them, maybe we would leave what was left of the world's deep forests alone. If that was true, it had worked. The wilder parts of the world have remained wild because humans fear the woods now. Hemlock stepped through his fold in the air, keeping silently hidden in the shadows of the trees and I gave him a moment, trying to be respectful, understanding he needed to assess the woods and make sure it was just us before he revealed himself. When he did, Esa sat down hard on a tree stump, his mouth hanging open and his bright blue eyes saucers.

"Esa, meet Hemlock," Desmond said laughing at the hilarious look on his friend's freckled face.

Once Desmond began to laugh, Nat and I joined in. It was impossible not to. We were on an adventure that could possibly end in death by Yeti, but we had eaten magical candy canes, sasquatch mushrooms, and in the air, there was a feeling of Christmas. Somehow, despite where we were and what we were doing, we felt lighter than we had in our entire lives.

Once our laughter died down, and Hemlock and Esa had made their acquaintances, I told Hemlock what we had learned of the polar bear sightings and that we were hopeful it was Eylif. "Were you able to find anything from your forest friends?" I asked as I finished relaying our own information.

Hemlock's giant brow ridge raised, I think likely at the phrase 'forest friends' and I hoped I had not offended him. I suppose it may have sounded sarcastic, if sasquatches even knew how to use sarcasm. Hemlock, so far, had been deeply serious about everything he did. But my giant new friend did not give me much time to dwell on whether or not I had offended him because what he said next absolutely blew all of us away.

"The polar bear sightings have indeed all been Eylif, the polar bear. The trees have also shared with me where the Yeti has hidden our friend, Santa Claus." As the words, in Hemlock's rich, mossy voice, sank in, I think all our faces looked exactly as Esa's had just moments before.

For the second time, I threw myself around the giant sasquatch, my skinny arms not even reaching halfway around his vastness. His fur tickled my nose as I took in his wild, rainy-day scent again.

"Thank you, thank you, thank you!" I said. "Let's go!"

"Slow down, Eve," Natalie said. "Let's find out where he is first, and then we can make a real plan. I have a feeling I already know, and if I'm right, the Yeti has not made it so easy for folks to just stroll in and grab him."

"Natalie is correct," Hemlock agreed. "Santa Claus is well hidden and well-guarded. Your map, Natalie, the area you have pinpointed, is not the home of the Yeti. Rather, it is the location of where the Yeti has imprisoned Santa Claus."

Natalie nodded. "When you said the Yeti could move as quickly as you can through the world, I began to suspect," she said.

"Any human who has come too close to this spot, too close to discovering the prison of Santa Claus, has been dealt with by the Yeti. I believe it would be wise for us to approach this Eylif first. I have also ascertained her whereabouts. The more allies we have, the greater our chances for success on this endeavor."

"Wait, you found both Santa Claus and Eylif in the two hours it took us to put together that Eylif has been sighted and might be somewhere in the Arctic Circle?" I said and I did not even try to keep the incredulity out of my tone.

"I did," the sasquatch said simply. "My, mmm, forest friends were of great help to me." He placed great emphasis on the words I had earlier used, and I thought I may have caught a note of a joke in his rumbling voice. So, sasquatches did know how to be sarcastic.

"Your forest friends are amazing," Desmond said in wonder.

"The trees see all and can communicate with each other over long distances. They will help in any way they can. They have no great love for humans, but a world sunk into chaos can only mean their destruction as well. The trees will surely burn alongside you. They also have always loved Santa Claus and his wife. The Claus family spent a great deal of time exploring the wilds when not preparing for their holiday. They were always welcome visitors in the wilder places of the world."

I thought I was simply here to save a man from a Yeti and bring back Christmas, but I was learning so much about the world on this adventure. I felt a sense of awe, that I, a simple twelve-year-old girl with nothing really all that special about me, was being given this gift. I had found two new friends in Desmond and Esa, and I knew they would be mine always. I had also befriended a sasquatch and was learning the secret ways of this elusive creature. We were on our way to find a polar bear, probably one with some magic, and an animal thought to have been extinct for decades. I had to take a deep breath and let it all wash over me. This new world, this world of love and friendship, this world that held promise, not just Christmas promise, but wild woods and joy and a life beyond the grey of the city, this was a world worth fighting for. Somehow, despite the enchantment, I had always felt this world could exist, but now I knew, and I felt determined to share this gift, to unburden the people and give them back joy and happiness.

"I have studied the trees and how they communicate, and the books just do not do it justice," Natalie said. "Is it because you are a sasquatch? You said you speak many languages. Is it a language, what the trees do?"

"It is a language, but I believe you have a limited view of language," Hemlock said. "Another day, Natalie? You and I, we could speak for hours on the languages of the world. I would tell you the story of the capture of Santa Claus, now. We have much work to do. But I promise, if we are successful, I will let you ask all your human scientist questions."

Hemlock struggled to hide his scorn for the word scientist, but Nat did not seem to notice. I saw her begin to go to her gamma, as though she wanted to record the notes of all that was happening into the science journals she kept, but she did not. I was proud of her. The tale of Santa Claus was not one to miss. She nodded to Hemlock in agreement that they would have this discussion another day, and the fact that another day may not come for us was left unsaid.

"As you know, Santa Claus disappeared from the world eighty-two years ago, Christmas Eve of the year 2025. An enchantment was cast over the land causing all of humankind to forget the Christmas holiday and Santa Claus. I was a child then, but I remember the night well. Our friend, Santa Claus would come to us on Christmas day with his wife, Santa Rosa, and their young daughter Holiday. They brought sweet treats for the children, and they played all day. Holiday had a toy called a sled and she would let us all take turns flying down the snowy hills while the elders watched for the prying eyes of humans. On this particular Christmas day, Santa Claus did not appear. Sasquatches are not immune to enchantments, though it did not affect us as strongly as it did you humans. We did not forget Santa Claus, but we also did not go looking for him. Until you came screaming into my forest, shouting his name, he was just a distant memory. We noticed he did not arrive, but nothing more. We asked no questions, and after a few years he was mostly forgotten.

Simply hearing you call his name was enough to break the enchantment for my brother and me. He believed it was a human affair and we should not involve ourselves, but I remembered Holiday and her kindness. I remembered Santa Claus and his bright cookies. I remembered his wife, Santa Rosa, who would fly down hills with the young sasquatches laughing and shrieking. She was so loved by the animals of the forest, the birds especially. They would follow her, eat seeds from her hand, and sing to her as she would flit about the trees. The three of them were magic, set apart from the human world, full of love and laughter. And my friend, Holiday brought books. The written word is the one language sasquatches have never learned, but she was teaching me. She brought books with bright pictures so that I could learn more of the world than just the wild forests where the sasquatches hide. So, when the enchantment was lifted and I remembered all those things again, I knew I had to help you. For the world, yes, but also because they were my friends.

The ancient trees that grow in the farthest reaches of the north tell me the night Santa Claus was taken a great cry went out from the pines that grew in the North Pole, Santa Claus's enchanted home. The human world believed there was nothing but blocks of ice that melted into the sea, but this is not so. He had an entire village hidden there and when the Yeti sunk the village those trees and animals perished. However, before they were drowned in the icy waters, the trees let their sisters know that it was the Yeti, sworn to protect them, who had taken their lives and the lives of the many animals who had once called the North Pole their home. He had used a powerful spell that put Santa Claus, the elves, and the reindeer all to sleep. With the help of a few wolverines, he moved them from the North Pole to a cave in the wildest and coldest part of the Arctic Circle. They are trapped in this cave by the Yeti's cruel magic. He has enchanted the area so that if any come near, he will know and he comes from his home in the highest Himalayas, shrouded always in ice and inhospitable to humans, and he removes the threat."

"Removes the threat?" Desmond broke in, his voice stricken. I knew what he must be thinking. His parents had stumbled across the Yeti's enchanted border and paid the price.

Hemlock looked at Desmond with gentle, amber eyes. "Sasquatches do not take lives, little friend. The Yeti has changed, and I do not know if he is still bound by our laws. He has lost his way, isolating himself on the top of that mountain. But the trees have told me that there are more humans than just Santa Claus, asleep in that cave. I make you no promises, Desmond, for the trees do not see everything, but I believe it is possible that some of the people who have gone missing from the Arctic Circle, may yet be alive."

Natalie took Desmond's hand as his eyes filled with tears. He did not try to wipe them away this time but let them slowly fall down his cold cheeks. I could not imagine the emotions he might be feeling, the hope that had likely welled up in his chest, for some measure of it was now welling in mine for him. I also could not imagine being given that hope only to find your parents had perished, and I hoped and wished with all I had that we would find both the Carters alive and well when we found Santa Claus. Esa and I both went to Desmond now too, hugging him as he cried and hoped. Solving the mystery of the death of Desmond's parents had just turned into a possible rescue mission.

"The polar bear, Eylif, did escape the Yeti," Hemlock continued. "The trees do not know how. She came to shore on a ship, battling her captors and fleeing into the woods. She has hunted for him since then, even stumbling upon the cave that Santa Claus slept in without realizing it, for it is enchanted and will appear an empty cave to any eyes that wander past. She has fought with the Yeti more than once, when she could find him, but he avoids her, preferring to hide in the Himalayan mountains and wait out the years until he has won. She now hides herself on an island in Iceland, despairing because she knows she is out of time. The trees tell me she has given up and awaits the fate of the world there. They tell me she has been brave and valiant, determined up until now, but the enchantment, the sadness, is weighing on her. I will take you to Eylif first for I do not know if we should go to the Himalayas and face the Yeti or if we should go to Santa Claus and free him. We need time to make those decisions."

The Captain of the Guard and Her Puffin

This time we left Dad's borrowed auto behind. I patted the hood and promised Dad we would come back for it soon. I wondered if stealing an auto would put me on Santa Claus's naughty list, even though we had only done it to save him. I wondered if the naughty list was something Santa Claus really kept, or if it was something that parents made up to coerce their children into good behavior. For the second time we traveled via sasquatch magic, but the first time we had been in an auto that Hemlock had lifted and carried. This time we walked through what I can only describe as a fold in the fabric of the world and that is a poor description.

We came out on a rocky shore and there were birds everywhere. I had never seen so many. When I looked up, birds were circling and when I looked down, there were many more at my feet. I could not name a single bird, but I could see Natalie mouthing names as she looked around her. Then I looked at Hemlock, who appeared for the first time since I had met him to be nervous and I realized he was out in the open, exposed for the world to see and there was not a single tree in sight.

"Hemlock! No trees!"

He shook his head. "There are none on this island. I had no choice. But if we could stop gawking at the birds and find your polar bear, I would be very grateful. It is an anxious feeling for a sasquatch to be out of the tall trees. There are less than one hundred people living on this island and they inhabit the southwest side, opposite to where we have landed. Still, it is a small island, and I have taken a great risk. If any had seen us just appear......" he did not finish his sentence.

I knew the risk he had taken, bringing us here. Hemlock was as determined as we were, and just as willing to risk all to find Santa Claus and stop the Yeti. Out of nowhere a bird noisily landed on Hemlock's broad shoulder. She had red rimmed eyes, her beak was of the brightest orange, and if I had not heard Nat call her a puffin, her black and white feathers would have left me thinking she was some kind of penguin. The puffin made a noise, a throaty cawing that was so much deeper than I had expected. The bird calls I had heard were trills, songs, but this bird had a harsh squawk wildly different from the bird songs I remembered from home. However, the noises it made had Hemlock's full attention. Then he seemed to be speaking back to her and I realized the puffin and the sasquatch were having a conversation. After a moment he turned back to us to translate.

"This puffin is a friend to your polar bear. The bear is not well. She has been wounded, possibly by a hunter. The puffins bring her fish to eat and keep her company, but they have no skill at healing. She saw that I was a sasquatch and recognized me as a friend to all nature. She has hope that I can help her friend. She is not sure about you four, however."

I felt my heart sink. Poor Eylif. And there was likely nothing we could do for her. The puffin flew away, and Hemlock made to follow her. He beckoned for us saying, "Come. She will take us to the polar bear though the four of you have yet to earn her trust."

We made our away across the rocky ocean shore in silence. I was fascinated by the sound of the spray of water, the crash of waves, the strange honk of the puffins joined by all the other bird calls so that the island was a cacophony of water and bird. I had seen documentaries, heard these sounds, birds and crashing waves. But as we picked our way over the rocky shore I realized you have heard nothing until you have listened to these sounds with real wind on your cheeks, with real salt spray on your lips, the briny scent filling your senses, with the sounds swirling in the air all around you so that it is not background on your screen for the images you are seeing but it is real and live and all around you. I wanted to live this kind of life forever, real for me to touch and smell, away from the city and the screens. I wanted to see it all. I wanted to stop and throw rocks in the ocean and just watch these birds. I had to remind myself that we had a mission, and I needed to focus. But I did make a promise to myself that if we made it out of this alive and with the world intact that I would travel, I would see the wild places of the world.

We approached a dark cave and the puffin turned and squawked something at us then disappeared into the dark cavern.

"Ing would like us to wait here. She believes surprising Eylif with four human children and a sasquatch may end in disaster. Eylif is, after all, a wild animal, and a polar bear at that."

I supposed that made sense and my friends all nodded in agreement. Hemlock lowered himself to a rock as though sitting could shrink him or make him less noticeable. I did not tell him that there was nothing that would make him less noticeable. He was a giant, black furred sasquatch with nowhere to hide on this wide-open island. Only Christmas magic could keep human eyes from seeing him now. The puffins, for their part, seemed to love him, and gathered round him, perching on his shoulders and his knees. I thought maybe, if another human were to approach it would be the mass of puffins gathering around him that would keep him magically hidden.

Ing returned shortly, her tiny bird figure waddling comically from the cave. She puffed out her little white chest and squawked and I could almost make out the words "Eylif will see you now." Hemlock confirmed that she had indeed told us we would be given an audience with the polar bear, and we followed the protective and important little puffin into the cold damp darkness of the sea cave. I heard the polar bears belabored breathing before I saw her. It was hard to tell in the dark cave, but there appeared to be blood matted in her white fur near her back hind leg.

The polar bear spoke first, raising her head and staring us down with her dark, almond-shaped eyes. They looked pained, but whether she was hurting physically or was simply sad I could not say. Likely, it was both. Her voice rumbled deeply and reverberated richly throughout the cave.

"You know where Santa Claus is?" she questioned. "I have been searching for him for nearly eighty-three years now and my puffin friend tells me you have found him."

"The trees have given me the location of his prison," Hemlock answered.

"And these children, sasquatch? Why have you brought them here?" she asked, her nut-brown eyes narrowing as she took us in.

"On the contrary, it is they who have brought me on their adventure," Hemlock answered her. Technically, he had brought us to this island, and we never would have found Eylif without him, or least not so quickly, but I was grateful to him for giving us some measure of the credit. "These children have freed themselves from the enchantment of the Yeti, which has caused all humankind to forget Christmas completely. They found me and brought me out of the cursed fog I was in as well. It is their wish only to save Santa Claus and Christmas and heal the world. In his letter to young Eve," he waved a hand towards me as he said this, "he mentioned you may have escaped and that you could be trusted to help."

The polar bear's eyes came to rest warily upon me. "He wrote you a letter? How has this come to be? How were you able to break the Yeti's enchantment? Santa is awake then?"

"I suppose I should start at the beginning," I told the polar bear. I told her the whole tale, touching briefly on Grams the Great and the years of no one being able to remember or hear my stories, writing

Santa Claus a letter just to see what would happen, waking Nat and Desmond with magic candy canes, and Santa Claus's response to my letter. I let Eylif read the letter herself, laying it on the floor so that she could hold it down with a long black claw and angle her giant head so that her close-set eyes could see the page. When she finished she slid the paper back to me, and I believe there were tears in her dark eyes, though I still do not know if polar bears can cry. I continued the story of how we fled our city, found Hemlock in the Alaskan wilderness, made our way to Esa in Helsinki, and finally here to this island belonging to Iceland that lies just barely within the Arctic Circle.

"It seems that all the pieces have just been falling together for us, so long as we believe they will. Eylif?" I then asked her because I thought she would be able to answer the question better than any other living soul, "is Christmas magic real?"

"Very," she rumbled nodding her head.

"Eylif, how did you escape the Yeti? Why were you not affected by the enchantment?" Desmond asked her. It was a question we had all been wondering.

The polar bear hung her heavy head. "It is my great shame, to have not been with him. He was expecting the Yeti to attack the humans near the North Pole on that Christmas Eve. He knew the sorry creature was plotting something, but the Yeti was too clever. He knew how Santa Claus loved all people. He knew if he made Santa Claus believe he planned to harm the humans, that he would send aid there and leave himself vulnerable. Santa Claus sent me away to the town of Longyearbyen, where he believed the Yeti was about to attack. I was to gather a force of polar bears and prepare to face down the Yeti. We did not know the magic he had found. We assumed he planned to attack the town while Santa Claus was distracted delivering gifts and that a Yeti and a few disgruntled wolverines would not be more than my bears could handle. We did not know the Yeti had become something more, betraying the wilds and the magic that had been given him to become something terrible, something sinister and unimaginable. We did not foresee that the attack on Longyearbyen was a ruse. By the time I realized we had been fooled and that the North Pole was being ambushed, it was too late. When I arrived, Santa Claus was gone, and our home was melting into the sea. But because I was in the North Pole, unknown to the Yeti, when the enchantment was cast, it did not affect me. The North Pole ice is nothing but Christmas magic and so I was saved. At least from the enchantment. I flew away from there as the last of the ice disappeared, exhausted, thinking only to find my family, Santa Claus, Santa Rosa, Holiday, the reindeer, the elves. I did not know where the Yeti had taken them. I did not know if they were even alive. I was so distraught that a ship spotted me and pulled me from the sky in a net. I battled and escaped them once we reached the shore and I have been searching the Arctic since."

"Wait? From the sky? You can fly? How can a polar bear fly?" Natalie asked, and I could not believe that was her first question after hearing Eylif's sad story.

"Christmas magic," Eylif responded. "I can do a great many things other polar bears cannot. For example, I am speaking with you."

The scientist in Nat was furiously calculating the physics of a flying polar bear, I was sure, but if we believed reindeer could fly, why not polar bears? I looked at Eylif's sad eyes and understood now why they held such deep grief. She had been alone for nearly eighty-three years, her entire family lost, her home melted away, and she had done nothing but search.

"It is no shame, Eylif," Desmond said and moved towards the bear, laying a hand against the white fur of her cheek, her wildness seemingly forgotten. "My family, my parents were also taken by the Yeti while I was not with them. I have searched for answers for years now, and only recently have I allowed myself to believe they may still be alive. If not for these friends here with me now, I would have searched alone, and I cannot imagine that burden. Come with us, Eylif, we will help you find your family. And if we never find them, you can be one of us. We can be your family." He turned to look at us, with question in his eyes, hoping he would find that we did consider him our family and that we would love the polar bear too.

Natalie, Esa, and I immediately went to him and wrapped ourselves around our friend and the polar bear. "Family," we said. "Always." The polar bear's puffin squeezed herself into the hug, making herself a part of our family as well, clearly deciding we could be trusted. And then suddenly we were all wrapped in the embrace of a giant sasquatch, who had been extraordinarily uncomfortable every time I had ever hugged him before. A sasquatch hug is something intense, powerful, and I believe even magical, though the magic part may have just been the strong emotions I was feeling. Either way, we were now a family of seven, bonded for life, I was certain, and just as soon as we saved the world, we would bring the rest of our families into the fold as well.

"There is only one problem," Eylif said. "I was attacked by hunters hoping to bring in the elusive, last living polar bear. It has been very difficult since the first spotting to remain hidden, for now the humans search for me. My brothers and sisters have all disappeared from this warming world, so that the white fur of the polar bear stands out. The humans have hunted me relentlessly and I was wounded. I cannot walk. My puffin friends have brought me fish, otherwise I would have starved and perished weeks ago. But I believe there is still a bullet in my leg. I would only slow you down." She hung her great head in sadness. "I have waited so long, fought for so long, but it is not my fate to see Santa Claus and my family again. I can only be grateful, knowing that you will go on to save him. My time left on this earth is not long."

"I believe I may be able to help you with your wound if you will permit me to examine it," Hemlock said gently.

Eylif eyed the sasquatch. "I do not think there is much that can be done, but I have heard that the sasquatch holds great magic," she said and nodded her ascent. Hemlock knelt gently down by her injured hind leg.

My eyes had adjusted to the dim cave, and I could see the matted blood now. Hemlock's large hands took on a glow and as the darkness around the polar bear lifted, I could see the angry wound in her hind quarters that had not yet taken her life but would have starved her to death if not for Ing and the other puffins. Ing now hopped protectively over to her charge and tucked her much smaller body under the bears chin, craning her neck to watch every move the giant sasquatch made. She honked at Hemlock, who gently reassured her that he meant no harm and even gave the little bird a gentle pat with his glowing fingers.

I was witnessing the magic of the world at work now. Hemlock had said the sasquatch had been charged with protecting and caring for all of nature. This was his magic, to care, to heal. I thought of the beauty of the Alaskan wild where we had found him. It was still there, whole and undestroyed by humans because Hemlock and his family were there to heal it and care for it. Now Hemlock, outside of his own forest, placed his hands, so enormous but so gentle, over the angry wound festering on Eylif's leg. The polar bear growled, but not an angry growl. Hemlock rumbled a sound I had not heard him make before, and somehow I knew it to be the language of the sasquatch, too wild for my human ears to understand. There was a clunk that echoed loudly in the sea cave. Ing startled and moved to the spot where she picked up a small torpedo shaped bullet in her bright beak. It was coppery and ugly, so small, yet it had wrought so much damage when fired at high speed from the rifle of some hunter who was not hungry, but only wanted to win the prize, the claim to fame of taking down the last polar bear. Ing let it fall from her beak back to the cave floor, squawking angrily at the piece of metal. On her peaceful, isolated island, I thought she may not know the danger of guns and bullets, but she knew that small piece of metal was the cause of Eylif's pain.

The golden glow faded from around Hemlock's hands, and he stood, though not to his full height as the cave's size would not allow it, and he moved slowly away from the polar bear, watching her closely as he did so. I wondered how much effort it had taken for him to heal another living creature. He looked exhausted, weariness filling his golden eyes.

Eylif's almond shaped eyes widened at the sensation of being suddenly pain free, and she rose slowly, cautiously, testing her newly healed leg. She turned to the sasquatch. "You have not only healed my wound but restored the strength to my weakened body. You have my deepest gratitude, friend."

Hemlock bowed his head to her. "Though we have not met before this day, I have heard your legend. I know your loyalty to our friend, Santa Claus. We will need your strength, I believe, if we are to win this battle. It was my greatest honor to return you to health."

Ing carried the bullet she held again in her beak to the polar bear. Eylif indicated a red pouch she wore around her neck, and the puffin dropped the bullet into it. I could not see what else she carried in her bag in the dark, nor could I understand why she would want to keep that bullet, but I guess those were not things I needed to know. Eylif stretched her body and shook out her fur, which in the darkness of the sea cave looked greenish. She then darted from the cave, and we watched her run up the shore, scattering birds, testing her speed, her strength, her agility. She stopped at the edge of the shore and loosed a fierce roar, startling the birds there who shot into the air and away from the reach of the fierce polar bear. Then Eylif, Captain of the Guard, turned and looked proudly upon us.

"My friends. Let us go and rescue Santa Claus."

Christmas Magic

Hemlock folded the air and we stepped away from the cold, rocky, bird filled beach and into a thick grove of trees. As their boughs surrounded us, I saw the tension melt immediately from the sasquatch's broad shoulders. Ice covered the branches surrounding us like little jewels decorating the green of the trees and red berries brightened the whole scene. As we appeared out of nowhere a snowy white arctic hare darted across our path in fright. It all felt like a holiday to me, though we had not saved Christmas yet.

"Friends, welcome to the taiga," Hemlock said. "This boreal forest is just south of the Arctic Circle. We are close to where the Yeti has hidden Santa Claus, but not so close that he will be alerted through his magical wards. We shall rest here, out of sight from human eyes and make our plans." He looked around the forest with a somber look on his face. "Many years ago, this time of year, this forest would have been blanketed in a thick cover of snow. If we are successful, the snow will return, and you will see more than frost and ice covering this barren ground. We will once again see the beauty of white drifts of snow."

The ground was indeed dusted with a coating of frost and even thick patches of ice in places, but no snow. In our research of the Arctic Circle, we had discovered that so much of the region's wildlife had gone extinct or dwindled in numbers with the disappearance of the snow. There were places in the world covered in white where the snow had never melted. It was hard, packed ice that had been there frozen on the highest peaks for eighty-two years, but since the Yeti cast his enchantment, not one single snowflake had fallen from the sky. I considered that he was hoarding it all for himself in the Himalayas, the highest peaks, the unvisited, uninhabited places where he hid his miserable self, where it had still not melted, where humans did not venture.

"The taiga makes up roughly 31% of the world's forests, a larger percentage than it was one hundred years ago, but we have lost so much forest. Humans cannot bear the cold here well and so it has fared better than some of the other forests of the world. There was a time when the winters here could drop as low as -60 degrees Fahrenheit, but now it rarely drops below -40 degrees. This was once the home to many of the world's reindeer, now extinct. You can also find moose, wolves, a great number of birds, bears and in some parts of the taiga you will find the Siberian tiger. Oh, and wolverines. Are they all on the Yeti's side, the wolverines?" Natalie asked, looking to Hemlock for the only answer she did not have.

Natalie was rattling off facts again, which meant she was nervous, or, and I believe this was the case in this moment, putting things together, thinking them through, figuring them out. Natalie was planning. Natalie was thinking about weather patterns and wolverines and trying to make sense of it all. We had a magical sasquatch, a flying polar bear and four children for this fight we were setting out to take on. Could the six of us manage an army of wolverines and a Yeti who had embraced the crueler magics of the world? Nat's wheels were turning, I was certain of it. She was trying to find us some advantage, some tactic, some plan that would bring us success.

"Wolverines are very solitary creatures," Eylif spoke up. "There are those the Yeti has enticed, corrupted, and brought over to his side to do his bidding. They share his desire for solitude and ridding the world of humans may be a common goal, especially as humans encroach more and more on the wolverine's habitats. Wolverines are of the weasel family but have the strength of a bear. They are aggressive, territorial, and sly, which I believe is why the Yeti chose them to work his cruel and persuasive magic on. An animal of strength, not afraid to engage in battle, and a common desired outcome for the world. And yet, there are still wolverines in the world who choose to remain apart. No, he will not have the loyalty of all, but those who have chosen not to join him will neither ally themselves with our side. They will maintain their neutrality and solitude. We must also be prepared for him to have other allies, friends we had not counted on. We do not know what plans the Yeti has hatched, what creatures he has enticed over to his side, over the last eighty-two years."

"Yes," Hemlock agreed. "I believe we will find few allies in this forest."

"Take heart my sasquatch friend," Eylif said. "We may yet find a few friends here. The wolves are about, and they have no love for the Yeti. The birds of the forest still sing songs of dear Rosa, who was friend to their ancestors. The Yeti will not be the only creature with friends."

Just then there was a honking at our feet, and we all looked down in surprise to see that Ing had followed us through Hemlock's fold in the world.

"Ing," Eylif rumbled shaking her great head. "You should not have come little one. This adventure will be fraught with danger. Hemlock, can you send her back?"

The puffin honked angrily at Eylif, puffing out her small chest and flapping her wings. She flew up and landed on Esa's shoulder, the orange of her beak very nearly matching his fiery hair. Esa smiled at the bird.

"You should let her stay," he said. Esa had been quiet, mostly observing, and I wondered why he was weighing in now. "She deserves to fight for our world. She is as brave as any of us. She kept Eylif alive, led us to her. She is a part of all of this," he said. The puffin nipped Esa's fingers and nodded approvingly. Eylif rumbled, looking distressed. I saw that she loved the little bird but knew that Esa was right.

"I can return her home, but we need all the allies we can get, even the smallest of creatures. And this little puffin has proven herself to be brave and true," Hemlock said.

I looked around at this odd group of friends, gathered together to save the world. We were an army of seven ready to do battle, but we had also become a family. A family made up of human children, a sasquatch, a polar bear, and a puffin. I wondered if there were still more friends to be made on this adventure. I wondered what more beauty we would find in the world that I had never known existed. I also wondered how this small army with no plan was going to defeat a Yeti with such strong magic and cunning he had been able to thwart Santa Claus and his captain of the guard, Eylif. I told myself to keep believing in Christmas magic, that all was going to fall into place, as it had our entire journey, but I could not imagine what our next steps needed to be. We had been lucky so far, and I knew I needed to keep believing in our luck, our good fortune. But there were moments of such great fear, fear so strong it I felt the weight of it in my chest, and I hoped I could continue to find the strength to keep pushing forward.

"If we go straight to Santa Claus, or anywhere within ten miles of where he is hidden, the Yeti will know. He will come immediately, and we will have to fight him. And we do not know what magic he has?" I was questioning Hemlock and Eylif, looking for their expertise, and they both nodded their heads. "We also do not know how to free Santa Claus and the rest from the enchantment. The trees can get us to the cave he is hidden in, but we do not know if we can get him out, correct?" Again, they both nodded. "We could surprise the Yeti by going to him in the Himalaya's, but then we are fighting him on his own turf, in a place very inhospitable to humans."

"I have researched the Himalayas, and I think it would be very unwise for us to go there," Natalie said. "From what I know of that region, we could go there, never find the Yeti, and still not make it out alive."

"I do not know that I could even find him "I do not know that I could even find him there. I could get us close, but he has magic, wards, even a few twisted trees who are on his side. I too think it would be folly to go to him," Hemlock added. "Natalie is correct. You humans could die of exposure before we ever found him."

"So, we have only one option, then? Go to Santa Claus and hope for the best?" I wondered out loud. I was ready for it. Ready to just show up there. But still, the thought was daunting.

"Can we create some kind of distraction?" Desmond wondered. "Some way to keep the Yeti away from Santa Claus while we rescue him?"

My fingers itched beneath my thick gloves, and as I thought about what kind of distraction we might create, I removed them to scratch at my fingers. The wind chilled my bare skin, but it felt good to free them for a moment. I let my fingers run along the frosted silvery bark of the tree I was leaning against, and, for the briefest moment, I thought I heard the voice of the tree. It sounded like a greeting, though not in any language I understood, but it was there, barely, and then it disappeared.

"Are you okay, Eve?" Natalie asked and I realized the shock of what I thought I heard must be painted on my face. I nodded, not sure if I should share what had just happened to me. Why had my fingers itched just then? Why had I felt the need to take my glove off in these subzero temperatures? I looked to Hemlock and found he was searching my face, knowing in his amber eyes. But he said nothing and so I kept quiet as well. I touched the cold bark of the tree once more before I put my glove back on my hand, but this time I heard nothing. Had I imagined the voice of the tree? I thought the cold and lack of sleep were finally catching up to me, but I could not fall apart now. I had a world to save.

"Fine," I told Nat. "Just cold, itchy fingers."

"Okay," she said suspiciously. Still, how could I explain to her that I sort of thought a tree was trying to speak to me. Natalie looked away from me as I remained silent and continued. "A distraction is a good idea, Desmond. If we could create some kind of distraction, something to draw the Yeti away from the cave where he has hidden Santa Claus, if we could free him before the Yeti finds us, our numbers will have grown. With Santa Claus and all his magical friends, plus Eylif and Hemlock, we could defeat the Yeti."

"Sasquatches do not take lives?" Esa asked. "You said that before, right?" He was directing his questions to Hemlock.

The prominent ridges of Hemlock's brows raised as he studied Esa, pale and small with fiery hair. "That is correct," the sasquatch confirmed.

"Let me be your distraction. I'll enter the circle first. I'll set off his alarm. He'll come for me, probably put me to sleep, eh?" Esa said, his English strongly accented, his blue eyes bright and brave. "Probably bring me to the cave where he's been stashing all those poor folks, but by the time he gets there with me, sound asleep and all, you will have freed Santa Claus and his friends, and we will have an army to battle the Yeti. Course, I'll be asleep, so I won't be much good, but you can wake me up again, with your magic and all. Right?" Esa looked at Eylif and Hemlock as he said this, hoping the two magical creatures in our group would confirm that they would indeed be able to wake him again from the Yeti's sleep.

I had underestimated Esa. I thought he had come along for the ride, just to see some magic and be involved, but he had just offered himself as bait for an evil Yeti. He was willing to sacrifice himself so we could have a chance, so the world could have a chance. It was a ridiculous notion, but I felt warmed by the fact that I was surrounded by such noble and good people, and I hoped only that I could show as much braveness as Esa just had. I put my arm around Esa and gave him a squeeze, but I was shaking my head as I did so. I could not let him sacrifice himself in that way.

"Absolutely not!" Desmond said before I could say a word. "There is no way we are going to risk your life like that!" No one argued with Desmond. While we were all impressed with Esa's offer, grateful even that he was willing to try, it was far too dangerous.

"Young warrior, you are very brave," Eylif said. "But your plan comes with far too much risk. The Yeti has lost his way. And even assuming he did only put you into an enchanted sleep, there would be no guarantee we could wake you."

Hemlock nodded in agreement with Eylif. "The Yeti has strayed from the ways of the sasquatch. We could not safely assume he would not take your life. Especially if he discovered your plot and was angered. You are brave, Esa, but we cannot allow it."

Esa shrugged. "It's on the table," he said almost nonchalantly. "If we cannot come up with a better plan, the offer will stand. If the world will burn anyway if we cannot save Santa Claus by tomorrow, you may as well let me try to distract the Yeti. Either way, it's lights out, right?"

Tomorrow. Esa was right, I realized. Christmas Eve was tomorrow. We had been awake so long, I had not realized how much time had passed. How long since we had slept? Stepping through folds, changing time zones, being only in the dark all this time had left me confused. I had lost track of the days. The wind was biting despite our many layers, I was exhausted, and I looked at my friends and saw weariness on all their faces as well. Only Eylif, freshly restored by sasquatch magic, looked as though she had any energy left. Hemlock looked especially exhausted, and I wondered how difficult it was to fold the world and bend it to your will, how much healing another body had taken out of him. I wondered where we would all be if not for the sustaining mushrooms from Hemlock's forest. But tired as we were, we had no choice but to carry on.

"It's a good plan," Nat said suddenly, surprising us all. She had dark shadows circling her green eyes. "What?" she responded to the looks on all our faces. "We have no other plan. And Esa is right. If we do nothing, it's lights out for all of us anyway. I will go with him."

"No!" Desmond and I both shouted at once.

"Listen. Eylif and Hemlock will be needed to free Santa Claus. Hemlock is the only one who can get us right to the cave he is imprisoned in. Beyond that, I think we will need their magic to free him. Desmond has strength, Eve you have all the belief in Christmas, so Esa and I can go. We can be the distraction for the rest of you. We're scrawny and probably wouldn't be much use in a fight anyway." She looked over at Esa, her cheeks coloring a bit. "Sorry, but....."

Esa shrugged. "It's true."

"No, no, no, no, no!" I shouted. They were all there because of me. Every last one of them was there because I stirred this up. There was no way I was letting Esa and Natalie risk their lives in that way. There had to be a better way to draw out the Yeti and save Santa Claus.

Desmond, at least was on my side, shaking his head and arguing with the two of them that it was the worst idea he had ever heard. "I don't care how good you think this plan is, we are all staying together!"

"It is an idea," Hemlock said reluctantly, deep uncertainty in his rumbling voice, "that we may have to at least consider. An option only if no other plan presents itself."

"We have one day until doomsday," Esa said in his quiet, carefree manner. "That's all I'm saying. I could go right now."

"I will go with him. Natalie can stay here with you. I can help keep him safe from the Yeti," Ing said.

"You are a very brave bird, Ing," I said. "But what can you do against a Yeti?" Then I realized that everyone was looking at me strangely, and after that I realized that I had understood every cawing noise that came out of Ing's bright beak, though they had not been any kind of words a human had ever spoken. "No one else understood that?" I asked looking around at my friends.

"I can understand the Puffin," Hemlock said. "The sasquatch speaks all languages. But I do not know how it is that you can understand her."

"I too understand the puffin. I have been gifted Christmas magic," Eylif told us. "Eve, is it possible you have been given this great gift?"

"Christmas magic gives you the ability to understand puffins?" I said stupidly, but also thinking about the tree I had placed my cold, bare fingers upon only moments before.

"Puffins, among other living things," Eylif said.

"Eylif, what else can Christmas magic do?" Nat asked the polar bear. I was still a bit speechless, but my cousin knew something I did not. I could see that immediately.

"There are four fundamental properties of Christmas magic. The first property is happenstance, meaning circumstances that happen for you purely due to chance, coincidence, even serendipity. Natalie, I believe you could tell us the root word for happiness?" the polar bear said. She had spent very little time with my cousin, but she already knew who to turn to for the studious answers.

"The root word for happiness is hap, which simply means luck, or chance," she answered without even needing to think about it.

Eylif's head nodded and if a polar bear could smile, I was sure she was doing so, but it was in her expressive, dark eyes that it showed. "Yes. Chance. Human happiness depends so much on luck, on chance, on happenstance. When you have Christmas magic, your luck changes. It can be that the things you need to happen, by luck, or chance, happen for you. For example, landing in the very right place in the Alaskan wilderness where possibly a sasquatch who was once dear friends with the daughter of Santa Claus lived and so he was sympathetic to your cause. It may also be a serendipitous occurrence, one you were not looking or hoping for but changed the course of your life. For example, a chance meeting where a young boy happened to have moved to the city in which you live, happened to enroll in your same school, and even happened to be sitting near enough to you to overhear your conversation and become a part of your adventure. Tell me, Eve. Do you feel your luck has changed in any way over any certain period of time?"

I thought about my life. In the last few weeks so many things had happened. Chance things. The things Eylif had already mentioned, but also, I remembered tripping and falling flat on my face in the library and, humiliating as it was, I had just so happened to land right in front of the Christmas book section. I thought of the serendipitous fact that Ms. Snow was the librarian at my school in the first place, the only librarian in the country who still valued a bound book and kept a collection on shelves in an old-fashioned library. I remembered seeing the flash of a letter from Santa Claus stuck to the bottom of Mom's shoe box. I thought of Desmond's delayed plane. I thought of Nat needing to use the bathroom just as we flew over Hemlock's forest.

"Yes, I believe I have been lucky for some time now. I think I could even say that the luck came at the exact same time that the Yeti's enchantment lifted for me. In fact, it was happenstance that I stumbled upon the candy canes at all," I said to the polar bear, and it was true. It had been luck that led me to the magical peppermints under my grandmother's bed, and I had been lucky ever since. Small things until now, but the more I thought about it, the more incidents I thought of that could have gone so very wrong, but I had been lucky. Grams the Great had driven Dad's auto relatively accident free for goodness' sake. That alone was a Christmas miracle.

Eylif nodded again and continued. "The second property of Christmas magic is the magic of empathy. Words and language and the way they are used to express love and beauty, and not just in the human world, but in the animal world as well, define who we are, create deep connections between us. From the beautiful songs of the birds to the chirps of the tiniest insects, all of nature needs to connect. We can all hear it, but Christmas magic gives the ability to truly understand other forms of communication, other languages. For those who were poets and storytellers, whose gift was already language, for those already strongly inclined to feel empathy for others, this ability is greatly increased. There are some who, like the sasquatch, can even speak the language of the trees and plants. It is a magic granted only to those with a true heart, those who will do no damage with the gift they have been given. Eve, you can understand the puffin. Is there more?"

I thought of when my bare hand touched the bark of the tree, and I knew I had heard it greet me. "A tree," I confessed, looking sheepishly at my friends, and now wondering why I had not already shared this with them. "I took my glove off and touched the tree and it, well it said hello, I think. I didn't t say anything because it sounded so crazy. I thought I had imagined it."

"Crazy?" Hemlock questioned. "Do you think I am crazy. Did I not tell you the trees have their own language. I wondered when I saw your face. Eve, you must learn to trust yourself. It seems you have been granted a rare gift. Do not squander it with secrets and mistrust." I looked down at my feet, feeling ashamed. Hemlock was right. I met his eyes and nodded to him in assurance that I had heard him. I apologized to them all for not sharing what I had heard sooner.

I had another question for Eylif as well. "Is the sadness I feel when others are sad, is that Christmas magic, the magic of empathy?" I was thinking about the ache I felt every time I looked at Desmond.

"That is normal, Eve. Most creatures have some form of empathy. Some feel it more strongly than others. But when you are gifted Christmas magic, yes, you may feel it more strongly than before because you can really understand and not just guess at the pain another might be feeling. It is not just languages but emotions that you will understand with the gift of Christmas magic," Eylif answered. I thought of the many times I had been selfish, ignored what Desmond and Nat might be feeling, to push through my agenda and I wondered if this gift had been granted to me mistakenly. But I could not dwell on that. I only nodded and asked what the third property was. I was eager to find out what other magic I might have available to me.

"The third property of Christmas magic is long life. No one knows how many years those with Christmas magic will be granted, but most live longer than is expected." I was stunned by this, but then I thought of Eylif roaming the Arctic Circle for the last nearly eighty-three years, still a seemingly young and strong polar bear. I thought of Grams the Great. She was 127 years old. Was it Christmas magic that had gifted her such a long life?

You said there were four properties," said Natalie. "What other gift will Eve be granted?" I could tell her wheels were turning. I could tell that she was searching for some gift that would help us in our quest to defeat the Yeti.

"The fourth property of Christmas magic is, of course, flight." Eylif announced and I think that pronouncement shocked even Hemlock. Only Natalie showed no surprise.

"What?! I can't fly!" I shouted. The whole notion seemed completely absurd to me, even crazier than living a longer than normal life.

"Not yet," Eylif said. "But it will come. If you have Christmas magic, and I believe you do, then the ability to fly will eventually be granted to you as well."

"Why flying?" I asked thinking that it did not really go with the other elements of Christmas magic.

Eylif rumbled a laugh. "Because flying is fun! Magical. A rare gift that fills the soul with joy! And Christmas is joy!"

"How will I know when it comes?"

"That is a good question. It is different for all. But for most there is a moment where you simply must let go and believe. Step off that cliff and fly."

I tried to imagine flinging myself off a cliff and believing I would not plummet to my death. I thought I had gotten pretty good at believing but I was not sure I would be able to take a flying leap from any height. The trees had spoken to me though. The more I thought back on it, the sillier I felt for ignoring them and shoving my glove back on my hand. And if I could talk to puffins and trees, if good luck followed me wherever I went, then why not flight? Yet, it was a thing I could not even begin to imagine.

"So, Eve has Christmas magic. How did she get it?" Natalie asked, always the one trying to solve the mystery, put all the puzzle pieces together. I could practically see the gears in her bright mind turning.

"That is a good question," Eylif said. "It is a rare magic. Santa Claus has the gift. His wife and daughter. The reindeer of course, and the elves. For me, the gift was granted after I risked my life once to save Santa Claus."

"Can it be magical objects?" Natalie questioned. "Eylif, do you think it could have been the magical candy canes?"

Eylif thought about this for a moment. "It is possible that an enchanted food could open the way. It broke the enchantment. But it would only open the way. Christmas magic is not a thing you can eat. It is a thing granted only to those with true hearts, the purest of spirits, the bravest souls. If Eve had eaten those candy canes but had been an ill-tempered child with a cruel and broken heart, she would have been given no Christmas magic. But because of the love in her heart, her strong belief in what she could not see, and her bravery and determination, she was given this gift."

Natalie was thoughtful. "We've all eaten the candy canes. I had wondered. If we had magic, defeating the Yeti would be easier." She sounded disappointed and I couldn't blame her. I had no idea why I had been given this gift, yet my friends, who were as brave and true and pure of heart as I ever dreamed of being, had not received the gift.

"Christmas magic is not given to make things easier," Eylif said gently.

"So, Eve and Eylif have been gifted with Christmas magic. Hemlock has forest magic. That's all wonderful. It's great. Really. But. We still have no plan. So, with no other plan, it's decided. Ing and I will be the

188

distraction." There was no question in Esa's voice when he said this.

Desmond looked at his friend with pained eyes. "It's too much Es."

"Nah. You are my brother, Des. I would do anything to help you save your parents. But this is bigger than that, bigger than your parents and our friendship. This is the whole world. Something must be done and so far, this is all we can think of. And, I'll have Ing." The puffin's feathers ruffled, and she nipped Esa's fingers in solidarity, cawing affectionately at him as she did so.

"It's a good plan," Nat said. She looked at Esa. "I don't like it, but it gives us a real chance. Only a human will draw the Yeti. I don't like it, but it's all we've got right now."

"Right now, sleep is what we need," Hemlock said, and I was glad he had not agreed to letting Esa sacrifice himself. "The human body does not function well on so little rest, even with my forest mushrooms still sustaining your bodies. It has been at least twenty-four hours since you three have slept," he said of Natalie, Desmond, and me. It was late, and I was becoming more exhausted by the second, but I was so enthralled by Eylif's tale, so enamored of my newly realized Christmas magic, I had not noticed the weariness I was feeling. I felt too heavy to stand, let alone fly. Hemlock looked like he was about to fall asleep where he stood. "I too need rest. Travel and healing have taken their toll. I do not think I could even take us to Santa Claus now, weak as I am."

"Do we have time to sleep?" Desmond asked.

"We must, young one," Hemlock said. "Just a few hours to regain our strength. I know you are anxious to see this thing through, we all are, but if we exhaust ourselves, we will not beat the Yeti. He has strength you cannot imagine."

"I will keep guard," Eylif said. "I am freshly healed by sasquatch magic and feel as though I could stay awake for days."

"Thank you," Hemlock told her gratefully. I could see the deep weariness painted across the bold features of his face. "I need but an hour, maybe two, and my strength will be restored."

Eylif stood ready with Ing perched on her great back. "We have four hours until midnight and the dawning of Christmas Eve. I will wake you then. Rest well friends. You will need all your strength."

I was frightened that we still had no plan other than Esa's back up plan, but I had never been this exhausted in my life. I did not think I could remain standing for even five more minutes. We'd been awake for days. Hemlock's mushrooms had seen us through. But they were wearing off and all the exertion of the last few days was catching up to us.

We began to unfold our thermal blankets, looking around for a place to spread them, but before we could, Hemlock performed another extraordinary feat. He placed his large hands on the bark of a nearby spruce tree, and the tree, and several others around it began to bend into a rounded enclosure leaving an opening just large enough for us to crawl through. Somehow, I knew, or heard, that it was not his own magic, but that he had simply asked the trees to aid us, provide us warmth and shelter. We spread our blankets on the frozen ground, over top of the soft pine needles the trees had shed especially for us. Sleeping all close together for warmth, we snuggled beneath our blankets, too exhausted to think. I placed my hand on the tree and thanked it for sheltering us, hoping it had heard and understood me.

"I am happy to keep you warm, little human. Remember, we are on your side. The Yeti cannot win, or the world is doomed. We will help you in any way we can. We ask only that when once you have saved the world, you do not forget the trees. Do not forget the wild places of the world, for without forests, the earth will not survive." Her voice was mossy and gnarled, a voice that seemed to creep like roots through your mind, a voice you could not imagine until you have heard it. I promised her solemnly I would not forget the wild places of the world so long as I lived.

Hemlock seemed to radiate heat in our little tree fort and though we were on the ground in the subarctic taiga, on a bed of frost in below zero temperatures we were not cold. It was magic, I knew it now. Sasquatch magic, Christmas magic, the magic of the trees, any doubts I had once carried were fully gone. As I lay amongst my friends, no, my family, protected by the trees, a magic polar bear standing guard, warm in the taiga, safe, and loved, I felt ready to fight the greatest evil the world had ever known. I felt ready to take on the Yeti.

Luna

We had slept only a few short hours when we were awakened to the sound of Eylif's polar bear growl and shouts for us to wake. I sat up with a start and saw my friends had done the same. Hemlock looked worried. There were more growls and screams outside our shelter that did not belong to Eylif.

"Wolverines," said Hemlock. "Remain hidden." The sasquatch left our magical tree fort, going to Eylif's aid, and it grew instantly colder inside.

"Wolverine attacks against humans are rare, even in the days where humans spent more time in the wilderness," Natalie said, and I knew she was trying to calm herself more than she was trying to educate us. "They do not view us as prey."

"Yes, but wolverines are solitary animals and there is definitely more than one out there," Desmond said. "I have a feeling these wolverines are friends of the Yeti. They may not view as prey, but they certainly view us as enemies."

We could hear a skirmish begin and not one of us had any intention of hiding inside a tree fort while Eylif and Hemlock fought. Our eyes met and without any discussion, we burst from our shelter ready to battle. Several of the wolverines were down but we were now surrounded by at least ten more and Eylif's muzzle was bleeding. I was not sure what we thought we could do against these wild beasts, but the four of us stood our ground. Ing perched on Esa's shoulder looking for all the world like she thought she could protect us. The growls of the wolverines were guttural and deep as they crept closer to us. If Eylif and Hemlock were not with us, I think they would have rushed in but in the face of the huge polar bear and the even larger sasquatch they were coming in cautiously. We all picked up the nearest stick or rock and waited for the onslaught.

Then a different howl broke the night. It was a long, high-pitched howl that should have been frightening, but somehow I found it comforting. The howl of the wolves was a long, sad, song. It held many emotions that I could not find human words for, but I understood it and it carried no aggression, no animosity, at least not towards us.

"I think they're here to help," I told my friends seeing the looks of worry on their faces. "I think the Yeti frightens them, and I don't think many things frighten wolves. Also, I think they do not like that the wolverines have thrown in their lot with the Yeti." All of this, I could hear in the howling song they were now throwing up to the bright, silvery moon overhead.

The wolverines had frozen at the sound of the wolf song. They were looking around with wild eyes for the creatures they knew could best them in this battle should they decide to join it. But my friends, like me seemed to be comforted, rather than frightened by the howl of the wolf. It was a sound we had been taught all our lives to fear, but we had changed since we left our city. We had seen so much, learned so much. The wolves, we knew, were coming to help us.

"I know this pack" Eylif said, relief in her voice at the sound of the song that now grew louder and closer.

The wolverines seemed to decide they needed to take us out before the wolves arrived and charged, with most heading for Eylif or Hemlock. My legs felt like jelly as I watched the one rabid creature that had decided to come after us, but I held my stick tight, ready to swing. I had no thought in my head, no strategy, other than to stand my ground. But seconds before the beast reached us he was knocked off his path by a flash of shining white fur.

Two other wolves came crashing out of the trees, throwing themselves into the fray. Between the three wolves, the polar bear, and the sasquatch, the wolverines were put down or scattered into the dark forest, back to their solitary dens below the frozen ground. We four children and Ing found we had to do nothing, and I was relieved because the glinting, long, sharp front teeth of those beasts had been terrifying under the starlight. Ing cawed her best caw at their retreating backs, telling them not to return, and I let my stick fall to the ground in relief.

When the threat was gone, the largest of the three wolves stepped forward, touching her nose to Eylif's in greeting. She was beautiful, with thick white fur and brilliant green eyes that gave off a light of their own in the night.

"My friends, meet Luna, the leader of her pack. She has been a friend to me for many years as I have roamed the arctic searching for Santa Claus. She has even spent time helping me in my search, and we have had many adventures together," Eylif said.

We all then gave our names and our heartfelt thanks to Luna and her pack for their help. I think Eylif and Hemlock could have handled a few wolverines, but there had been more than a few, they were vicious, and we had been outnumbered. Without the wolves we would have been in trouble.

Luna was looking intently at Esa, her green eyes reflecting the moonlight. "My sentinels have been watching you," she said. Her voice was softer than I had expected. I looked at my friends to see if they had understood her, but I did not think so. "We have seen the damage the Yeti has done. Many of our wolf brothers and sisters have lost their lives due to his negligence. The polar bear and the reindeer have disappeared from the world. The snow and those whose existence depended upon it are gone. The earth suffers at the hands of the Yeti, who was supposed to be its protector. You have come to free Santa Claus and stop the Yeti and we have come to offer our assistance. My sentinels are impressed with the boy with hair of fire. Wolves fear little in this world, but fire is among those few things. This boy must be a formidable human, indeed, to have hair of flame. They say he is brave and has offered to sacrifice himself for the good of the pack. They will accompany the boy and the brave little puffin to draw out the Yeti. They will do all in their power to ensure his safety and his success. With the help of my sentinels, perhaps we can delay the Yeti further."

Esa, with his hair of fire, had so impressed the wolves that now, if we decided to use his plan, he would at least not have to go alone. Luna's two sentinels sat on their back haunches, just behind their leader, awaiting her instruction. One had jet black fur and yellow eyes, the other was silvery gray and looked like he was trying very hard not to wag his tail. Hemlock told the others what the wolf had just said, and Esa nodded gratefully to Luna and the two wolves behind her.

"I would be honored to accept the help of your sentinels," he said formally. I wanted to laugh a bit, because formality was not Esa's way, and I could tell he was being extra serious for the benefit of the wolves. He also looked relieved to know he would have more help than a puffin, not that he was not grateful for Ing as well.

Desmond tried to argue, but the wolf silenced him with a bark that said it was not for him to decide. Her bark told Desmond that this act of bravery was to be honored, not taken from the boy with fire for hair. By the way Desmond's eyes widened at the bark, I wondered if maybe some Christmas magic had rubbed off on him as well. Had he understood her, or had the bark just frightened him? And so, with the arrival of the taiga's wolf pack, Esa's plan to sacrifice himself to the Yeti as bait, was solidified. I do not think any of our party, other than the wolves, felt entirely sure that it was the right thing to do.

"The rest of my pack, other than our pups, will accompany you to free Santa Claus. We will be ready for battle when the Yeti arrives. He will surely bring more of his wolverines, and you will need our teeth. With my two sentinels gone, there will be only six of us, but six wolves are a great many in a battle," Luna told us.

"Thank you, Luna. We are so grateful for your help" I said to her. She did not seem surprised that I had understood her words without translation from Hemlock or Eylif and I wondered how long the wolves had been watching and listening to us. I wondered if either the polar bear or the sasquatch had been aware of them. Hadn't Eylif mentioned the wolves?

"Come," the wolf said to all of us. "Join us in our den. We will eat and rest and prepare for the pending battle. She shook the frost from her shiny white coat and her sentinels followed suit. The two wolves who had volunteered to go with Esa, now that their leader was not speaking, bounded towards my friend with fire for hair, licking his hands and playfully jumping all around him. I had always imagined wolves would be serious and even sinister animals, but the wolves, at least in this pack, were more like playful puppies. Triple the size of a playful puppy, to be certain, but all three wolves frolicked and played as they made their way to their den. It was Luna who surprised me the most as she barked and played around Eylif's four furry legs, rekindling the friendship she had long shared with the polar bear.

The den of the wolves was a cave. It was dim and cold, but it did not seem to bother the wolves. A jumble of wolf pumps came rollicking up to us as we entered the cave. We all received licks in the face and playful nips to our gloved fingers as they tumbled about. Luna, who was their mother, nipped and played and let them climb all over her in greeting, but eventually shooed them away to give us room to rest and plan. I laughed as I watched the rollie balls of fluff eventually make their way back to us, scooting in quietly on their bellies, so that we each ended up with a fat, fluffy puppy in our laps. Even Hemlock and Eylif were snuggling a little wolf pup. And Ing was snuggled between the thick fur of the two wolf sentinels, whose names we had learned while we walked were Jacy and Tungi. Their home was a joyful one, and I was glad the Yeti's enchantment had not seemed to touch the world of the wolves. I could think of no better place to regroup before we launched our plan to defeat the Yeti.

Natalie's Secret Book

W e only have half a plan. Esa," Desmond said
when he had finished the granola bar he'd
grabbed from my backpack full of Mom's
ready to eat snacks. I had passed them around as we sat
huddled in the wolf den discussing our plans between
playing with mischievous pups. "How will we free
Santa Claus and whoever else the Yeti has taken in the
short time we'll have before the Yeti comes?"

He had been referring to his parents when he said
'whoever else' but their names were left unsaid. I think
he was almost afraid to hope that his parents would be
in that cave with Santa Claus, at least afraid to hope out
loud. I couldn't blame him.

It was then that Natalie shook the little black wolf,
who was diligently trying to lick her face, off her lap
and sheepishly pulled a book out of an inside pocket in
her coat. I looked in surprise when I realized it was a
library book. She held it before her so that we all could

see it. It was not one of the children's stories with bright pictures of Santa Claus and reindeer, but rather an ancient, tattered tome entitled *Christmas Magic: A Guide to Ancient Spells and Enchantments*. I did not remember checking that one out, but I knew it had to be one of mine.

"This book somehow ended up in my bag the day you brought all those books home from the library, Eve. I just could not read it or even realize I had it because of the enchantment. But I had been reading it when you and Grams showed up at my window, so I stuffed it in my bag just in case we needed it. I read it some on the ferry ride, but everything has been such a whirlwind that I'd forgotten about it until Eylif began to tell us about the properties of Christmas magic. Happenstance, I guess, that it somehow ended up coming home with me," she said with a small smile. "Well," Nat continued, "this book begins by laying out the four properties of Christmas magic, exactly as Eylif explained them, so I think we can conclude that it is an accurate book and no silly story as some of the others were. Once I came to that conclusion, I decided it was time to really read it and see if there might be any useful information. So, after you all fell asleep I read until I couldn't stay awake any longer."

"Who is the author?" Eylif questioned.

Natalie looked at the book. "Jack Frost," she said.

"Yes, I think we can trust the writings to be at least accurate," Eylif said cautiously, though she did not look as thoroughly convinced as I would have liked her to.

"Then I think I may know what we need to break the curse" Nat said. "It is just a small section, but it talks about curses against Christmas magic and what is needed to break them. The Yeti has cast an enchantment against Christmas Magic?" Nat asked looking to Eylif for confirmation.

"Indeed," the polar bear replied. "The ultimate enchantment against Christmas magic."

"Well, if I am reading this correctly, the enchantment has grown in strength over the last eighty-two years, and it will mature into a curse at the stroke of midnight on Christmas day. That is when it will become permanent. The world is enchanted now. If we do nothing the enchantment will become an unbreakable curse."

"That sounds like a Jack Frost kind of enchantment," Eylif said. "And it is the same information Hemlock learned from the trees and Santa Claus put in his letter."

"Well, according to Frost, in order to turn the enchantment that would hide Christmas magic from the world into the curse that would destroy Christmas magic completely, the Yeti had to become the opposite of Christmas magic. Christmas embodies merriment and joy. It brings peace and love. Most importantly, at Christmastime families gathered, and celebrated together. The Yeti embodies sadness and fear. He brings anger and chaos. War. The Yeti stands alone. On Christmas Day he will become the curse. It will be unbreakable because he will swallow the last bit of Christmas magic left and it will be gone forever," she explained to us. "It is an unbreakable curse because Christmas magic will no longer be hidden from our enchanted minds. It will be destroyed, and the Yeti will become it's opposite, Anti Magic. Not hate, not evil, just nothingness, apathy. No one will care and Frost says the enemy will win and the cursed world will slowly destroy itself until it ends."

"Does Frost tell us what we need to do to stop the enchantment from becoming a curse?" Desmond asked with a chill to his voice that I know all of us felt.

"Sort of," Natalie said, sounding a bit frustrated.

"Again, what you have read all sounds very much like Jack Frost. He would not have created this enchantment. He does not have that kind of power. But Frost likely discovered it somewhere and then made it all very confusing and jumbled, leaving everything to chance for any parties involved," Eylif told us. "I have heard of Anti Magic. The opposite of Christmas Magic. Friends, we cannot let this come to pass."

"Yes," said Hemlock. "Hate is an emotion. It can be changed because the heart still feels. It can heal. Apathy is far worse. Anti Magic means that magic is gone, caring and love are gone, and the world will suffer the consequences of that. Hatred and rage will overtake the world, because once planted there will be nothing that can heal it, no one to care."

Natalie nodded. "Yes, I think that is what the spell the Yeti used to cast the enchantment means," she said. "It was all there, in a strange and jumbled way. It says he had to evoke the power of the enemy. The process.....I do not want to go back over it, but in the end, at the stroke of midnight Christmas day, unless we can stop it, the Yeti embodies Anti Magic the way that Santa Claus embodies Christmas magic, and it is over for the world."

We all stared at her, too horrified to speak. How could any of this be real? I pictured Natalie, reading in the dark, learning all of this alone, and feeling frightened.

"Jack Frost goes on to say that in order to stop the enchantment the twelve spirits of Christmas must come together," Natalie went on. "The twelve spirits of Christmas can be anyone so long as they embody the true spirit of Christmas. He names Father Christmas and Mother Christmas. Obviously, that is Santa Claus and his wife. He then names the spirit of friendship, which I think could be Esa who is willing to risk his life for his friends. The untamed spirit, which I think is obviously Hemlock, who is the guardian of the forest and all things wild. I was not sure about this one, but I think Luna could be the spirit of joy. She and her pack saved us from the wolverines, but it is here in her den with her frolicking pups that you see their playful joy. There is the spirit of family, which I think could be Desmond, who is here fighting so hard to save his parents, who named Eylif his family in spirit because he shared her pain. The spirit of peace I think may be Ing. She did not know the hunter's bullet, she could not hurt a fly. She is a caregiver, a protector, a peaceful friend to all. Eylif is the spirit of Christmases present, searching every day for Santa Claus, fighting every day to keep Christmas alive in the hearts of all. She embodies Christmas spirit in every present moment she lives. And maybe, well, I might be," and here Nat blushed a bit, "the spirit of wisdom. Only because nothing else fits me," she said. Poor Nat was always so humble.

"It all fits you Nat," said Desmond. "Just none so well as the spirit of wisdom." I knew that had there been any daylight at all we would see that her cheeks had gone a deep red. I also knew she had been working this puzzle out for some time, and I was fairly certain she had it all right.

"Finally, Eve, I think you are the true believer. It says the True Believer, or the Spirit of Belief, is the most important role for without belief there is nothing." Natalie finished. At these words I felt my own cheeks flush, but before I could question her, Esa spoke up.

"Didn't you say twelve. Twelve spirits of Christmas? Who are we missing?" he questioned.

Natalie nodded. "We need two more. The spirit of Christmas Past and the spirit of Christmas Future. I just don't know who those people might be. In fact, I could be wrong about all of it. I'm not sure if any of us count for the twelve spirits Frost names. And he does not really say what these spirits will need to do, other than be present together to stand against the curse."

"Jack Frost," Eylif began cautiously. "I am not sure how to say this. I think we can trust the information in this book to be true, but the sprite, himself, was not trustworthy. He was a creature of mischief. He wanted to create chaos in the world, and not just through winter winds and snowstorms."

Nat shuddered. "Yes, well, there are a lot of words and phrases I don't quite understand in the curse, but what the Yeti had to do, what he had to become to win all that power for himself, and to cast such a large blanket enchantment across the whole world, I don't know why anyone would write the curse down in a book for any to find. But in the end, and the Yeti would have to have known this, if we are successful, Frost says the earth will rise up and swallow the curse and its caster, and the joy of Christmas will be restored."

"I would not find it surprising if it were Jack Frost himself who put the book into the hands of the Yeti," Eylif said. "It was the kind of creature Frost was. Complicated and strange, not necessarily evil, but neither was he a true and trustworthy soul either. He was put on this earth for the sole purpose of creating turmoil, and it would appear that in this book, with this enchantment, he has found the ultimate chaos."

"Sasquatches do not search out human books," Hemlock added. "In fact, most do not read the written word. It would make sense that an outsider was involved in setting the Yeti on this path. However, he was only susceptible because of what had already become broken and twisted inside him."

"So, how do we do this? Esa and the wolf sentinels draw the Yeti out. But we still have not figured out how to free Santa Claus. Only that we need Santa Claus to break the enchantment and stop the curse. Does it say how we do this?" Desmond asked. I could tell he was trying to keep the impatience from his voice. He was so close to learning what had happened to his parents, to possibly seeing them again, that he was past caring why or how the Yeti had cast the curse. He only cared how to lift it, and I could not blame him.

Natalie shook her head. "I can find nothing in the book about how to free Santa Claus. I've read the entire thing now. There are other curses. But nothing about imprisoning people or enchanted sleeps. I'm sorry, Des. I tried. It seems that the Yeti imprisoned Santa Claus with a magic separate from the enchantment. I think he may have been given this magic, these abilities, when he struck his deal with the enemy in order to cast the enchantment. I'm really sorry, Des."

"Don't be sorry, Nat. It's okay," he told her. "If not for you we would know nothing. Thank you."

I took a deep breath. "So far, everything has fallen into place for us. Christmas magic has been with us on this entire journey. I believe that will continue. What we need will come to us when we need it."

Desmond dropped his head and sighed. I wish I could give him a better plan than that. I could not blame him for wanting something more solid. His parents may be asleep in that prison with Santa Claus. His oldest friend was about to risk his life for our cause. We were trying to save the entire world, but we were winging it. I wanted a better plan as well, but with so little time left, there was nothing else for us to do but show up at the enchanted cave where we knew Santa Claus to be hidden and believe we could find a way to free him.

The Yeti

We had talked about Esa, using him as bait, and none of us had really wanted to do it, but somehow it had become our plan. Now the time had come. Esa, Ing and the two wolf sentinels, Jacy and Tungi, were ready to go. We could stall no further, but there was an unease in our group that could be felt in the air.

As the four of them waited for Hemlock, who was conferring with the trees to make sure he found the right location, Tungi was playfully nipping Esa's fingers and smelling his hair as though to check that it was not actually made of flame. Ing was perched on Jacy's back looking very serious. Hemlock, finally certain of where to send them, stepped forward and folded the air and without hesitation, Esa and the three animals walked forward.

"Hey, Des. If I don't come back and you lot manage to save the world and all that, look out for my parents, will you?" Esa said as he readied himself to step through, to become the Yeti's bait.

Desmond looked stricken and he wrapped his friend in a bear hug. "You'll be back Es. You'll be back and we'll take care of our families together."

I felt the chill air through the fold when Hemlock opened it, somehow even more frozen than the subarctic taiga. Natalie and I both hugged Esa and patted Ing on the head. Then Tungi lowered his silver furred body for Esa to climb onto his back and they shot through Hemlock's folded air and into Yeti territory with Ing flying close behind. Jacy disappeared after them in a flash of shiny black fur and just like that they were all gone. The Yeti's territory and our friends disappeared from view as Hemlock's fold smoothed and became the taiga again.

We all stared for a long time at the place our friends had been standing, alive and well only moments before. I was numb and still unsure how we would free Santa Claus once we arrived, but we were running out of time, and we had to do something. Hope was all we had, and a belief that we would prevail. Christmas magic would beat Anti Magic. It had to. I had to believe that, especially now that our friends had given themselves as bait in the Yeti's territory. I stared at the empty space they had once occupied, and I believed as hard as I could that Christmas magic would see them safely through this.

Hemlock had sent Esa and company to within a mile of the Yeti's magical wards, which meant we needed to give them about ten minutes to breach the barrier and then maybe a few more minutes for the Yeti to arrive. None of us really knew how much time it would take the miserable creature to realize Esa was there, but our friend now carried the white stone Hemlock had given me to call him. Once Esa rubbed the stone, we would know the Yeti had come and we would go immediately to the cave where Santa Claus was imprisoned. That was as far as our plan had gotten. We had no idea how much time we would have once we reached Santa Claus's cave, but we did know that the Yeti, like Hemlock, could reach a place almost instantly. We were assuming that he would get to Esa, Ing, and the two wolves quickly, and we hoped the four of them would be able to give us at least a few minutes to make something happen.

It felt like time had stopped moving, and Desmond was the first to stand and demand we go. "What if the Yeti got him before he could activate the stone?" he said, and I could hear the panic in his voice.

No one could argue with him, but then Hemlock held up the other half of the magical stone and we saw that it was glowing brightly in his hand. "It is time," he said, and he folded the air.

Eylif stepped through first. She had insisted that if there was trouble waiting for us on the other side, she should be the first one through to face it, being the warrior of the group. We did not argue. It was a comfort to know you had a giant polar bear standing between you and any danger when you stepped through to the unknown. Luna went next for the same reason, barely letting Eylif get all the way through before she bounded after her. Nat, Desmond, and I walked through together, our hands clasped, followed by the rest of Luna's wolfpack. Hemlock was the last to come through, to protect us from any danger from behind. His fold fell away behind him, the taiga was gone, and we were in the Yeti's territory, deep within the Arctic Circle.

It was the coldest air I had ever felt. We were dressed in the warmest clothes, but the air slapped and bit at my exposed cheeks and lips and seeped into my weatherproof clothes. It was still dark, and there was a full moon above us, and soft, gentle rays of moonlight wrapped itself around the entrance to a bleak, rocky cave surrounded by ice. We could hear the Arctic Ocean behind the cave, breaking softly against the shore. Behind the cave the aurora borealis lit up the black sky, a sight I had longed to see since I first heard it existed, and though its beauty astounded me, I had no time to enjoy it now.

"Welcome curse breakers," came a resonant and solemn voice. "Saint Nicholas and his family are waiting." Perched above the cave was a giant white bird, glowing serenely, but whether the glow was his own or created by the moonlight around him I was not sure. He was watching us intently with shining eyes.

Hemlock dropped to one knee and Eylif, Luna and all the wolves dropped into a low bow, so I did the same. Nat and Desmond sank down beside me.

"Mighty albatross," Eylif said. "We are grateful to you for being here and bringing your luck to our side."

The enormous bird bade us all to rise so we came to our feet. The albatross then extended its huge wings so that we could see the full length of his wingspan, which I think was as wide as I was tall. "I have watched over this cave for many years now waiting for the twelve warriors of Christmas to arrive. Now that your spirits are together this enchantment can be lifted. You are missing two spirits?" he questioned. "The boy and the bird?"

I wondered how he had known about Esa and Ing, but hope was rising in my chest as I realized that Natalie had been right. We were the spirits of Christmas.

"They have gone to draw out the Yeti," Desmond said. I looked at my friend with raised eyebrows. This albatross was not speaking like Eylif and Hemlock spoke. He was speaking to us in his own bird language, and yet Desmond had understood him.

"It is important that they return with the Yeti, but I will leave that to Christmas magic. And the other two will be here soon," the mighty albatross said looking up into the night sky, his white feathers gleaming in the glow of the moonlight.

"Who are the others? Do you know how we can free Santa Claus?" I asked, my questions running together. I expected the Yeti to burst through a fold in the air any moment and I had no patience for reverence and awe no matter how regal the bird was or much he glowed.

"Christmas spirit will free him," the bird answered. "I believe you have brought yours with you?"

"What do we do though? Who are the others," Nat questioned, repeating the questions I had not received answers to. She was nervous, I knew. My cousin needed a decisive plan of action, steps laid out that we could follow, but we were flying by the seat of our pants. It was a feeling I was used to, but not Natalie. And even I felt like one should not save the world flying by the seat of her pants. I knew we had Christmas spirit, but what exactly did that mean? How could we use it to free Santa Claus?

The albatross folded and unfolded his great wings and lifted into the air. "I must leave you now. I have a task to perform, and time is short. You must simply show your Christmas spirit and Santa Claus will be free." The albatross then rose into the air and flew out over the ocean leaving us to ourselves in the darkness. The streaming rays of moonlight seemed to follow him as he went.

"What does that mean?" Desmond asked with a touch of panic in his voice. "We came prepared for a fight. We are exhausted, and, well, to be honest, I am terrified, and we have no idea what we are doing. How are we supposed to show Christmas spirit?" He approached the entrance of the cave, his hand fell flat against the darkened entrance, and no matter how he pushed he could not breach the entrance. He balled it into a fist, and I knew he wanted to try and punch his way through.

Nat took his hand, pulling it away from the cave, her face sad and frightened. I could see she had no ideas either. Then it hit me. She had no ideas about how to show Christmas spirit because she had been doing nothing but reading tomes on how to cast and break enchantments and curses. But what had I been reading? Children's books. I had been spending my time with my nose in a brightly colored children's book. Not only that, but I had also had years of sitting with Grams the Great hearing all the stories of Christmases past. It was a day of feasting, celebrating, gift giving, and love. I searched my pockets. I had nothing. I looked at the ground beneath my feet. Ice and rock. I had to make this real, but I had no time. I searched for the prettiest rocks I could see in the darkness. I found five, as quickly as possible.

"Merry Christmas!" I shouted to my friends, and I think I shocked them. I do not think they realized why I was acting so jolly, but what else could I do. "A Christmas present from me to you," I said handing my cousin, my best friend for life, and my confidante in this world, a rock because she was my rock. My person. I had never imagined that the first Christmas gift I would give would be a rock, but I swallowed the feeling that it was a completely insufficient gift for this person that I loved so much, and I placed it in her hands.

Then I gave Desmond, Hemlock, Eylif and Luna each a rock as well because they had become the most steadfast friends anyone could ask for and what better to represent our solidarity than a perfect, beautiful, solid, arctic rock. They were dark, cold, smooth, and they had stood the test of time, just as I had to believe we would all withstand the Yeti.

"I love you all," I told my friends. "I hope you accept these humble gifts from me, though they are not wrapped in pretty paper, and they are not valuable. I hope you love them, and I hope they remind you always of our first Christmas together. Merry Christmas!"

Natalie smiled as it dawned on her what I was trying to do. She tucked her rock into her pocket. "I will cherish it forever," she told me. "Merry Christmas, Eve."

Eylif tucked her rock into the red pouch she wore around her neck which also carried the hunter's bullet. She placed Luna's there as well, promising to return it to her den for safekeeping as soon as she was able. Desmond put his in his coat pocket and they all shouted Merry Christmas. Eylif roared what I think was supposed to be a jolly roar and Luna lifted her head toward the moon and howled.

Hemlock squeezed his rock tightly in his fist. "Sasquatches do not keep trinkets or items, Eve, but this I will take with me back to my wilds and I will give it a home where I can always visit and be reminded of this Christmas with my friends. Merry Christmas!" he shouted with so much enthusiasm in his rumbling voice that I felt his own Christmas spirit wash over me. I felt genuine joy and laughter bubble forth.

And when I laughed the earth trembled a bit beneath our feet. I looked at the cave, expecting Santa Claus to burst forth, but he did not. My friends were looking at the cave as well. The gifts had not been enough. I thought of my books again. We could not decorate a tree, we could not feast, we had no sugar plums or candy canes. We could celebrate though. I pictured Grams the Great shuffling about my house in soft red and green socks humming on her way to bed. Christmas carols. It was all I had left. I grabbed Natalie's hand and drug her to the cave entrance shouting for the rest to follow us. I made them all join hands. Desmond wrapped an arm around Eylif's shoulders as she sat down on her haunches and then he grabbed Natalie's other free hand. Hemlock took my hand. Then I sang. My singing voice had never been impressive, but I put all the Christmas spirit I had into that song. I was not sure the words were right, but I started with a song Grams sang all the time.

DECK THE HALLS WITH BOUGHS OF HOLLY
FALALALALALALALALALA
TIS THE SEASON TO BE JOLLY
FALALALALALALALALALA

I only knew snippets, just pieces of songs, so I sang them over and over until the others learned the words and joined in.

JINGLE BELLS, JINGLE BELLS
JINGLE ALL THE WAY
OH, WHAT FUN IT IS TO RIDE
IN A ONE-HORSE OPEN SLEIGH, HEY

RUDOLPH THE RED NOSED REINDEER
HAD A VERY SHINY NOSE
AND IF YOU EVER SAW IT
YOU WOULD EVEN SAY IT GLOWS

SILVER BELLS, SILVER BELLS
IT'S CHRISTMAS TIME IN THE CITY
HEAR THEM RING, RING-A-LING
SOON IT WILL BE CHRISTMAS DAY

THOUGH IT'S BEEN SAID MANY, TIMES MANY
WAYS MERRY CHRISTMAS TO YOU

We held hands and we sang. Luna and her wolves howled behind us, their wolf song blending perfectly with our voices. Desmond's voice was strong and clear, Nat's voice soft and sweet, Hemlock's was low and rumbling, and Eylif's held something of a growl. It was not perfect, but it was joyful, and it filled the night sky and the earth below us rumbled. It was working. Santa Claus and Desmond's parents and all those Christmas souls trapped in that cave would burst forth any moment now. I could feel it. I felt so happy, so joyful, so full of song and life and love and laughter, I knew we were going to free them, we were going to win.

But then there was a terrible screaming from behind us, a snarling roar that chilled me to the bone. I turned and a creature more horrible than I could ever have imagined came into view. He was howling mad, with angry red eyes. His fur, which I think may have once been white, was matted and filthy. The stench that came from him burned my nostrils, a putrid, acrid smell of sweat and filth. I wanted to vomit, but whether it was the fear or the smell that made me feel so ill I was not sure. The reverberations of his roar left me paralyzed, they rattled me to my very depth, and I felt I could not move. I had thought Hemlock's brother was terrifying, but I did not know terror until the Yeti stepped into my presence. He had a limp body thrown over one shoulder and the flash of flaming red told me it was Esa. The silvery form of Tungi was slung over his other. Ing and Jacy were missing. This huge, formidable creature was carrying an enormous wolf like it was nothing. He tossed both his loads into the cave entrance, and as they disappeared into the black, cavernous mouth of the cave the air rippled behind them, and we saw nothing more. At least, I was now certain we had the right cave.

But Esa. Limp and lifeless, and Tungi as well. Please let them be asleep. Please let them be unhurt. I could not believe the strength the Yeti must have had to toss a wolf like it was nothing ten feet into the mouth of a cave. And where were Ing and Jacy? But I had no time to dwell on the state of my friends.

Eylif raised herself on her hind legs, coming to her full height, and hitting the Yeti with a roar of her own. Unlike the Yeti's roar, hers restored my bravery. The paralyzed feeling, the inability to move, was broken by the strength of the magical, untamed wildness of that polar bear roar. Eylif launched herself at the Yeti and the battle for Christmas and the world began.

"You again," screamed the Yeti for they had battled many times over the years. The polar bear and the Yeti rolled and tumbled and clawed at each other as a pack of wolverines poured through the fold the Ycti had created in the air.

Hemlock took a stand in front of Desmond, Natalie, and me, but Luna and her wolves threw themselves against the wolverines. There was snarling, hissing, howling, and gnashing of teeth. The wolves were faring well against the wolverines, but Eylif was losing. The Yeti was twice her size, and he was angry. Hemlock looked back at us, and I knew he was torn between leaving us alone and helping the polar bear.

"Go! She needs you!" I shouted and he was off with a sasquatch scream of rage that I did not know he had in him, though I had heard it from his brother before.

Desmond chased after Hemlock, gathering rocks as he ran and throwing them at the Yeti. I doubted the enraged creature felt a single rock, but at least Desmond was doing something. Nat and I stood dumbly, clutching each other's hands, not sure how to help against a giant Yeti and the squat, wild, snarling wolverines. But then a group of those wolverines burst through the ranks of the wolves and rushed toward us. They were huge, by some Yeti magic, larger than a real wolverine should have been, with sharp teeth and muscled legs that ended in sharp claws, and they looked like they wanted to do nothing more than eat two delicious children.

Without thinking I launched myself backward, jumping higher than I had thought I could. Higher still. I looked down at my feet and realized I was ten feet above the ground. Christmas magic. I was flying and I had not had to throw myself off a cliff after all. I pushed

217

myself towards Nat and grabbed the back of her shirt pulling her into the sky with me just as one of the wolverines launched itself at her. It's claws barely missed her as I pulled both of us into the sky. She was heavy, but I was not going to let go. I looked around for Desmond, but to my astonishment he too was gliding through the air.

I wanted to follow Desmond, to help fight the Yeti, but I needed to get Nat somewhere safe first. She seemed to be growing lighter in my arms as I flew toward a towering tree. I was thinking I could deposit her there where she would be safe from the heat of battle while I joined the fight. But, suddenly, I realized she weighed almost nothing.

"Let go, Eve," she said excitedly. "Let go." I removed my hands from around her waist and she stayed in the air, laughing as she kicked her boots around, testing what she could do. "Come on!" she shouted and dove back down to the earth.

I watched my cousin grab as many rocks as she could carry and then launch herself back into the sky. She began pelting wolverines with the rocks she had gathered. Her aim was terrible, but she hit one and it dropped to the ground, out cold, because even though Nat's arms were as scrawny as mine, she now had gravity on her side. I followed suit, launching rocks as quickly as I could at the wolverines all the while trying to make my way to the Yeti.

But just as I got close, I saw a swarm of locusts from the dark sky come flying toward us. Eylif had mentioned the Yeti may have other allies, but I had no idea how locusts could live through this arctic cold. In fact, I think many of them did freeze and drop before they made it to us. The Yeti had brought them here as a mere distraction, knowing the cold would kill them. They swarmed at the same time another horde of wolverines burst forth from the trees. We tried to stay in the sky to keep safe from the wolverines, but the locusts dive bombed our eyes, our mouths, everywhere, making it hard to see and creating chaos. We were outnumbered, vastly outnumbered, as more and more wolverines and locusts came to the fight.

As I batted away the locusts, many of whom were dropping to the ground frozen, the wolverines nipped at my feet. I saw the wolves were being bloodied and overtaken. I looked at the cave where Santa Claus was being held, hoping for him to burst forth, but I was disappointed.

Santa Claus did not come, but something else amazing happened. From the trees came flocks of birds, all different kinds of arctic birds. They pecked at the eyes of the wolverines, they scooped locusts from the sky and swallowed them whole. They created more chaos, but this time it was for our side. Even more astonishing than the birds, was Hemlock's brother, slipping through a fold in the air. I remembered how he had once terrified us in the forest, and I was glad he was on our side. The red furred sasquatch was followed by several others, and they launched themselves with a growl at the wolverines. With the arrival of these new allies the tides began to turn. We were winning.

Nat and I flew toward the Yeti, joining Desmond in showering rocks down upon his head. Eylif was in the air, flying above the raging creature, clawing and biting at him. Hemlock's arms were locked around the Yeti, and I thought we would have him soon. He could not withstand our joined strength for much longer. But then I saw Hemlock suddenly drop to the ground. I flew to the sasquatch. He was, thankfully breathing. I knelt beside him. He had a gash across his face and blood in his fur on both his arms and legs, but he was alive. I looked around and saw that many of the wolves had dropped to the ground, though no wolverines still fought.

What was happening? My friends had defeated the Yeti's wolverines and locusts, and yet they were collapsing one at a time to the cold ground. I watched in horror as Hemlock's brother and his sasquatch friends toppled next. The Yeti was using his magic to put my friends to sleep. It had to be the same spell he had cast on Santa Claus.

He had gone for Hemlock first because he likely viewed him as the largest threat, but I saw Eylif fall from the sky and land with a thud on the cold ground. Reluctantly, I left Hemlock. I needed to help my friends before the Yeti had put us all to sleep. Luna went down next. It was all happening so quickly. Where was Natalie? Desmond was still pelting the Yeti with rocks, dodging about in the dark sky. I could not find Nat. Panic was sinking in. Then I saw my cousin lying in a heap on top of Eylif. At least she had landed in a soft place. I flew to them. I had to know that they were still alive. When I had confirmed they were still breathing, I looked for Desmond and flew towards him. But just as I reached the last of my friends still standing, I saw his eyes roll back in his head and he began to drop from the sky. I tried to catch him, knowing a fall from that height could kill him, and while I could not stop him from falling, I slowed him down enough that when he hit the ground, he was not hurt. At least I hoped.

There were none left. Neither a wolverine to aid the Yeti for the wolves and sasquatches had taken them all down, nor a friend to aid me. Sasquatches, wolves, birds, Nat and Desmond, they all lay sleeping on the ground. There was blood everywhere, the frozen bodies of locusts lay in heaps, and the forest was eerily quiet. It was a terrifying sight, an ominous silence, and a great terror overwhelmed me. It was just the two of us. The Yeti and me. My biggest fear had been going on this adventure without Natalie and Desmond. I had not thought I could do any of it by myself, and now here I was, alone, with no one left to fight the Yeti but me.

My back was to the creature as I crouched over Desmond, and I did not want to turn around. I did not want to see him, but I could not go down without a fight. I stood to my feet, staying on the ground, knowing if I flew, when he put me to sleep I would crash to the frozen ground and likely never wake again with no friend to stop my fall. What would happen? Would we all sleep eternally in this cave with Santa Claus while the world burned?

I could hear laborious, rasping, breathing behind me as I turned and there he was. The Yeti. His eyes reflected red in the moonlight, and I could feel an evil emptiness emanating from them. He was demon-like and terrifying. And huge. He made Hemlock feel small. I thought he was easily ten feet tall, and standing this close to him, the smell I had noticed earlier was even stronger, acrid, and burning my nostrils. He was a demon, and I was a little girl.

But I stood my ground. What else could I do? My heart was like a drum in my chest, so loud it was all I could hear. Behind the Yeti the aurora borealis lit up the sky, and I let it comfort me as I awaited my fate. Any moment now I would drop to the ground and join my friends in their slumber. The Yeti threw back his head and screamed but this time, though it did seep under my skin and into my bones, it did not paralyze me. I had come all this way to fail, but I had given it everything I had. I had made friends I could never have dreamed of. And I would not have to live to see the world burn. It was okay.

The Yeti's glowing red eyes looked into mine and he shouted, "Why will you not fall asleep?"

What? I had not even felt him trying. Hope rose in my chest. If he could not put me to sleep, could I still win? Certainly, I could not beat him with strength, but there had to be something I could do.

"A true believer! This is not possible!" shouted the terrifying, giant beast. His voice grated and rasped. His breathing was ragged. He was bloody and stooped over. I knew the fight my friends had given him had drained him. I remembered Hemlock saying how much using his magic had exhausted him. The Yeti, I could see, was exhausted.

Then the words he had spoken sunk in. A true believer? That is what Natalie had said she thought I was. The spirit of Christmas. The True Believer. The Yeti looked at me with his red eyes, full of rage and anger and what else? Fear? He could not be afraid of me, could he?

"If I cannot put you to sleep, then I will have to take care of you another way," he roared and with those words the Yeti came flying towards me.

Santa Claus

I had forgotten I could fly and so instead I turned and tried to run. But you cannot outrun a Yeti and I felt his long arm reach out and swipe my feet out from underneath me, his long, clawed fingers ripping through my thick, lined winter pants and cutting into my leg. Frozen tundra feels like cement when you fall flat upon it, and as pain wracked my body and blood poured down my leg, I knew my fate was going to be worse than a good, long sleep. I braced myself for the claws and teeth I knew were coming, but at that moment two shapes shot from the trees. The wolf sentinel, Jacy, with snarling teeth was on the Yeti's back, biting and clawing and Ing was flitting about his face squawking and pecking at his eyes. I reached for the closest thing I could find, a large stick, and I began swinging. I hit his legs, his gut, I threw all my meager strength into it, but the Yeti, battle weary as he was, was still stronger than the three of us. Jacy and Ing were dropped in sleep within moments, but they had bought me time and now I ran. The Yeti rested, stooped and gasping. His use of magic was wearing him down probably more than any physical battle was.

I remembered finally that I could fly, and I shot into the air, which enraged the Yeti enough that he chased after me now. He had no intentions of letting me get away. I had no thoughts in my head, no plan, only adrenaline racing through my body and a will to live, because as long as I stayed alive there was a chance that I could still save my friends. I flew to the top of the cave entrance that held Santa Claus and I landed there. If I could just finish what we had started. If, somehow, in all this chaos and disaster, I could show true Christmas spirit, and set Santa Claus free, then we could still defeat the Yeti and lift the curse.

The Yeti was coming now, climbing to where I was perched. "You cannot win true believer. Your friends are gone, Santa Claus is imprisoned, and you are running out of time. This enchantment will become a curse that will destroy your race and there is nothing you can do about it. You are alone and helpless. I do not even need to catch you. I only need to await the stroke of midnight."

"Why are you doing this?" I shouted back to him in frustration.

"Why, little human? For thousands of years your kind has done nothing but destroy. You call it progress, but you are careless and greedy. You destroy forests, you take lives, you pollute, and you tame. You want to tame everything. But the world is not tamable, and your people are about to learn that."

"If this curse becomes permanent you won't just destroy the human race. The entire earth will sink into despair, and nothing will be safe. It will all burn."

"Possibly. Your race, with broken and twisted hearts, will become even more destructive and the earth will suffer. But eventually you will destroy yourselves and the earth will be wiped clean of you forever. The wild places will regenerate themselves and future generations will be free from the scourge of humanity. And I will rise to the top, no one will be able to hurt me, my power will be complete, and I will never suffer at the hands of a human being again."

He did not care that the wild places would burn with the humans. He did not care that the animals and trees would suffer. He wanted an earth empty of humans that could grow into something new.

"You might die too! Don't you care? There will be nothing but suffering on this earth and it will be your fault!"

"I have suffered already! I had a family once, little human. I was not always the only yeti in the Himalayas. What do you think happened to them? Do you see my little child by my side? My wife? Seen by humans and called monsters. Abominable. They died one hundred years ago today at the hands of your race. Men are the real monsters, taking a child from his father on Christmas Eve. I mourned on my mountaintop, but when I went to take my revenge upon the people who had destroyed my world I was stopped. Santa Claus would not let me destroy the humans. Santa Claus sent me back to my mountain. Even before the deaths of my family, Santa Claus protected the humans from me. I only ever wanted to keep them away. But when they took my family, I wanted revenge. I wanted every human to suffer as I had. But Santa Claus and his polar bear guard foiled every plot. Then Jack Frost paid a visit. Jack Frost, who was tired of Santa Claus having all the best Christmas magic, tired of Santa Claus stopping all his best tricks. Jack Frost gave me what I needed to destroy Christmas and destroy all of you greedy, selfish, nasty humans. You will all pay the price now."

My heart broke for him. It broke into a million tiny pieces. His heart was not evil, it was anguished. He was in pain. But he was also still coming for me, still trying to climb, to reach me, to destroy everything I loved, and though I was deeply saddened, I could not let him win. I could not let him destroy an entire race because of the heinous crime committed by one. As the Yeti drew closer to where I was perched, I launched myself into the sky again and landed in a tree. My glove had torn, and the bare skin of my hand brushed against the frosted bark.

"Eve, we are here," the tree reminded me. "Use us, Eve." Her branch wrapped itself into a circle, full with thick evergreen needles and dotted with bright berries. She let the circle, frosted with white, drop into my lap. I stared at it for a moment. A wreath? A Christmas wreath. She was reminding me that I needed Christmas spirit.

I held up the wreath. I took a deep breath. The Yeti had dropped down from the side of the cave he had been climbing and he was now loping toward the tree I had flown to. A low, angry growl rumbled from his belly as he moved. I knew what I needed to do. He was a poor creature. He had experienced tragedy, and he had no one to love. He had let all his sadness become twisted anger and rage, and after that he had let it become emptiness. Apathy. Apathy for the world. But he had not become Anti Magic yet. He felt something still. He had enough twisted hate and rage to want to end the human race. And Hemlock had said that hate was still emotion. It could be healed. I flew to the Yeti, Christmas wreath in hand, and careful to stay out of reach I dropped the wreath. He caught it, not knowing what it was.

"Merry Christmas, Yeti," I said softly. "It is a gift for you." And I meant it. I wanted his Christmas to be merry. I wanted his pain to end.

The sorry creature with angry eyes and twisted heart sat down on the ground and howled, but it was not the same rage filled roar that had filled the night only moments before. This sound was filled with all the sorrow and agony of deep loss. Loss, but not remorse. A Christmas wreath could not heal years of pain and sorrow, and the Yeti stood, faster than I realized he could move and throwing the wreath to the ground he jumped and wrapped a hand around my ankle and ripped me from the sky.

But I was not to be eaten by a Yeti on Christmas Eve, for at that moment a man dressed in red with a beard of white burst forth from the cave with a deep "ho, ho, ho" and the Yeti tossed me aside and turned to face who I knew to be the man we had come to save. Santa Claus. Free now from that last bit of Christmas spirit, that gift given in empathy to one less fortunate, the greatest Christmas spirit there is.

Santa Claus. My heart filled with joy at the sound of his voice, at the sight of his face, at the twinkle of the bluest eyes I had ever seen. He was not the chubby old man described in books, but rather he was regal and elflike. His hair and beard were white with hints of red and his face was strong and bright. He was a giant of a man, strong and lean, clothed in a red suit with a garland of green and red berries atop his head. The Yeti stared up at Santa Claus with fear in his red eyes as I looked up at him in wonder. In the moonlight, I saw him wink at me and all the terror I had been feeling only moments before left me. I felt only peace and joy.

"It is over Yeti," Santa Claus said as two enormous reindeer came from the cave to stand by his side, pawing the ground while their breath steamed.

I looked around as my sleeping friends began to awaken. The wolves were rising to their feet, Luna was the first and she had come to kneel before Santa Claus. My heart nearly burst as I saw Hemlock sit up. Desmond rose next, slowly, groggily, and probably painfully, considering I had only been able to slow his fall. Eylif rose and nudged Nat. When my cousin finally opened her eyes and sat up, the polar bear whispered something to her and Nat remained upon Eylif's back, looking weak and tired, as the polar made her way toward Santa Claus.

The Yeti simply stared, panting, fuming, and growling angrily at Santa Claus. I thought we had won, but the Yeti dashed my hopes. "It will still come, Santa Claus. You are awake but you cannot stop the curse. You are missing two of your party."

Santa Claus looked up at the night sky, at the twinkling stars, and he had a smile on his face. The silhouette of the albatross darkened the moon and Santa Claus laughed a deep belly laugh and looked at the Yeti with sympathy in his eyes. "No Yeti, I think they have just arrived."

An auto then flew behind the albatross and as it came closer, I realized I recognized it. Mom's auto. Was my mother coming? But when it landed it was not my parents who stepped from the vehicle but Ms. Snow. She launched herself from the auto, her red hair streaming behind her, and threw herself into Santa Claus's arms. As she did so another figure burst from the cave, a woman dressed in purple, with shining, plum dark skin, dark, wild, flowing purple locks of hair and wings that glistened like sugar in the moonlight.

The fairy wrapped her arms around Santa Claus and Ms. Snow, crying "Holiday, my daughter" and soft tears glistened in Santa Claus's eyes.

I was confused only for a moment before I realized that my librarian was Santa Claus's daughter, and this fairy must be her mother. Happenstance. Christmas magic. We were all connected. I looked at my mother's auto and wondered why Ms. Snow was driving it, when none other than Grams the Great stepped out, a broad smile across her wrinkled face.

I was staring around me in disbelief when Esa emerged from the cave, walking between two people who I instantly knew to be Desmond's mother and father. Desmond was running towards them, and Esa stepped away as the three embraced, crying and clinging to each other. In fact, Esa did not step away, he rose from the ground, his eyes looking wild. He was flying. All four of us had the gift of Christmas magic. Esa smiled and waved at me before he turned a somersault or two in the air and then joined Jacy and Tungi, who had been reunited and were licking each other's faces and rolling around on the icy ground.

I looked again to the Yeti, his wild eyes looking as though they were deciding who to attack first, when the tree I was leaning against reminded me not to worry. They were on our side. She leaned her long trunk over, and she wrapped the Yeti in strong arms just as he was about to launch himself toward me. He cried in outrage, but he could not free himself. A tree is the strongest creature on this earth. Not even a Yeti can stand against the strength of a tree.

I went to Natalie, who was still rubbing her eyes and struggling to stand to her feet. I looked around and saw Desmond and his family, Hemlock embracing his brother, the wolves licking the faces of their brothers and sisters who were still trying to wake up, Eylif nudging tiny Ing awake. Grams the Great. Ms. Snow. I felt so much Christmas joy I thought I might burst.

For the second time, Santa Claus winked at me. "We have very little time friends," he said. "We must lift this enchantment and stop the curse of the Yeti."

He took his wife and daughter's hands in his. The rest of us seemed instinctively to know what to do. Grams the Great, leaning heavily on a cane, joined us and took Ms. Snow's hand, then mine. Hemlock, Natalie, Desmond, Eylif, Ing, Esa, and Luna all joined the circle. We stood, hand in hand, wing to paw, the twelve guardians of Christmas. As we joined together, the soft golden glow of magic surrounded us. The moonlight, the starlight, and the aurora borealis all lent their light as well. We twinkled and we glowed, and we were filled with warmth and peace and love.

"Friends, we have come together to lift this enchantment begun by the Yeti. We are the twelve spirits of Christmas. We are its guardians. I am Santa Claus, Father Christmas, guardian of the children and spirit of childhood. Mother Christmas, Santa Rosa, the Sugar Plum Fairy, the Spirit of whimsy and delight. My daughter, Holiday Snow Claus, the Spirit of Christmas Future, who will carry on when I cannot. Carol

230

Blackwood, who holds the wisdom of the ages in her heart and mind, the Spirit of Christmas Past. Eylif, my great captain, the Spirit of Christmas Present, the warrior who safeguards our North Pole home every day, ensuring that I can always bring Christmas to the world. Hemlock, the Untamed Spirit, and protector of the forests, without which our world would perish. Natalie Blackwood, the scholar, and Spirit of Christmas Wisdom. Desmond Carter, who never stopped searching for his parents, who embraces all he loves as his own, the Spirit of Family. Ing, gentle and loving, the Spirit of Peace. Brave Esa Salo, willing to sacrifice himself for his companions, for the world, the Spirit of Friendship. Luna, who takes delight in the world around her no matter the circumstances, the Spirit of Joy. And Eve Farrington, the true believer, and guardian of all Christmas spirit, the Spirit of Belief. Friends, find it in your hearts to forgive the Yeti, fill your hearts with the joy of Christmas. Let nothing but goodwill towards all fill your hearts and then this enchantment will truly be ended."

We bowed our heads. I thought of how difficult it might be for Desmond to forgive the Yeti after what he had done to his parents. I thought of the eighty-three years Ms. Snow had lost with her parents. I wondered how much of her childhood they had missed. I did not even know how old she had been when the Yeti had raided the North Pole. I did not know what he had done to her or how she had ended up living in the mortal world as enchanted as the rest of us. Only I had heard the Yeti's sad story, but I shared it with the circle. If they knew what he had been through maybe they could more easily forgive. And as I finished, I felt their forgiveness, their love, their compassion wash over me.

I let peace, joy, goodwill, and love fill me. There was nothing but warmth and joy in our midst. We encircled the Yeti who had fallen to all fours as the tree let him drop. I let the love inside me pour out towards him, for he was nothing but a poor, pitiful creature who had let rage twist his heart into a knot of hatred. The ground began to move around the Yeti. The roots of the trees were stirring. The frozen ground was softening beneath us. Earth and roots rose up around the Yeti who screamed his wild scream. He fought the roots, but they wrapped themselves around him and slowly, just as Natalie had described from her book, the earth swallowed him, swallowed the curse whole, and was healed. I shuddered and turned away because I did not want to watch any creature, not even this horrible one, suffer. Tears streamed down my cheeks as I listened to the last angry howls of the Yeti before he disappeared beneath the frozen tundra.

"What was broken is now whole. Turn Eve, and watch," Santa Claus said. I turned, reluctantly. Where the Yeti had once stood, was rich loamy soil and as I watched the spot, small bits of green began to rise, and a tiny sapling unfurled herself from the ground.

"The Yeti is at peace. The curse has been swallowed by the earth and the good that was left in the Yeti now grows here, a Christmas tree, born on Christmas morning, to bring joy to the world." For it was now, midnight, and for the first time in eighty-three years Christmas had come.

The Yeti was at peace. The enchantment was lifted. No curse would blanket our land with sorrows. It was Christmas morning. As joy and laughter filled me, I raised my face to the starry sky and something soft and cold landed in my eyelashes. Santa Claus let forth his booming belly laugh, a ho, ho, ho so bright and jolly there was not a soul in our circle that did not smile. Snow was falling on Earth, and I held my hands up to the sky in victory, lifting my face so that the soft cold flakes could fall upon it. If the rest of the world could feel half as happy as I felt in this moment, it would be enough, more than enough, to change the grey sadness that had filled it for so long.

"Come Dasher, Dancer," Santa Claus shouted to the two reindeer who had first joined him from the cave. "There are gifts to be delivered to the children of the world and we are getting a late start. A sleigh pulled by six other reindeer emerged from the cave and Dasher and Dancer joined their ranks.

"I've been sitting in that cave since Eve's letter arrived with nothing to do but make toys," Santa Claus roared. I saw his sleigh was being filled with gifts by a crew of tiny elves dressed in green. Another Christmas miracle. For the first time in eighty-three years the children of the world would know toys. "Hemlock, will you and the other sasquatches see these people back to civilization?" Santa Claus asked, waving his arm toward the handful of confused explorers who had emerged from the cave. Hemlock agreed, and Santa Claus was off in a dash, his beautiful red sleigh taking off into the starry sky, his booming voice shouting to his reindeer.

"On Dasher, on Dancer, on Prancer and Vixen, on Comet and Cupid, on Donner and Blitzen! Merry Christmas my friends!" he roared to us as he disappeared into the night through a fold between the stars and the aurora borealis.

And us? We reveled. We danced. We sang. We celebrated. We frolicked in the first snow the earth had

seen in eighty-three years. I had brought back
Christmas, just as I had set out to do.

The North Pole

As the revelries began to die down, I sat down next to Grams the Great, who was wrapped in so many layers I could only just see her watery green eyes. We sat perched on a wide, flat rock watching the falling snow accumulate around us.

"You did it plum pudding," Grams said with a twinkle in her eye and pride in her voice. "You brought back Christmas. I knew you were the right kiddo for the job!".

"I had help."

"I know! My other favorite granddaughter!" She was so pleased with herself it made me laugh.

"And Desmond, Hemlock, Eylif, Esa, Luna, Ing! Even you Grams. We could not have broken the curse without the Spirit of Christmas Past! Grams, I would not have even known Christmas existed without you."

"Well," she said very softly. "Well, yes. I am Grams the Great after all."

"Grams, tell me, how did you get here? How did you know where to come?"

"Ah. Well, miss Holiday there," she said nodding towards Ms. Snow, "showed up at our door shortly after you left. Your poor mother and father could not understand a word of what she was saying, enchanted as they were. She said you had left a candy cane tucked in a book you had come to return to her after school hours. Christmas books she had not even realized were in her collection! She said she was not sure why, but she ate it, and suddenly remembered everything. Can you imagine? Taking a bite of a peppermint and realizing you are Santa Claus's daughter. So, of course, I told her you children had gone off to save Santa Claus. Well, then your parents got really angry, thought we were both crazy! They asked poor Holly to leave immediately. I could not have the poor thing out on her own, not knowing where to go, so when they were walking her to the front door I snuck into the garage, stole your mother's auto, picked the traumatized thing up off the street and we decided together to come looking for you. Of course, Holly felt terrible about the auto, but I assured her your parents would forgive us when we brought back their daughter."

I was amazed. I had left a candy cane behind. Happenstance again. Christmas magic doing its best work. If I had not quarreled with Nat and Desmond and gone to Ms. Snow feeling guilty, if Ms. Snow had not then gone to see Grams the Great, we could not have broken the curse.

"But Grams, you did not tell me how you found your way here," I reminded her.

"Christmas magic, Eve!" she laughed. "We had no idea where you would be, so we decided to head toward the geographic North Pole. Holly said with a little Christmas magic things might work out for us. She was right. Just when we thought we would have to head back to the city, the albatross showed up. Took us straight to you. Auto is definitely dead now. Not sure how we are going to get it home. Your poor mother. But we made it just in time. Christmas magic, my darling. Christmas magic."

I laughed at my grandmother, who seemed more alert than I could ever remember her being. Then a feeling of guilt washed over me. We had been reveling, dancing, celebrating and all that time Mom, Dad, and Uncle P.J. were likely worried sick over where we all were. Our gammas had no service in the Arctic Circle, but I don't think any of us would have thought to call even if we could. I felt an ache as I thought of them and realized how much I missed my family. I had lost track of how long we had been gone, but I knew it was long past time to go home.

"Grams, how were my parents and Uncle P.J. when we left?"

"Hmm, those old grumps! Stomping around, shouting at me, demanding I tell them where I had sent you. Pretended to forget and when you get this old, people believe you when you pretend to forget," she said, winking at me again. Then she grew more serious. "They were not doing well when I left. They were very worried, Evie Pie, but they'll be okay. And they will forgive us when they hear all you have been through, when they hear how you and Nat and your friends saved not just Christmas, but the whole world!"

"I wish they were here to see all this," I said, feeling guilty again. "It's so perfect, the only thing that could make it better would be to have them here with us."

Grams did not answer. She was looking up at the sky. I saw the silhouette of Santa Claus's sleigh before I heard the twinkling of the harness bells. It had to be close to morning, but it was still dark. It would be many more months before the sun would shine where we were. The snow continued to gently fall, the sparkling white confetti of our Christmas party. We could not feel the biting cold, which the Sugar Plum Fairy had explained was part of her Christmas magic. We were at peace, surrounded by wild snowy beauty, in the company of wild creatures. Few humans have ever been given a gift so great as we had.

The Sugar Plum Fairy, Santa Rosa, Mother Christmas came to stand by our side. "Santa Claus returns, and I believe he is bringing you the very gift your heart desires," she said to me. Her earthy purple skin shone in the moonlight and her sugared wings, tipped with glittering gold were the most beautiful thing I had ever seen.

"The only gift my heart desires is to see my parents and my uncle, for them to know we are safe, and to be here to see this," I told her.

I had thought I wanted a toy crafted by elves, but I understood now what I really wanted. All those stories of gathering with your loved ones in celebration, that is what I longed for. I longed for them all to feel joy and happiness. I could not wait to see what the peace of Christmas would look like on them now that the enchantment was lifted. I was not naïve enough to think that Mom would ever stop worrying over my grades, but I wondered what a real laugh would sound like coming from her lips.

As the sleigh descended and came closer to landing, Santa Rosa lifted her arm. She wore a purple gown trimmed in white fur that rippled as she pointed to the sleigh. "My darling, Santa Claus knows your heart. Look at what he has brought you."

I squinted in the dark as the sleigh touched down in the soft snow. Behind the pawing reindeer I could see that there were five figures seated in the sleigh with the tall, bearded man. I took off flying, hearing the laughter of Grams the Great and the Sugar Plum Fairy behind me. I would know three of those silhouettes anywhere. The other two, I assumed belonged to Esa as the woman had a head full of fiery red hair that matched my friend's perfectly.

They were mine. Mom, Dad, Uncle P.J. My family. I heard Nat squeal with delight and found she was next to me in the air, because flying was the fastest way to get anywhere. The next thing I knew I was being scooped up by my father and Nat by hers and my mother, grumpy and mean as she could be, was crying and laughing at the same time and had pulled all four of us close to her. We hugged and laughed. We cried. There was even some scolding, though not half the scolding we deserved for stealing Dad's auto and running away to the Arctic Circle. It would seem that Santa Claus had explained much to our families on the sleigh ride here. And then my 127-year-old grandmother floated down from the sky, commenting how much easier flying was on her hips. My family was surrounding me, and my Christmas wish was complete.

Santa Claus gave us a booming "Ho, ho, ho, Merry Christmas," and then left us to tell our parents our story while he went to his wife and daughter.

With no enchantment weighing us down we felt more happiness than any of us had ever felt in our lives, any of us that is except Grams, but I could see in her eyes how elated she was to feel this joy again, and to see her family reveling in the joy she had longed for them to know.

"I remember this feeling," she whispered. "This is what it feels like to really be alive. Merry Christmas, my beautiful family."

"Merry Christmas Grams," we all told her.

"I believe it is now time to go home," Santa Claus said. "Eve, Natalie, Desmond, Esa, and of course, Grams the Great, you will join me in my sleigh. Hemlock, in one hour's time, the place you would once visit us will be restored. Bring the rest of our friends."

We loaded into the sleigh with Santa Claus, Ms. Snow, or Holiday Claus now, and the Sugar Plum Fairy. Santa Claus shouted to his reindeer who tore off through the snow that had already grown deep and thick and gradually we were borne into the sky, the sound of Christmas bells and 'ho ho ho's' ringing in our ears.

I had dreamed of this for so long, flying in a sleigh pulled by magical reindeer. On the edge of my seat, I leaned over, seeing the Arctic Ocean below. The North Pole had melted into the sea eighty-three years ago today. I was not sure where Santa Claus planned to land this sleigh, but I had learned to trust in Christmas magic. It felt like only moments, though I knew we had been in the air for much longer, when we began to circle over a certain spot. The Sugar Plum Fairy unfurled her sugar gold wings and flew down over the water. I watched as she circled, flying faster and faster, stirring up the ocean, a cloud of luminescent snowy gold dust trailing behind her. She had created a churning, spinning whirlpool before she rose into the air, her arms working in a pulling motion as though she were working an invisible rope.

"My beautiful wife," Santa Claus said, gazing at her lovingly. "Plum, show them what you can do." The beautiful fairy rolled her eyes at her husband but flew from us toward the ocean with a smile on her plum dark face.

I leaned further out of the sleigh that continued to fly in wide circles, staring in wonder. Santa Rosa flew just above the frigid, rolling water, unphased by its wild coldness. At a wave of her arm, a mass of ice formed over the top of the ocean, cracking and spreading, in circles around a center point.

"That is the North Pole, the very most northern point of the earth, and the most magical place in the world. My home," Santa Claus explained to us. Ice continued to circle in a beautiful whirling pattern until a giant mass was formed and Santa Claus guided his reindeer down to the ground.

The Sugar Plum Fairy landed softly beside us and with a wave of her arm snow began to fall gently all around us. "Santa Rosa, my plum, it is beautiful," Santa Claus said as he put his arm around her. The ice continued to spread until it had grown so far out into the ocean we could not see where it ended. Santa Rosa waved her arms again and evergreens began to emerge from the ice in a circle around us. When the trees were full sized, the fairy threw little, twinkling balls of Christmas lights into their branches, and that is when Hemlock appeared, with all our families, Luna and her wolfpack, Ing, Eylif and all the elves. They streamed through Hemlock's dimensional fold, laughing and tumbling about in the snow that had already begun to accumulate on the icy surface.

Then there was a final wave from Santa Rosa, and before our eyes, tiny homes began to rise from the ice. They had bright, red roofs and swirling carved details. Windows appeared, and twinkling bright light filled them. The same fairy lights that adorned the trees now lined the eaves of the tiny homes, candy canes lined the lanes, and the elves began to dance in and out of the houses. In the center of it all one large cabin unfolded itself from the ice. Santa's workshop. It was all more beautiful than I had ever imagined it could be. The books, the pictures, the descriptions, nothing could have prepared me for what had appeared before my eyes, this delight of fairy magic. The North Pole, home of Santa Claus had been restored by the Sugar Plum Fairy. It was a winter wonderland, and I was dazzled.

"Home," Holiday Claus sighed beside me, and I felt a pang of loss knowing that the best part of Ad Prima Academy would be leaving. I couldn't blame her, though, as I looked around at the snowy beauty of the North Pole. It was a perfect village of wonder.

Santa Claus entered his newly restored home like a king entering his castle. He looked around, smiling and twinkling and jolly, as our rather large party milled in after him. Even Luna, Jacy, and Tungi had followed Santa Claus inside, though they looked uncomfortable to be surrounded by walls and a ceiling and they stayed very near the door.

"There is one thing the Yeti took from us that we can never get back," Santa Claus began once we were all settled. "Time." He looked at his daughter who had lived for eighty-three years among mortals, never knowing why she could not age, enchanted and alone.

He looked at Desmond and his parents. Desmond had been shorter than his father when they had last seen each other, but now matched his lanky height. The Yeti had robbed them of so much. "Eighty-three years of Christmas's that will never be celebrated. But we will move on in joy. I will rebuild the North Pole, and my family and I will continue to spread the joy of Christmas to the people year after year for as long as humanity survives. And thanks to these brave children and their companions, I believe we have many more years to celebrate."

Santa Claus then looked to Luna, Jacy, and Tungi. "Brave wolves of the boreal forest, I would like to invite you and your pack to live here at the North Pole. Jacy and Tungi who so bravely accompanied young Esa, willing to sacrifice themselves for the good of the entire world, Jacy who traversed ten miles in just twenty minutes, running at her top speed for far longer than any wolf should have been able to, saving Eve from the Yeti, Tungi who lunged at the Yeti, stopping him from taking the life of young Esa, and Luna who risked her whole pack to save these children from the wolverines and fought so bravely against the Yeti alongside Eylif and Hemlock. I would be greatly honored if you would replace my lost polar bears and work with Eylif as the North Pole Guard."

"It would be our great honor, Santa Claus, to live here with you in this magical place," Luna said as her puppies, who Hemlock must have gone back for while we flew in the sleigh, tumbled and frolicked just outside the door to Santa's workshop.

"Hemlock, you and your brothers and sisters who came to our aid, will always be welcome here. I know you will never leave your forest, but I hope you will visit often," Santa Claus said to the giant sasquatch, who was sitting next to Holiday. My friend promised he would return as often as he could.

"And Eylif, the captain of my guard, you will, I hope, return to your post?" Santa Claus said with a twinkle in his blue eyes.

"If you will have me, Santa Claus," said the polar bear. "I have but one request. Ing, the Puffin, whose heart yearns for peace and joy, but who is also a brave and fierce friend, should live here with us as my most trusted advisor."

"Your request is granted with great joy. And Ing, I thank you for your service today, helping the wolf sentinels to save not one, but two children on Christmas Eve," said Santa Claus. My heart filled with joy for the sweet, brave puffin, whose white feathered chest was puffed up with pride.

A wonderful warm smell had begun to fill the house, gingery and sweet. The elves were already at work in the kitchen, but they started the feast by bringing cups of steaming hot chocolate topped with peppermint sticks and piles and piles of whipped cream and shaved chocolate. It was magical cocoa, the kind that makes any other chocolate seem bland and boring by comparison and it filled us all with great warmth as we listened to Santa Claus speak.

"Follow me," Santa Claus boomed in his rich deep voice to my friends and me once his speech was over and our refreshments were gone. As we walked past the kitchen, Natalie and I both laughed and waved to Uncle P.J. who was standing in the middle of a circle of tiny elves with his sleeves rolled up helping to cook what I hoped would be Christmas dinner.

"Naps," said Santa Claus with a wink, "are an important Christmas tradition. After staying awake all night delivering gifts, I feel I deserve a lovely Christmas day nap, and I think you all have more than earned some rest as well."

He opened the door to a large room filled with very cozy looking beds. Jacy and Tungi crawled right into the bed next to Esa, wiggling hilariously and nosing down the heavy red quilt as they tried to figure out how they would all fit. Luna curled up in a bed all to herself, not bothering to disturb the blankets. Ing snuggled into her polar bear, who was already practically asleep on the floor while Hemlock fell onto the biggest bed in the room and was still too large for it. Nat, Desmond, and I each found a bed for ourselves as well. The blankets were soft and warm, the quilts on top were heavy and all reds and greens. I could not believe I was about to sleep away my first Christmas day, but I had never needed a nap more. I fell asleep thinking about Grams the Great and how many of her Christmas stories included my great grandfather's love of a Christmas day nap. She said he could fall asleep anywhere and you'd find often find him on the floor in a corner of whichever relatives house they were visiting snoring away. I thought of my great grandfather watching over me from above as I drifted off into my first Christmas day nap.

A Christmas Gift

O ur wounds had been healed by the sasquatches, we had been given our Christmas Day naps, and we were bathed and dressed in beautiful holiday clothes gifted to us by Santa Rosa. It was time for Christmas dinner, and it was everything I had imagined and more. Candied yams and mashed potatoes with gravy, breads and honied butter, green beans with herbs and spices, a roasted turkey and a ham, collard greens, sweet potato pie, pecan pie, pumpkin pie, sugar plums, fig pudding, food I did not even have a name for. There was so much food on the table I did not think I could find room to taste it all. But eventually I did. I had a bite of everything. Desmond had multiple bites of everything. We washed it all down with sparkling cider and fairy nectar. When we finally left the dining table of Santa Claus and the Sugar Plum Fairy our bellies were so full we could hardly move. We were surrounded by family, the families we had grown up with and the family we had forged on this adventure, and we were happier than we had ever felt.

My parents looked lighter. Mom, especially, seemed to have lost some of her hard edges. She was even talked into a game of charades with a group of elves who had decided they liked her. It was, honestly, one of the most hilarious things I had ever seen, my no nonsense, somewhat grumpy, and always reserved mother trying to act out a hippopotamus for a group of tiny, confused elves. I don't think they ever guessed it and Mom's team lost horribly, but she was laughing in a way I had always wanted to see her laugh. Dad looked content and calm, just as I had pictured happiness would look on him. And Uncle P.J. had found his people in the kitchen elves. He had to be drug from the kitchen just to eat and he was back now, helping with the dishes while dragging recipes from his new best friends.

As I lazed under a brilliantly lit Christmas tree, taking in all the happiness, Grams the Great, who looked spryer and sharper than ever now, sat herself down next to me. "Evie Pie, there is something we should talk about," she said. "This North Pole air has cleared my mind. Even my body feels lighter. Holly has invited me to stay, and I think I will."

"What? Grams?!" I shouted, alarmed and then I felt guilty over my selfishness. I could see how good she felt, how happy she looked, how amazed she was to have her lost mind back. Some of the battiness was still there, but I think it had just become a part of her personality. So, I swallowed the sadness and told her it was okay. "But what does that mean? Humans can't visit the North Pole. Does that mean we will never see you again?"

Grams the Great shrugged her skinny, bony shoulders. "Up to the big guy," she said nodding towards Santa Claus. "Although, I get the feeling that wife of his really runs things around here. Maybe we should talk to her." She winked, and I had the feeling Grams the Great and the Sugar Plum Fairy had already spoken.

"I have a job to do here, Evie Pie," she said proudly. "Santa Rosa could rebuild all these buildings in a night, but Santa's books, his Christmas archives, Holly and I are going to rebuild those together. The Spirit of Christmas Past and the Spirit of Christmas Future, collecting the stories of Christmas through the centuries and preserving them for all the future generations."

As happy as I was for both of them, it occurred to me that two very important people were leaving my life. Ad Prima Academy would be a very different place without Ms. Snow and my house would be so quiet without Grams. I was happy for Mom. She would finally be able to get rid of that chair she so strongly disliked, but I did not think the new Mom would have cared much about it anymore anyway. Yet, with so much Christmas spirit and so much joy and happiness surrounding me, the sadness I felt that these two women would no longer be a part of my daily life simply did not feel that heavy.

"Evie Pie, my plum pudding, you do remember that I am one hundred and twenty-seven years old?" Grams said and I looked down, not wanting to hear where she was going with this. "I'm not immortal. Not like Santa Claus, Santa Rosa, and Holiday. I can't live forever. I have only been given an extra few years thanks to the gift of Christmas magic."

"Maybe you will be given even more extra years living here at the North Pole?" I said hopefully, thinking of just how much heartier she already looked, thinking that if she wasn't living in the room down the hall from me, at least I could picture her here, happily building a library with Ms. Snow, or rather, with Holiday Claus.

Grams the Great shrugged her shoulders. "Who knows. But thanks to you, Eve, I will live on as the Spirit of Christmas Past, and when my time comes I will pass on peacefully, knowing that my granddaughters brought back Christmas, and I will not be leaving them in a world of sadness and drudgery."

"You started it Grams, bringing back Christmas. It was your Christmas magic that started this all," I reminded her.

"I know," she said. "Watch this!" And my batty, old, gnarled, sleepy Grandmother who was still wearing fuzzy Christmas slipper socks, rose into the air, turned a few somersaults, and floated towards the ceiling to play with the elves, so full of Christmas magic that she had not even needed magical candy canes to break her enchantment. She had just needed to get so old she forgot to be enchanted.

As my grandmother floated away from me, Santa Claus approached carrying a parcel wrapped in beautiful green paper and tied with a velvet red ribbon. "I have something for you Eve," he said.

I smiled. This was my very first Christmas present. I did not care what lay beneath that paper. I looked up at Santa Claus in wonder.

"Open it," he encouraged.

It was hard for me to tear that paper it was so beautiful. I did so very slowly. I wanted to unwrap this gift forever, to always remember this moment. What I eventually held in my hands was a book with a white leather cover, the title etched in gold.

"I made the bookmark myself," he said as I opened the book and held the carved wooden bookmark in my hands. "This is a most important book Eve, a book that tells the story of Christmas. Read it and share it with all who will hear."

I felt goosebumps rise up on my arms and tears filled my eyes and I made Santa Claus the most solemn promise I could that I would bring all this joyous news to a world newly awakened from their enchantment. Armed with my new and beautiful book, and my new family, and a heart full of Christmas spirit, I promised Santa Claus that I would bring joy to the world. It was Christmas day at the North Pole, calm and bright, snow falling gently, family gathered together, but from now on the whole world would know this day too. I would make sure of it. A feeling of peace washed over me as I held my new book to my chest, praying that this joy I now felt would soon fall like fresh snow upon all the earth, washing away the heavy gray of the past eighty-three years.

Epilogue

Grams the Great lived out her unnaturally long life at the North Pole, fulfilling her duties as the Spirit of Christmas Past. She recorded volumes and volumes of everything she remembered in beautiful leather-bound books and Holiday Claus catalogued them and placed them neatly on the shelves of the North Pole library. She said she had always wanted to do something grand with her retirement and now she was doing the greatest work of all. When we left, I had been afraid I would never see her again, that I may never see any of them again, but Grams the Great had been right. The Sugar Plum Fairy promised me that we were a family now and she would see to it that our bonds were never severed.

And she was true to her word. Santa Claus would arrive on my rooftop on the first day of summer vacation every year. Mom had relaxed quite a bit, but she was still not about to let us miss a day of school, so our visits to the North Pole came in the summer. Santa Claus would gather Nat and me and then we would pop over to Helsinki to pick up Esa and Desmond and fly to the North Pole. It was hard having Desmond and Esa living so far away, but we did know a sasquatch who made regular visits a bit easier.

Ing was always in the sleigh with Santa Claus when he arrived and Eylif and Luna were always waiting to greet us when the sleigh landed. Luna and her pack now permanently lived at the North Pole, guarding its borders, though with the Yeti gone, there was little danger. Grams the Great was always there, excited to show us her latest volume and share hilarious tales of her hijinks with the elves. The elves seemed to be her very favorite people in the world with their mischievous ways and their love of baked goods. We would eat sugar cookies and build gingerbread houses, and we even learned toymaking. Our first week of summer was spent in cozy, bright sweaters, sledding, having snowball fights, drinking cocoa, climbing frosty evergreens and generally being merry. Hemlock would always eventually step out from the trees and scare us all before he joined in the fun. Sometimes, he even brought his brother, Linden, who turned out to be a fairly decent sasquatch who just had the unfortunate job of frightening away humans since he was so very large.

We learned everything we could about Christmas, and we spread its joy throughout the land. The holiday and its traditions came back slowly at first, with people accepting it as a long-lost tradition that some were trying to bring back. But it grew. Beginning in our little city of Spokane, it grew and grew until the world had embraced it again and every year we came together to give thanks for our many blessings, and in celebration of the love we shared and the joy of living. And with lighter hearts, the people even began to explore the woods again, hiking and camping and breathing in that fresh clean air. The world, with Christmas returned to us, with peace in our hearts, healed.

Eventually, we grew up. Nat, of course, became a brilliant scientist. She kept her promise to Hemlock, working to conserve what forests we had left, but also to regrow some of the wasted lands. Desmond, too, became a scientist, working with Natalie as a conservationist. The two were inseparable and it was to no one's surprise when they announced their engagement. Of course, Santa Claus, being a saint, insisted the wedding be held at the North Pole so that he could officiate.

It was a Christmas wedding. The Sugar Plum Fairy dusted the whole affair with glittering lights and fairy dust and Natalie was the most radiant bride I had ever seen in her creamy glowing dress, dusted with fairy magic, with all her radiant, twisted hair piled atop her head. She wore a necklace with a lovely arctic rock gifted to her on a certain Christmas Eve in a setting of silver and gold. The wedding party was the oddest assortment of creatures. A sasquatch and a man with hair of fire were the groomsmen. A polar bear, a wolf and a puffin were the bridesmaids. I was Nat's maid of honor, walking down the aisle with Esa to stand at an altar of sculpted ice, snow falling in our hair, and laughter filling the air. Elves sang, reindeer danced, wolves howled, and it was a most splendid affair. It was most definitely my favorite of all the Christmases I have been blessed to celebrate over the years. It was also at that wedding that I fell in love with the man I ended up marrying a few years later. Another North Pole wedding officiated by Father Christmas. I suppose you can guess who that man was, considering there were very few humans at that wedding, and I did not go on to marry a reindeer.

I became an artist and writer of stories with Grams the Great editing my first story, the very one you have just finished reading. In fact, this story was even added to the North Pole archives by Grams and Holly. My great grandmother, having always been my biggest fan, also read every other book I wrote up until the day she finally passed, peacefully in the night, as she had predicted, and though we all missed her greatly we also knew we had been blessed to have her for so many long years.

Many of my stories and works of art carried a Christmas theme. When one is gifted with Christmas magic, one must do all they can to spread that joy. But not all. I also loved to write stories of the wild things that roam this earth in honor of Hemlock, Eylif, Ing, and Luna. It was how I honored my promise to the trees, to remember the wild places of the world. The second gift Santa Claus ever gave to me, the first to be delivered under a tree in my very own house, was a beautiful set of wooden carvings. A sasquatch, a polar bear, a wolf, and a puffin. Now that I am an old woman myself, these toys still sit at my writing desk, an inspiration to me always and a reminder of a world outside the human world that must never be taken for granted.

Life is beautiful, it is to be treasured. Christmas, one day a year, is only a reminder to treasure all the days we are blessed to live in this wild world. I am a very old woman now, happily retired from the world though I will never stop writing and creating. In fact, Desmond, Natalie, Esa, and I have all retired and we are living out the end of our unnaturally long lives together at the North Pole, where we feel the joy of Christmas every day.

And so this merry tale comes to an end, but not before I say one last thing to you, dear readers.

Happy Christmas to all, and to all a good night!

This book is dedicated to four very magical children –
Landry, Isley, Ari, and Sylvie. May your days be merry,
bright, and filled with the joy of a life well lived.

Made in the USA
Monee, IL
20 October 2024

67969175R00152